A True Witch

Book 1

L.J. Fox

Artwork by: Wendy Frere

Copyright © 2025 L.J. Fox Australia

Australian (British) English

ISBN: 978-1-7644136-2-6

Version 1

I wish to acknowledge the Traditional Custodians of the land upon which we live and work and pay respect to Elders past and present.

...I do have to wonder what sort of childhood the Grimm brothers endured. They are not a merry bunch of storytellers, what with their children roasted by witches, maidens poisoned by old crones, and whatnot.

Libba Bray (2009). "Rebel Angels", p.51, Simon and Schuster

Chapter 1

NIAMH FLYNN 2018

You could smile, Niamh. It wouldn't hurt, you know," her mother said, disapproval dripping from her voice.

Niamh rolled her eyes. "I'm here, aren't I? That's enough. You don't get smiling as well."

They strode across the car park toward the nondescript red brick building serving as an aged care home when Niamh suddenly stopped in her tracks and looked around. Her skin was prickling and her hair felt electrified and standing on end, as if someone was watching her. Looking around, she could only see various vehicles in the carpark and the foliage of the outer garden. Niamh shook her head to clear the feeling and raced to catch up to her mother who was striding along, aware that time was precious. All Niamh could think of was that a family sized pizza for dinner tonight had not been sufficient to buy her attendance today and she should have held firm for a higher price.

As they entered the building, the odours of incontinent residents reached them, and Niamh gagged involuntarily.

"This place smells like shit," she announced, bluntly.

Her mother didn't respond, and Niamh realised she must have become accustomed to this potent smell. She visited this venue every week to spend time with Niamh's failing grandmother. Niamh had never been here and could barely remember her grandmother at all. She could vaguely recall an incident when she was a young child where she had been frightened by the old lady and her mother whisked her away quickly. No need to be frightened today. The old lady had stomach cancer and was dying, her mother had informed her and she had been coerced into visiting to say goodbye.

They navigated down various corridors, passed a few nurses and the odd escapee, until they reached palliative care, a door assigned number 24, where they halted. Niamh looked at her mother expectantly and saw her take a few deep breaths summoning up the courage to enter, then with a determined push, she opened the door and they entered.

Niamh immediately saw her two aunts in the room next to a large hospital bed. The aunts turned toward the newcomers and stepped forward, embracing her mother affectionately, "Hey, Luce."

The aunts turned from her mother and stared at her. "Hello Niamh, good to see you again," Bethany said.

"Aunt Beth, Aunt Bella," Niamh nodded her head at them in greeting.

"The boys are in the sitting room. They've said their goodbyes," announced Arabella.

The aunts were referring to their own children. Bethany had two sons and Arabella, one son. Lucky them, thought Niamh, getting the grandmother deed over and done with. She wondered if they had negotiated pizza tonight.

Niamh had barely ever seen the two aunts in her entire life, though she knew her mother saw them often, and spoke to them almost daily. They were almost strangers to her and she looked at them now, noting that other than different hair colours, the three sisters almost looked identical. They each wore their hair in the same cut, thick and straight and hanging half-way down their back. Her mother had red gold coloured hair, still natural as far as she knew, Bethany was strawberry blonde and Arabella's hair was a dark red.

She was aware of the two aunts sneaking glances at her now and again, and she wondered if they were trying to determine who she looked like. Niamh shook her own long, messy thatch of wavy, dark red hair defiantly, wishing she was anywhere else but there.

She stepped into the room further, looking at the figure in the bed and could hear the grandmother's raspy breathing. The woman in the bed lay with eyes closed and her face pale, almost grey in colour and if it wasn't for the sound of her breathing, she could have already been dead.

Niamh could hear the three sisters chattering as they always had when they were together. Each spoke very fast, and their voices overlapped frequently. Niamh found it difficult to listen to and understand what they were saying but she guessed the sisters had spent a lifetime talking in this manner and understood each other. She just caught a few words or phrases now and again.

"... not long now, the nurse said ..."

"... not conscious ..."

"... maybe she can hear us ..."

"... she hasn't passed it on ..."

"... what if she doesn't wake up ..."

"... what will we do ..."

"... May should be here"

Niamh switched off from the incessant chatter of the three women and stood as far back as she could from the bed. Her back leaned against a bookshelf, and she positioned herself in a relaxed stance ready to leave as soon as the option presented. Did they have to stay until the old lady died? She hadn't thought to ask that question. Could they just say goodbye and then leave? What if it took her two days to die? Surely, they didn't have to stay there and wait for that. Her three cousins had said goodbye and been excused. Surely, she could do the same.

The chatter stopped and she saw her mother approach the bed slowly and cautiously, as if any noise would wake the patient. Her mother reached out and placed her hand on top of the withered pale grey hand resting on the outside of the bed covers. She leaned down closer to the old woman's face and spoke to her.

"Mum, it's Lucinda. I'm here now and I'm with Niamh. Can you hear me?"

There was no response from the frail patient, and her mother leaned down and kissed the old woman on the forehead. Niamh watched and hoped she didn't have to do that, kiss an old stinky woman who she didn't know. Most of her friends saw their grandparents regularly and had great affection for them. Niamh knew nothing of her grandparents, or even if she had ever had a grandfather. Where was he? What happened to him? She had no relationship or attachment with this person in the bed. She briefly wondered why that was the case, that she barely knew people in her own family. Hell, she didn't even know her father. Most people would find that strange but to Niamh, it was just the way it had always been.

Niamh glanced out the large window next to the bookshelf absently. Again, that prickling sensation scored her skin, and she shivered involuntarily. Maybe she was just allergic to aged care homes.

The three sisters resumed their strange overlapping chatter again for ten minutes and then the three of them headed out of the room.

"Niamh, we'll be back shortly. We're just going to call May and have a word with the doctor," announced her mother as she closed the door, leaving Niamh alone with the dying grandmother. Briefly, Niamh wondered what or who May was but then she realised they had left her alone with the dying grandmother.

Alarmed, Niamh quickly looked back at the figure in the bed, imagining a zombie apocalypse where the grandmother rises from the bed and tries to attack Niamh and eat her flesh. She felt a shiver run down her spine and chided herself on being so melodramatic. This old lady wasn't going anywhere. She probably didn't even have any teeth.

A strange gurgling sound coming from the woman reached her ears and she strained to pay attention. Sure enough, along with the raspy inhaling and exhaling, there was a slight choked sound like her throat was closing. What should she do? Was this normal? She glanced at the door, alarmed, hoping the three sisters would return but there was no sign of them. Maybe it was just her imagination, she decided.

Then, she heard it again, a bit of a rumbling sound. Shit! Niamh stood up straighter, trying to decide whether to venture closer to see if there was a nurse button or something she could press. What if the old lady needed help? She didn't want to help her but maybe she could call someone.

Gingerly, Niamh stepped closer to the grandmother, step by step until she was next to her. She looked down, noting the pale withered flesh stretched across the bones of her cheeks, giving her a skeletal look. Niamh thought she could tell exactly what her skull would look like without skin or flesh.

From a distance, she had thought the old lady looked grey but in close proximity, she could see a pale yellow tinge to her skin. Her mouth was sagged open in an exclamation of surprise. Niamh looked at her facial features and wondered if she had ever been a pretty woman. Did she once look like her daughters or her granddaughter? Was her hair once red, whereas now it was white? There was no way of knowing that now. Had she ever seen photographs?

She couldn't hear any sounds coming from the grandmother, other than the raspy breathing as she studied her face. Did she feel anything for this withered woman who shared her blood? She knew she should feel something but was not sure she did. Was she heartless not to feel something for this person, a blood relative of hers?

Suddenly, something grabbed Niamh's wrist where her hand had been resting on the side of the bed. She gasped in shock and looked down to see the old woman had reached out and was clenching Niamh's wrist in her withered hand, which suddenly felt incredibly strong. She could see the ligaments and muscles bulge and strain as the hand gripped her wrist in a vice-like grip. She quickly looked up at the woman's face and saw the grandmother had turned her head toward Niamh, opened her eyes and was looking directly at her.

Her eyes were a haunting grey colour and they pierced into Niamh's soul. Niamh couldn't move, couldn't turn away or speak. The eyes held her riveted, hypnotised and immobilised. Instantly, she felt sweat break out across her forehead, chest, armpits and lower back. The eyes bore into her and the hand gripped her wrist, painfully. Prickling swirled over her whole body in waves, and she wondered briefly if she was about to pee herself.

Faintly, she could see a ball of golden spinning shapes above the bed of the grandmother, but she reasoned that this twirling mass of light could not be real. Was she hallucinating?

Staring into the grandmother's eyes, she could hear distant music, folk music and she could see a vision of green grass, rolling hills and distant mountains. People were dancing and singing, and she could see large bonfires. Niamh wanted to scream, 'WHAT IS HAPPENING?' but she was spellbound and couldn't move.

The music faded away, but the grip continued, and the stare continued. Niamh could see the old lady's mouth opening and she knew the grandmother wanted to say something. She saw her jaw move, and her throat restrict as she tried to form words. Niamh found herself leaning closer to hear what the grandmother wanted to say.

"You. It is you. I knew it! Lucinda. What have you done? Hahaha, Brilliant!"

The old lady gave a small laugh, feeble and ironic. Her gaze never left Niamh's eyes and bore into them, seeking answers. Her face broke out in a smile, a soft warm smile and for a moment, Niamh could see the grandmother as a young woman, beautiful and with dark red hair.

"You. Niamh. I bestow it upon you. You are the one."

The voice came out whispered and coarse, like someone thirsty and dry. Niamh stared at the woman with no understanding of what she had said and acknowledging she had just used her name for the first time.

"You, Niamh. You are the one. I bestow it upon you."

The light in her eyes disappeared as if a light switch had been flicked off. Niamh saw the light go, extinguished, kaput. She felt the grip on her wrist loosen and she looked down at the hand which no longer grasped her by the wrist. Gingerly, she pulled her hand loose from the withered hand that had held such a tight grip on her. She looked back up at the grandmother's face and the eyes were open and staring, her head turned toward Niamh, her mouth open and it was clear the grandmother was dead.

Niamh shuffled backwards, staring at the grandmother's face until she backed into the bookshelf she had earlier leaned against. She could hear a noise outside somewhere that sounded like wolves howling and she was aware of something outside that was not normal. The baying of the wolves and her body tingling all over, she wondered if she was going to faint.

The door to the room opened and the three sisters entered, still chatting. Their chatting stopped immediately upon seeing their mother on the bed. There was a moment of shock and stillness, then they rushed over to the prone woman only to realise she had passed. Arabella started crying softly, and Bethany held the grandmother's hand, the very hand that had just moments ago gripped Niamh's wrist. Her mother touched the grandmother's face tenderly and Niamh could see a tear trickling down her cheek. This continued for a few quiet moments.

"Luce," said Bethany. "She can't be gone yet. You know, she hasn't given it to anyone."

The three sisters stared at each other silently, puzzled, eyes searching each other.

“What happens now?” asked Arabella, wiping her nose with a tissue. “She can’t go without bestowing.”

“I don’t know what happens now. Has this ever happened before?” asked her mother.

Suddenly, her mother swung around and looked at Niamh suspiciously. She looked down at Niamh rubbing the red welt-like marks on her wrist on the side of her jeans.

“Did you go near her? Did she say anything to you?” she asked firmly, her voice stilted and almost angry.

Niamh, still in shock from her experience, was speechless, rubbing her wrist and staring back at her mother. She became aware of all three sisters, standing up, eyes wide and staring at her and then the three of them started walking toward her silently.

Chapter 2

BRIDGET CONLON 1969

The rock hit Bridget on the side of her head. She cried out in alarm and pain, falling to the ground as countless stones and rocks rained down on her, some hitting their mark and others falling short. Laughter from the young boys followed and the sound of fleeing feet as they bolted, pleased with their target practice. Bridget sent off a bolt of magic out of anger and it found its mark, tripping two of the boys up. They tumbled to the ground, landing hard on the stones and jumped to their feet with bloodied knees, eyes wide open at the thought that Bridget had caused the fall.

The woman rose to her feet, wiping the blood from the side of her head with her apron. Red streaks marred the cream fabric and smeared across her forehead. She sighed in resignation as it was not the first time the village boys had found her an easy target and it wouldn't be the last. She was thankful her daughter, Agatha, was not nearby and the target of the boys though it had happened to Agatha more than once. There was nothing she could do to prevent this from happening but if she ever managed to catch one of the little rogues, she'd whoop his arse with a stick until it bled.

She walked back to the cottage and looked across the hedge to the vegetable garden, spying Agatha with a basket collecting carrots, turnips and potatoes. Luckily,

Agatha had not been aware of the rock throwing incident and was calmly singing to herself as she collected the ripe vegetables. Bridget worried for her daughter's safety, more so lately as the attacks from the village boys was becoming more frequent due to the warmer weather, and the Garda would do nothing despite her pleas. She worried that these village boys would soon grow into men and potentially, the thought of them paying Agatha a visit when she was alone at night as had happened to her, was more than she could bear.

She had only just reached the house when a bell tinkling drew her attention to the front gate where a short, stocky woman had entered and was heading down the path to the cottage. Her high-pitched voice rang out as she reached the front door.

"Yoohoo, are you there, Caillieach?"

Bridget sighed again, knowing Mrs McCleary was seeking more of the love potion she had been buying weekly for the past few months. She desperately wanted a child, and her husband seemed to have lost interest in a physical relationship with her. These love potions were an attempt to woo him into her bed and there had been a small amount of success, though the amount of alcohol Mr McCleary consumed helped the situation enormously. Bridget silently thought that all the magic in the world was not going to improve the appearance, demeanour or sex appeal of Mrs McCleary.

The local village people called Bridget, 'Caillieach', the witch, as they had called her mother before her, and her mother before that. Her family had always been the witches of the county. The local villagers gossiped among themselves about the witches, of spells cast to cause injury and imagined ills that had befallen the town due to the close proximity of the witches. Of course, most of the gossip was sheer nonsense, but some spells were well placed and well deserved.

This was 1969 in Ennis, County Clare, Ireland and yet, for all the superstitious behaviour of the town folk, it could have been 1769 or 1669. Bridget had lived in this cottage on the small acreage fifteen minutes stroll from the village all her life, and her mother, and grandmother before her. She had no idea how far back the family had lived in this cottage or on this land, but it was far longer than anyone's living history.

Nothing had changed in the past two hundred years regarding the town folk's treatment of her family, and she knew that nothing would ever change. Yet, the very villagers who persecuted them were the first to visit when desirous of a remedy or potion.

Bridget donned a pleasant smile and chatted with Mrs McCleary telling her how fetching she was looking and taking the few shillings she charged for the love potion. After the woman had left, she squirrelled the money away with the rest of the money she had been accumulating in the tin under the hearth.

She had reached the momentous decision a few years ago that her daughter and herself needed to leave Ireland forever and move to America or Australia where no one knew them and the people were more modern and accepting. This was a grand dream and one that her own mother had whispered to her on her deathbed. There would never be a better life for them if they were to remain in Ennis with local legend and myths too deeply rooted. She was aware of her family history and had lamented at stories of ancestors tortured, burned, drowned and tormented for being a witch. The family graveyard just down the hill was full of these family members who had lives cut short by the town folk.

Now, although only in her forties, she knew she would not be leaving Ennis ever. She placed her hand over her abdomen and felt the large growth that was hidden under her apron. There would be no hospital cure or doctor intervention for her, and she was unable to use her magic on the disease without the help of other caillieachs. She had kept this secret from her daughter for many months, but now she could feel the growth becoming larger, and she felt tired and sick much of the time. Her time was running out.

Also, unbeknown to Agatha, she had arranged to sell the cottage and small plot of land to Mr Benjamin McAdam, the farmer who owned the land around the cottage. He had plans to lease it to his overseer and she would be paid handsomely. This money would be sufficient, along with her tin under the hearth for Agatha to enjoy a new life in a new country when Bridget was gone.

She looked around at the ancient cottage with its thatched roof which often leaked rain, the cobblestone floor that was always cold, and the stone of the walls that had stood for hundreds of years. A tear trickled down her cheek at the thought of her family no longer owning this special place. Above the door and the windows, hung trinkets to ward away evil and embrace good luck including Brigid's cross made from sticks and reeds. Agatha could take them with her to be safe in her new home.

It was time for her to be truthful with Agatha and tell her of this terrible sickness that would soon take her life. She didn't worry about Agatha as she knew the girl was smart, quick witted and tough. She had to be tough to live here in this cold place and suffer the taunting from the village people. How different their lives may have been had they not been witches, but there was no point thinking of that now.

Agatha appeared at the door with a basket of freshly picked vegetables carried on her hip.

"Agatha, come here child. I need to talk to you."

Chapter 3

NIAMH FLYNN 2018

Scratch, scratch, scratch.

Niamh roused from the deep sleep she had been enjoying and glanced at her bedside clock – 2.02am. She peered up at the dark ceiling and wondered what had woken her. The noise began again, and she listened, imagining it sounded like a plant scratching on the glass of her bedroom window in the wind.

Swearing under her breath, she threw the covers back and padded over to the window, determined to identify the guilty plant so she could chop it off first thing in the morning. She pulled the curtain back and was met by the darkness of outside. Looking up, she could see the moon was throwing filtered light into the night sky and everything looked surreal and like a painting.

Something moved low down near the window, and she jumped back in surprise. A flash of two eyes looked back at her and she realised it was a large rabbit or hare. He'd obviously rubbed against the window as he moved through the garden. She exhaled in relief and moved to close the curtain, but something made her pause. The rabbit was looking directly at her, unafraid and still. She stared back at the rabbit, waiting for it to take fright and move on. Was she dreaming? Had the incident at the grandmother's death bed rattled her more than she had realised?

Her eyes were becoming accustomed to the darkness, and she began to visualise the plants around the rabbit. As she looked further beyond the window garden, she became aware of at least one dozen sets of eyes staring at her. The eyes glowed a yellowish flash as they watched her in sets of two. One dozen rabbits perched on the grass of the front lawn, lined up neatly and staring at her window, while the one rabbit had ventured forward to scrape on the glass. It was an eerie sight, and she stood mesmerised as the rabbits paid her homage.

Climbing back in bed an hour later, she reflected on the day's events with the dying grandmother and later with her aunts. Her mother and two aunts had questioned her relentlessly for some time on whether the grandmother had spoken to her. The episode was unnerving, and she was still processing it in her mind. Their behaviour had made her more determined not to tell them anything. She refused to answer and eventually, walked off leaving them with their dead mother.

Her mother had tried talking to her several times since the event and Niamh had remained silent and sullen.

"Did your grandmother give you something?"

"Did she speak with you?"

"What did she say?"

"Did you touch her?"

"How do you feel?"

The truth was that she felt a bit odd and had ever since the grandmother had seized her wrist, as though a course of low-level electricity had passed through her. It had left her tingling and buzzing to a certain extent. This buzzing feeling had not left her all afternoon and evening, and even now, she could still feel the effects.

Why hadn't she told her mother what had happened, or her aunts?

She had felt angry at the time, forced to attend this morbid event of someone she didn't know, and she felt sure her friends would react the same as she had. Then there had been the shock of the grandmother grabbing her wrist and trying to analyse what had happened in her mind. What did the grandmother's words even mean? Bestow what? Why was her mother, Lucinda so brilliant? None of it made any sense.

Finally, she had been angry that her mother and aunts knew something and were not telling her. They were expecting the grandmother to give them something and it had not occurred and yet, they were not being upfront about what they were expecting and what was going on.

She still felt angry. The grandmother hadn't given her anything anyway. She had just acted weird and said strange things. She had said she was bestowing something on Niamh, but then didn't bestow anything on her. What was she going to bestow? Did she own a one-million-dollar house or some treasure she was going to bestow? Is that what the aunts were unhappy about, that she may inherit something that they wouldn't?

Why had her mother hidden her from the grandmother all these years? The grandmother had known her name, and she knew she had met her at least once as a small child. Her mother visited the grandmother every week and yet, never took Niamh. Why now? Why say goodbye when she never got to say hello.

She sighed and closed her eyes. Unless her mother and the aunts confided what was going on, then she wouldn't be telling them anything either.

Tomorrow she would confide in her best friend, Emma, regarding what had happened. She was sure to have a better understanding of family relationships than Niamh did. Maybe they could go hang out at the shopping mall for the day. It was summer holidays and the perfect time to shop, eat, hang out and socialise. She would message her after breakfast and organise it.

Day planned, she climbed back into bed ad drifted back into a deep sleep to dream of being surrounded by rabbits.

Chapter 4
AGATHA CONLON 1970

For an Irish girl accustomed to the cold, Agatha found Melbourne to be the perfect climate, though she was aware it was only autumn, and she had missed the heat of summer. With her pale skin, she was often reminded to keep out of the Australian sun.

Her mother, Bridget, passed away over winter, within six months of Agatha becoming aware of the disease. She had watched it eat her mother's body until there was nothing left but skin and bones. She had been able to numb her mother's pain with potions and herbs grown in the cottage garden but had refused to dose her with the potion that she craved, that would end her existence.

Despite feeling miserable and alone, she was relieved her mother's pain and suffering was finally over. Now she was truly alone in the world and unwanted in the local county, so the thought of setting off to Dublin and catching a Pan Am flight to Australia was an exciting and logical step. After an hour at the family cemetery saying goodbye to her mother and a last glimpse at the stone cottage that had been the family home for centuries, she left for a new life. She was excited for herself but also, that she was fulfilling her mother's dream of escaping this miserable existence.

Agatha had lived in Melbourne for only three weeks when she first became aware that there was someone else nearby with magical powers. Although she had experienced the hair standing on end sensation a number of times since being in Melbourne, it had taken her a few weeks to realise what it was. Her mother had told her about the sensation, but she had never been around other people with magical powers so didn't recognise the feeling.

Now she was aware of what the prickling sensation meant, she had no idea what to do with the information. Should she try to identify who this person was? Friend or foe? Her mother had told her that there were various other caillieachs around in different counties, and therefore, other countries as well as enemies, but it wasn't something she possessed any knowledge of.

Being a determined person, Agatha resolved to discover who this other person was. The curiosity was too strong to ignore. The sensation seemed to occur more often when she was at the shopping area, not far from where she was boarding, so she walked along the row of shops on the main street of the inner-city suburb, feeling receptive and openly inviting the connection. The sensation proved stronger at one end of the street than the other, so she turned a corner into a side street where the sensation was at its strongest and followed the strength of the signal. Two blocks up a slight incline, she turned to the right into a quiet, tree lined street, and walked slowly, the sensation so strong that she could almost see the hair on her arms standing straight up.

Ahead on the left, she could see a person standing at their front gate staring in her direction. Instinctively, she knew this was the magical person and they had felt Agatha moving closer and ventured out to greet or to warn. Agatha slowed and stepped slowly and cautiously toward the person. She identified it was a female around the same age as she was with short, wispy, bright red hair and a purple dress. She appeared friendly with a wide smile lighting up her face, so Agatha walked up to her and stopped. This red-haired woman was much shorter than Agatha with large breasts and yet, petite in many ways.

The two women stared at each other as the minutes ticked by, each waiting to see what the other would do. The red head still had a huge engaging smile on her face and gradually, with no way of preventing it, Agatha smiled as well. The two smiles were contagious and became two laughs, and within minutes, the two women were almost rolling around the ground in tears, laughing at nothing, laughing at themselves.

When they had recollected themselves and calmed a little, the red head opened the gate and gestured for Agatha to enter.

"I'm Maybelline," said the red head. "May."

"Agatha."

By the time Agatha left, four hours later, it was to travel back to the boarding house to collect her belongings and give notice to the landlord. She had a new place to stay and a new friend in Maybelline Connor. She wouldn't be lonely anymore and for the first time ever, she felt like she belonged somewhere, and her life had purpose.

Chapter 5

NIAMH FLYNN 2018

"So, you watched your grandmother die?" asked Emma, wide-eyed with interest.

"Yeah. It was pretty gross," admitted Niamh. "My mother bribed me into being there, then my mother and the aunts left me alone with her. She was making this choking sound, so I walked over to the bed and she grabbed my arm and said something weird, then just ... died."

"What did she say?" asked Emma, thinking how creepy if would be to watch someone die in front of you.

"Umm ... something like 'I bestow it upon you. You are the one. Lucinda's brilliant.' "Niamh shook her head to clear the image she had in her mind of the dying grandmother.

"Lucinda? Your mother?"

"Yep."

"Bestow it upon you? What did she bestow?" Emma asked.

"No idea. Nothing, but when my mother and aunts came back in the room and realised she was dead, they wanted to know if she had given me anything. They were really demanding and kind of ... weird about it," said Niamh.

"Really? Hmmm. Maybe she was going to tell you something important because she couldn't have had anything valuable on her. She was on her deathbed after all," reasoned Emma.

"Yeah. It couldn't have been anything tangible. You're right, and surely, she would have had a will for all her property and valuables," said Niamh.

The two girls were sitting in the busy food court at the local shopping centre with their chicken burritos in front of them, so far untouched. Niamh became aware of someone addressing her and she turned to the table next door to see an older couple. The woman had her head tilted on the side and was reading a tag on Niamh's backpack.

"N. I. A. M. H, that's an unusual name. Is it pronounced Nee-am?" asked the older lady.

Niamh looked down at the offending label poking out of her backpack, leaned down and poked it back out of sight, kicking her backpack further under the table, away from prying eyes.

"No. It's pronounced Neve like Steve," she answered in a well-rehearsed response, refusing to look at the woman with the roving eyes. The woman took the hint and didn't bother Niamh again.

"Why don't you ask your mother what the grandmother might have bestowed on you, if it bothers you?" asked Emma.

"The less I have to talk to my mother the better," answered Niamh sullenly. "It doesn't bother me anyway."

"Well, it must bother you a bit or you wouldn't be telling me about it," said Emma with a raised eyebrow. "Why do you hate your mother so much?"

Niamh paused to think on her answer. "I don't hate her. I just ... don't like her very much," she finished.

"Well, I think your mother is nice. Nicer than mine, anyway, and she's pretty and kind of cool. You know, in an older kind of way. Did she ever tell you who your dad is?"

Niamh pursed her lips in refusal to acknowledge this statement. Was her mother pretty? Who cared if she was or wasn't? She shrugged it off. "No. She had some short passionate affair. That's all I know."

"You could do a DNA test, you know and see if there are any other relatives out there," Emma picked up her burrito and Niamh thought it a good time to change the subject.

"Are you really going to Torquay for a few weeks?" asked Niamh, voice forlorn.

"Yeah. Leaving tomorrow with the parents and brother. Chill out on the beach for three weeks. Suntan, here I come!" Emma joked.

Niamh sighed. "What am I going to do without you?"

"Text me lots," Emma answered.

Emma had always been Niamh's closest friend. Niamh was aware that she was considered aloof by her peers and didn't have a huge amount of friends. She didn't really know why but guessed it might be because she was so much taller than all the other girls and didn't fit in with the normal activities and banter of teenagers. She convinced herself that she didn't care and she didn't need other people anyway. The thought of being totally alone when Emma went away was a little depressing and she wondered what she would do with herself. There were a couple of other girls she could tag along with, but it wouldn't be the same.

It was early January, that stagnant time when secondary school is over, but an adult life had yet to commence. She didn't feel ready for an adult life yet and still felt like a child, trying to find herself and not wanting to face anything serious in life. Both Emma and Niamh had been accepted at the local university for a Bachelor of Arts degree, but Niamh knew she had only applied as Emma had. Emma was interested in pursuing a career in social work, and Niamh felt she was so fortunate to know who she was and what she wanted to do. Niamh felt at that moment that she would forever be an angry child in a world she didn't understand.

Chapter 6

AGATHA CONLON 1970

May unwrapped a wooden plaque she had purchased and showed Agatha the inscription, 'The Coven' and they both laughed. It was the name they had decided to call the house they were renting. May announced it was to hang on their front door. They already had Brigid's Cross and a number of home-made charms hanging above various doors and windows. May had a few basic charms already hanging in her house, but Agatha explained the importance of the Brigid's Cross and how they needed to protect themselves. She guessed the Irish were more wary and suspicious of people than others.

Neither girl had employment so a plan was hatched that May would become 'Marvellous Maybelline' as she was the one with the better people skills and Australian voice, and they would begin a small business selling potions and remedies, conducting readings and healing illnesses. May had already been growing herbs and flowers in various pots and containers in the back garden and between the two of them, they had a vast knowledge of potions, tonics, pain killers, aphrodisiacs and natural remedies.

May's magic included the ability to move objects without touching them, boil water, light a fire, cause it to rain but her biggest talent which had nothing to do with magical abilities, was her likeable character, quick humour and dry wit. People couldn't help but want to be in her presence and laugh with her. May was everyone's favourite cousin, or niece or sister and Agatha quickly became attached to her and considered her a sister.

May had caught the ferry across to Melbourne from Tasmania and left her family behind a few years earlier. Somehow, she was born a true witch despite having no witch heritage that she knew of. She swore she must have been adopted, and her parents never admitted to it, and Agatha privately thought this assumption was probably correct. As far as she knew, a true witch could not randomly be born to non-magical parents. Even with just the one magical parent, not every child was born a true witch.

Agatha was the stronger of the two regarding magical abilities and could also heal wounds or mild afflictions, though not a serious disease like what her mother had suffered. What May found fascinating was that Agatha's magic was tied up with her emotions. If loud thunder was heard, May often found Agatha was in a bad mood that day. In anger, she could cause a fire or an explosion and May swore she wouldn't want to be Agatha's enemy.

Between the two of them, they determined that they would advertise in the papers for customers and May would be the public face of the business, but Agatha would also work with creating potions, healing the sick or whatever was needed.

MARVELLOUS MAYBELLINE
Clairvoyant, witch, fortune-teller
Trinkets, potions, tarot reading.
Call for appointment

The advertisement ran in the Melbourne newspapers every Friday and within a few weeks, the appointment book was filling up and the girls were busy. Widows wanted to communicate with their recently departed husbands, men wanted to know if they would meet a new partner or how they could make themselves more attractive to future partners, girls wanted love potions, middle aged people wanted to know what their future held, and a range of people were seeking natural remedies for illnesses they were too embarrassed to attend a doctor for including herpes and flatulence.

A few customers were difficult such as the young couple with a little boy dying of leukaemia who were looking for a cure. May gently explained that she could not cure him and that they were best seeking medical treatment, but she could give them a natural drink full of vitamins and minerals that would help the little body to fight.

One man became aggressive when May explained that she could not talk to the deceased, and Agatha had to step in and subdue him with magic, as she had with a few men with views to assault or rob May. These hostile customers found themselves sitting on the pavement out the front of the house, unsure how they had ended up in that position with sore behinds as if they had been kicked up the arse.

Between the two of them, Agatha and May managed to find a way of providing each customer what they wanted without over-stepping boundaries or giving false promises. Marvellous Maybelline became well-known in Melbourne and within a few months, a journalist wrote an article on the success of the small business. The article was written, tongue-in-cheek with good nature, after the journalist had visited May undercover pretending to be a love-lost middle-aged customer. May had immediately identified he had a wife and children, and his ruse had not been successful. He had laughed with the two witches about the true nature of his appointment and left as a friend with daisy-chain necklaces for his daughters.

Being successful was unexpected and exciting for the two young women but any semblance of a normal life became remote once the article was published even though the address was kept private. Word travelled and people started turning up at the door, day and night, requesting a reading, or a potion or an illness cured, and the phone never stopped ringing. Even with signs on the gate and front door asking people to make appointments, it was still a problem.

The women were forced to move to a more secure property with a larger fence and gate out the front, and with high fences around the boundaries at 14 Liddle Street in Coburg, north of the city of Melbourne. After living in this house for a few years, May was able to purchase the property after a rich customer left her estate to May. Without any attempt to encourage bequeathments, Agatha and May occasionally found themselves the recipient of a lonely old person's will when they passed on.

The biggest problem with all the publicity regarding Marvellous Maybelline was that it attracted the attention of the Grimm family.

Chapter 7

FLYNN SISTERS 2018

The three sisters sat in Lucinda's lounge room discussing the funeral for their mother, and to organise the financial affairs. Paramount in their mind was whether their mother had died without waking and whether Niamh had been the recipient of the bestowment.

"What do you think, Luce? Have you seen any signs?" asked Bethany.

Lucinda paused and considered the question. "Well, I don't know. She's at an awkward stage at the moment, very rebellious and angry all the time. Doesn't want to talk to me, barely at all. I just don't know." She shrugged apologetically, hoping this deflection was an adequate response.

"If she does have it, don't you think it could be dangerous, considering as you say, she's angry all the time?" asked Arabella. "Who knows what she could do?"

"But also, you're forgetting about the Grimm's," said Bethany. "They might be aware of what's happened."

Lucinda looked alarmed and all three contemplated this thought. Niamh was almost a stranger to Bethany and Arabella, and they wondered why Lucinda was not more aware of her own daughter with something so serious.

Bethany gave a concerned look around the room. “Where is she?”

“She left this morning and said she would be at the shops with Emma, her friend,” said Lucinda,

“What if she doesn’t have it?” asked Arabella. “Does that mean it’s gone forever?”

“Is it possible one of us has it without knowing?” asked Lucinda.

The three women looked at each other thoughtfully then dismissed the idea simultaneously. Another quick thought that was also dismissed was whether one of them had it but was deliberately keeping it secret from her sisters.

“I’m pretty sure none of us has it,” said Bethany and the other two sisters nodded. They felt they would know if one of them had it, and why pretend not to have it anyway?

“Why do you think mum never bestowed it on one of us? Do you ever think about that?” asked Lucinda.

The other two considered the question for a few minutes. “I have thought of that lately, since she’s been in care,” admitted Arabella. “If I were braver, I would’ve asked her outright.”

The other’s nodded acknowledging the unsaid, that their mother was intimidating, and none of them were brave enough to make a stand or say something that could potentially make her angry. Not that she had ever raised a hand to any of them or spoken out of turn. She didn’t need to, and the three girls had been in awe of her, even as a sick old woman on her death bed. There was also the thought among the three sisters that they had been born just normal people and had disappointed their mother, or so they thought.

"Do you think none of us were suitable, or up to the task?" asked Bethany. "Or maybe, that's what she thought."

"Then why would you think that Niamh would be," asked Lucinda.

The question hung in the air and none of them knew what their mother thought. In truth, Lucinda had kept her daughter away from her mother nearly all her life, since an incident when Niamh had been five years old and saw how her mother was reacting to the child. She had deliberately kept Niamh away from all of them, away from all-seeing eyes.

Lucinda looked at her two sisters, thinking how lucky they were that they only had sons. Sons were inconsequential and her sisters were free to be loving mothers to them without the stress of whether they were magical or a normal person or may be chosen and bestowed. How different would her life had been if she had bore a son instead of a daughter. Would her son have loved her and showed her affection, unlike her surly daughter? She would never know the answer to that.

The sound of the front door opening stopped them in their tracks, and all three pair of eyes turned as Niamh walked in.

Chapter 8

AGATHA CONLON 1970

According to the appointment book, the next appointment at 10am was a new customer named Dora Grimm. As the two girls always did, particularly with a new customer, Agatha planned to stay nearby in the kitchen while May entertained in the drawing room. This worked well as there were two girls handy should the customer become aggressive or try to get out of paying. A new customer was an unknown factor, and it paid to be cautious.

May had peered out of the window in time to see a shiny black car pull up on the other side of the street and park. May was naive with cars, but she could see that this car was expensive and well cared for. A woman emerged from the driver's side and stood staring at the house. She appeared to be in her thirties with pale blonde hair in an up-style with designer clothing and boots. May was giving a running commentary to Agatha in the kitchen when she stopped, aware that Agatha had walked up next to her and was also looking out the window. The guarded, haunted look on Agatha's face made May pause and then she realised she had a prickling sensation.

The two girls stared out the window at this woman, both with the knowledge that this woman had magical abilities. It was a surreal moment as other than each other; they had never encountered another magical person before. Agatha turned and headed for the front door with May on her heels. She opened the front door and the two of them stood on the front porch only twenty metres from Dora Grimm. So far, Dora Grimm had not moved but now she slowly slung her handbag over her shoulder and with another smug look up at the girls on the porch, sauntered slowly across the road toward the front gate.

Without a sound, Agatha and May walked down the two steps to the front path and down to the gate. They stood side by side with no inclination to open the gate and invite Dora Grimm in. Dora Grimm stopped on the footpath, with only three metres and the front gate separated her from the two girls. Her liquid brown eyes stared into the cool grey eyes of Agatha and then slowly moved over to stare into the blue eyes of May. A slight smirk was apparent on her face as if she was finding the situation humorous.

Instinctively, Agatha and May knew this woman was not a true witch without needing to be told. Her aura was dark, not the colourful and playful one like May, or the bright, illuminous aura like Agatha. They could feel darkness and evil emanating from her as if she was a dog shedding fur. For the first time in their lives, they knew they were facing an enemy and yet, Agatha didn't feel fear. She felt an ingrained anger and aggressiveness she had never known.

May was the first to feel a stabbing pain in her forehead and although she never said a word, a change in her breathing alerted Agatha who glanced quickly at her and pushed with her mind. The pain stopped and then Agatha felt the stabbing pain across her forehead. She pushed harder and she heard Dora Grimm inhale loudly.

Agatha had thrown the pain back at her as if tossing an unwanted basketball which had scored a goal.

Dora Grimm stared at Agatha, realising she was the stronger of the two. The smirk had practically disappeared from her face. Agatha paid attention to the liquid brown eye colour for the first time and that her eyebrows were quite thick and dark which was not fashionable for the time. She was attractive and yet, not classically beautiful.

Dora Grimm looked down at the gate, paying attention to the small sign which read 'Marvellous Maybelline' and then her eyes slid to the protective charm sitting next to the sign. It was one that Agatha had brought with her from Ireland and was hand-made from sticks and reeds with hair from Agatha's head threaded through. Dora Grimm furrowed her brow in a frown as she stared at the charm designed to ward off evil.

It was Agatha's turn to smirk, understanding that Dora Grimm was hesitant about entering the property despite having an appointment which was equivalent to an invitation.

"We rescind your invitation. You are not welcome," Agatha said firmly to her.

Dora Grimm looked back at Agatha thoughtfully. "Irish," she stated though not as a question. She looked at May as if expecting May to speak but May kept her mouth shut. Dora took a step backwards with her eyes still on the two girls. Agatha could see Dora was trying to decide what to do and hadn't expected this turn of events. She guessed that Dora Grimm had seen the advertisement in the paper and been curious, wanting to know who Marvellous Maybelline was. Perhaps, she visited all mediums or fortune-tellers who advertised to judge whether they were real or fraudulent. She wouldn't have expected to find two true witches when she turned up for this appointment.

With another glance at both girls, the smirk returned to her face, and she turned and almost sauntered back across the street to her car. With one last glance at the two girls, she sat in the driver's seat and drove off.

Agatha put her arm around May and sighed. She instinctively knew that this was not the last they would see of Dora Grimm. She was some sort of magical enemy that neither girl had encountered before, and where there was one, there would be more. This episode was just the beginning.

Chapter 9

NIAMH FLYNN 2018

Feeling eyes on her, Niamh walked self-consciously into the living room and stopped, glaring at her mother defiantly. Why did they have to treat her this way, she wondered? Why couldn't her mother be like other mothers, and just yell out, 'How was your day, love'?

"Niamh, the funeral of your grandmother will be Friday," her mother informed her.

"Right," Niamh responded, non-committedly.

"Can we talk to you for a minute? Would you take a seat?" asked her mother indicating the free lounge chair.

Niamh looked at the vacant chair, contemplated refusing the invitation and then turned and sat on a kitchen stool, forcing her mother to half turn her body. She dropped her backpack to the floor at her feet and then ceremoniously turned to look at her mother.

Her mother glanced at her two sisters for back-up and then took a deep breath. "I know we've asked you a few times if your grandmother said anything to you before she died, and I want to explain to you why we need to know."

Niamh continued to stare at her mother waiting and not showing any emotion on her face. She noticed her mother looked very uncomfortable and almost a bit embarrassed. She hadn't seen her mother behave in this manner before and concluded that her mother was embarrassed in front of her sisters that there was a problem communicating with her daughter.

"Your grandmother, Agatha, was from Ireland, Ennis in County Clare. Our family had lived in Ennis for hundreds of years and has always been ostracised by the people of the town."

Niamh raised an eyebrow. Ostracised? Stange term to use.

Arabella continued, "Agatha's mother, Bridget, saved money for many years and wanted her daughter to start a new life in a new country. After Bridget died in 1970, Agatha immigrated to Australia. The three of us were born here in Australia. None of us here have suffered the harassment that our ancestors in Ireland did, as the Irish are very traditional and superstitious."

Bethany could see the confusion on Niamh's face. "The town people called our ancestors, 'Caillieach' which means witch. Our family have always been witches."

"Witches?" said Niamh, her voice derisive.

"Yes. Witches," her mother confirmed. "Not all of us are true witches, of course."

"What's a true witch?" asked Niamh, trying to keep a straight face.

"Well, your grandmother was, and her mother was. They had certain abilities, like ... the ability to move objects, cast spells and heal people. None of us three have those abilities though we do know the basics of how to make potions and spells," said Arabella.

"A true witch must bestow the magic to another before she dies. She cannot take the magic with her when she passes," said Bethany.

"What happens if she does take the magic with her when she dies?" asked Niamh.

The three sisters looked at each other. "Well, we don't know, really."

"And you think the grandmother bestowed this magic on me?" asked Niamh.

"Maybe ...," said her mother. "Did she? It could be dangerous if you do have it, and don't know how to use it."

Niamh looked at her mother's serious expression, and then at her two aunts. Was this a joke? Surely, they couldn't be serious. Her family were a bunch of witches in Ireland and left Ireland because they were given a hard time by the people in the town. Immigrating to Australia gave the family a chance to live without the superstition of old Ireland.

Niamh shook her head as if to clear it. She looked at the three faces in front of her, all waiting to hear her announce that she has been bestowed.

"You know," she started. "I think they were ostracised not for being witches, but for being totally fucked in the head."

With that, she scooped up her backpack and left the room.

Chapter 10

DORA GRIMM 1970

Dora Grimm entered the kitchen, agitated and threw her handbag on the sideboard where it knocked a vase over. The sound of crystal hitting the marble startled her husband as he sat sipping his cup of tea at the table. He glared at her in annoyance and waited to hear the details of her latest rant.

"Well .... It's finally happened," she said, pacing over to the kitchen sink and spinning to face him. "I just came face to face with two witches."

"You WHAT?" he said, sure he had misheard.

"Two of them. Strong witches too. Strong enough to push me back," she said.

George Grimm was sitting upright now, cup of tea left on the table, staring at his wife in surprise. "Where?"

"It was one of those ads in the paper. I made an appointment to check it out, like I always do. Nice house in Coburg. I didn't even get as far as the front door. Two of them felt me coming and came out to the gate."

"But ... who are they?" he asked.

"Hmmm .... Irish, it sounded like. Must have just arrived or we'd have known about them sooner," she said, thoughtfully.

Neither of them had encountered a witch before although their respective families had spoken of it. Both were deep in thought trying to remember snippets of information they had gathered from their family over the years.

First rule: witches were the enemy, always had been, always would be. The Grimm family had originated in Europe and lived in Germany for the past few centuries until two branches of the extended family immigrated to Australia in the 1870's. They hunted witches and been instrumental in the witch hunts, torturing and eliminating thousands over time. That was their primary mission in life, to hunt down and eliminate witches. Their entire existence was based on killing witches, a line-bred trait.

The witches were so obvious in their magical abilities and such an easy target back in the dark times of a past era. They didn't hide their talent and often helped the villagers or cast spells for rain to fall, or crops to succeed, or in the latest case, even advertised their abilities. If only the villagers of the bygone era had known that the Grimm family were also magical, then they would have been on the receiving end of the torture as well, but the Grimm family were not obvious and too clever to be caught. They recognised that magical abilities equated to power, money and status and hid their skills whereas the witches used their abilities for healing, well-being and in their opinion, nonsense.

Of course, there were differences in the magical abilities and the Grimm family knew that the witches were more powerful than they were, however, the witches lacked the sheer guts, determination and dirty tactics required to win a war. The Grimm's had evil in abundance and were proud of it. They had never lost against the witches. EVER!

As far as George and Dora knew, there had never been a witch in Australia before, or at least in Melbourne. Dora's branch of the family had settled in Sydney and George's family in Melbourne and the two families intermarried to keep their blood pure. George and Dora had been married for six years and already had three children.

"I'll call my mother later and ask what she thinks," said Dora, waking George from his thoughts.

George nodded. He wondered what harm there would be to leave the two witches alive and well and co-inhabit Melbourne alongside them. His modern mind of the 1970's told him that this was possible and quite logical. Afterall, whoever heard of a witch hunting down a Grimm and torturing or eliminating him? But an inner inherited urge to wipe them off the face of the world kept bubbling to the surface. He thought of it like a cat and dog inhabiting the same house in an uneasy truce until the dog chases the cat away.

He wondered what his wife was thinking as she stood with her back to the kitchen sink, staring into space. She would be the one most likely to want them out of the way, and what exactly did that mean? Banish them from Melbourne? Banish them from Australia? Murder them?

Chapter 11

NIAMH FLYNN 2018

Niamh flopped down on her bed and searched for her phone. She quickly typed a message and sent it to Emma.

> *Mother and aunts ambushed me. Turns out grandmother was a witch from Ireland. Could have bestowed magic on me. Now we know.*

She only had to wait a few minutes before a ping notified her of a response from Emma.

> *No way! Is it a joke?*

> *No. Serious. I'll check the broom cupboard. Might be able to visit you down the beach.*

She smiled at her off-hand joke about being a witch and riding a broom. Did witches ride brooms? What did witches actually do? What the hell even was a witch? Did they wear black with tall hats and have warts on their nose? Perhaps, hang around a boiling cauldron, throwing in toads and lizards?

She fired up her laptop and searched Google for 'Ennis Ireland witch'. She learned that Ennis in County Clare had a long history of witchcraft and a few famous witches. She wondered if any of the famous witches were related to her. Did she have an ancestor burned at the stake? What was it that her aunt had said, oh yes, that their family had lived in Ennis for hundreds of years and always been ostracised by the people of the town. That sounded like they may well have ancestor burned to the stake as witches.

This whole event unfolding was so bizarre that she couldn't wrap her head around it. In the modern age, who ever heard of witches or believed in them? Surely, that was for the superstitious people of the past, where the unexplained was put down to witchcraft. With greater knowledge and science, the unexplained became logical and expected.

She remembered reading a story that in the 17th century in the United States, a paddock of cows started acting strange and walking in circles, trembling and convulsing. The villagers blamed the owner's wife and accused her of witchcraft and casting a spell on the cows. She was burned at the stake but in recent times, scientists discovered that the cows were suffering from rye grass poisoning.

How could there be room in modern society for witches?

Google informed her that there were many types of witches; black witches, white witches, green witches, wicca and she realised witchcraft is taken very seriously by some people. For a family of witches from Ireland, she found it odd that her mother never talked about witches or witchcraft. Why was she only hearing about this now?

She shouldn't have been surprised about her mother and aunts when all the signs had been there. When you are brought up a certain way, you don't question it. You assume that the way you have been raised is normal and other people's way of life is not normal. Her mother and two sisters were not the traditional maternal type of women that she knew from the mothers of children at school. They dressed in a unique and striking way with colourful Bohemian type dresses and spent a lot of time in their gardens and in the kitchen, brewing and cooking items that she had never bothered asking about but she was sure wasn't edible, some sort of herbal remedies. They had various trinkets and objects scattered around the house and were always making weird charms out of natural products, and they had unusual interests and topics of conversation.

Emma had always thought Niamh's mother cool due to her uniqueness, but Niamh often wished she had a normal mother, more like Emma's. She had seen Emma hug her mother and give her a kiss on the cheek. Niamh could never remember that type of affection from her mother before. She had always felt that she was kept at arm's length as if her mother was unsure what to do with her and she was her mother's dirty little secret.

In truth, she had always felt very alone and hated herself for feeling like a victim. She wondered what it would be like to have siblings and felt envious of Emma having a brother. She was eighteen years old and an adult though she didn't feel like an adult. There was no room in her life for playing a victim and whatever her childhood had lacked, was no longer relevant. She closed the laptop lid with an audible snap and looked out her bedroom window. She could see her mother saying goodbye to the two aunts. The three of them looked so similar with their thick long hair of different shades of red.

It was true that the grandmother had said she was bestowing something upon her, but nothing had happened. No sirens had gone off, no fireworks had lit up the skies and no sudden magic powers had appeared.

Niamh was still just Niamh. They were just meaningless words and there was no need to feed the superstitions of her mother and aunts by admitting to what the grandmother had said. Her solution was to simply ignore what had happened, bury the grandmother next Friday and pretend nothing had happened.

Niamh opened her bedroom door and sauntered out to make a quick bite to eat and watch a few shows on television. She knew her mother would not bring up the subject again so soon after the earlier conversation. If nothing else, her mother was not confrontational.

Chapter 12

DORA GRIMM 1970

Think of your children, Dora," came the exasperated voice of her mother down the phone.

After discussions with George, Dora had begun to think they should let sleeping dogs lie and leave the two witches alone provided the witches left them alone. Now, after speaking with her mother she was beginning to change her mind.

"Don't you realise that they will breed like rabbits and Irish, you say? We all know how the Irish breed. Your children will be in danger. Don't you realise that?"

Her mother's kill or be killed mentality was wearing Dora down. Mentioning a witch to her mother was like waving a red flag at a bull, and two witches meant her mother was already a charging bull.

"I'm not sure what we should do," Dora said.

"Take charge!" Her mother demanded. "Do we have to hold your hand with everything?"

That remark cut Dora, and she winced, hoping her mother didn't hear her intake of breath. She knew what her parents felt about George and how they spoke of him being ineffectual and weak. Having to hold her hand in everything referred to George's inability to hold her hand at all.

After the phone call, Dora relayed the conversation to George and the two of them spoke of the logistics of eliminating the two witches. For one thing, neither of them could enter the property uninvited and she wouldn't be holding her breath waiting on an invitation any time soon. The only option was to eliminate them outside the property which was difficult. Coburg was a built-up area so anything they tried in public would most likely be seen by people. It wasn't as if the two of them would be just walking in the middle of the road in the dead of night waiting for Dora or George to run them over in the car.

They were also busy people, George with a full-time job managing the local TAB shop and Dora was looking after three infant children under 5 years of age. Stalking the two witches would take time and waiting for the right opportunity to strike. George purchased two hunting knives in sheaths to carry, Dora's one fitting neatly in her handbag. Dora found that with every phone call with her mother, she was constantly making excuses for why they had not yet succeeded in hunting down the witches, or even meaningful stalking.

Armed, they began alternating driving past the house, or parking in the street and watching the house. This activity continued for many months and involved hours of their time. Mostly, they witnessed customers walking onto the property and rarely, one of the witches leaving. It was possible the witches were leaving the property during the times neither were able to watch but the venture proved more difficult than they had imagined, as well as boring.

There were a few close calls where George had followed one of the witches to the shops, his hand twitching to use the knife. He was well aware that if he got too close, they would be able to detect him, and the taller witch had much better senses than the shorter one. If they sensed him each time he stalked them, he felt he would never be able to get close enough to use the blade on them.

On one of these occasions, he had followed the shorter witch and watched as she entered a corner store. He had witnessed her visit this shop regularly and knew she would exit the shop with a bag containing milk and bread, or similar daily staples. She always walked back the same streets to return to her house, and he had found a great place to hide where he would not be seen. It was a small lane that ran between a brick garage and the next-door neighbour's garden. The small lane was overgrown with branches from the garden and was obviously used by locals to cut through from one street to the next street without having to walk all the way around.

Standing in the lane, he was hidden from the street she would be walking along, and he could wait for her to walk past, then jump out behind her. Slowly and silently, he pulled the knife from the sheath, kept in the pocket of his trousers and held it at the ready in his right hand. His confidence level was high, and he knew this was the perfect opportunity. If she sensed him but couldn't see anything, she may assume she imagined it.

Peeking around the corner, he saw her walk back on to the street from the corner store and head his way. He stepped back into the lane and became invisible, waiting. He could feel sweat dripping from his forehead and down his chest and realised he was nervous. He knew he was bred for hunting witches. This is what his family did, what they had done for centuries, but so far, he hadn't ever hunted a witch. He'd never felt a blade slide into flesh and experienced the blood gush. He tried to imagine if he would enjoy it, or gain some satisfaction from it, or if it would be akin to squashing a cockroach with his heel.

She was taking too long. She should have reached the lane by now. He wasn't game to peek around the corner again in case she was right there and would see him. Damn! Seconds ticked by and his hand felt clammy, holding the knife handle.

"Hey mister, what're you doing?"

He swung around in shock and standing behind him in the lane was a young boy of about eight years old, peering at the knife suspiciously. George quickly pushed the knife back into the sheath and let out a deep breath in frustration.

"Nothing," said George gruffly, and movement caught his attention. He turned back around and saw the red-haired witch walk past the lane. He had missed the opportunity due to the interference of this local boy. Angrily, he looked back around but the boy was heading down the lane the way he had come from.

George decided to head home for the day. Although unsuccessful, he thought the laneway was a good place to try again on another day.

Chapter 13

LUCINDA FLYNN 2018

Lucinda climbed into her comfortable bed and lay staring at the ceiling for hours. She was so tormented by the current situation with Niamh and knew she was not handling it very well. In fact, she was aware that she had never handled Niamh very well. She had no idea how to treat her daughter and had always tried to protect her. In doing so, she had completely alienated her and now Niamh treated her as if she were the enemy. Tearfully, she wondered if she would be considered an inadequate mother.

It was really bad luck that she was the one that produced a daughter. She knew she needed to stop thinking this way. Nothing could change it and she was grateful to have such a beautiful, although feisty daughter. Niamh was heir apparent, and they all knew it. Her sisters didn't know if Niamh was a true witch or not, but Lucinda knew. She had known from the time Niamh was born and had even been told beforehand. She had kept the child hidden from her mother for five years, knowing that her mother would immediately realise what she was.

She thought back to the time her mother had finally met Niamh when she was five years old. She had been dreading this day but knew it was inevitable and thought it amazing that she had managed to keep her daughter isolated for five years. From the time of Niamh's birth, she had let her mother think that she had been embarrassed to bear a child out of wedlock, ashamed to show the dirty little secret to her mother.

Bethany and Arabella were not true witches, just as she herself was not, but her mother was a true witch, and she would recognise it in Niamh instantly. Lucinda knew this and she feared for the safety of her little girl if her status of true witch be known. They had already lost family members due to being witches. She was not prepared to lose Niamh as well but on that fateful day, her mother had turned up at her house unannounced.

Just as she had always feared, her mother knew instantly that Niamh was a true witch. The biggest shock was that Niamh at five years of age, recognised it in her grandmother too. She remembered too well, the words her mother had said to her. They would haunt her for the rest of her life.

"What have you done, Lucinda? Oh my! What have you done? I'm right, aren't I? No wonder. No wonder you have kept her hidden from me. You knew I would see it, didn't you? She is so precious and special, but she is in danger. Don't you see that? You must bring her to me and let me teach her to protect herself before they get to her. Let me help her."

Lucinda wiped a tear away from her face. Could she yet admit that she had done the wrong thing by refusing to let her mother teach Niamh, and instead, hid Niamh away? No. Not yet. She couldn't accept that mistake just yet. She also felt her mother had realised more than just the fact that Niamh was a true witch. She had seen the deeper secret Lucinda had been suppressing.

Did her mother recognise Niamh in her final moments? Had she bestowed the gift upon her?

Que Sera Sera. Whatever will be, will be.

Doris Day had sung that song but to Lucinda, the words were from a lazy person who couldn't be bothered trying to change anything and could just sit back and let things happen.

Is that what she needed to do? Sit back and see what happened? She was adamant that she needed to make amends with Niamh and repair their broken relationship. At eighteen years old, Niamh could leave home for a life on her own at any time and she would be lost to her. She needed to reconnect with her daughter before it was too late. She so desperately wanted to be friends with her daughter.

A sound caught her attention, and she lifted her head off the pillow to listen. She heard it again, a strange, giggling sound. Giggling ... at 2.10am in the morning? Did Niamh have the television up too loud? She sat up and looked around the darkness of her bedroom.

The sound seemed to be coming from the outside window, so she pulled the bed covers back and tiptoed over to the curtain. She heard it again and the sound was definitely coming from outside. Very gently, she pulled the curtain apart just a little to see outside without being noticed. A strange sight greeted her and her breath caught in her throat as she scanned the scene in front of her.

Hundreds of pairs of eyes flashed in the darkness of the night like sparkling jewellery. She slowly turned her head from one side of the garden to the other and realised that there were hundreds of animals sitting on the grass in front of the house. She could see wild rabbits mostly, but also foxes, a few dogs and cats, and even owls. As her eyes adjusted to the dim light, she noticed there were just a few wallabies at the back near the front fence, possums on the fence, and a few other animals she couldn't identify. These animals were all sitting quietly side by side and their focus was on one area.

Lucinda adjusted her position to peer to the left to identify what the animals were focused on and she saw a figure. In the dim light, the figure appeared ghostly pale and she could see the figure moving and the frequent sound of giggles. With shock, she realised that the figure was Niamh, and she was dancing naked in her front garden in front of hundreds of wild animals.

The dancing was completely natural and unrehearsed, in time to some unheard music tempo. The pure pleasure in the dance moves and the giggles moved Lucinda and she wished she could join in. She felt a great pleasure in simply watching this spontaneous event as it was unfolding in front of her eyes.

The dance went on for a considerable amount of time, and then suddenly, Niamh stopped. She appeared to bow down to the animals as if thanking them and then she turned and headed around to the back garden and into the house. Lucinda saw the animals begin to disperse slowly into the dark of night.

Now she knew for certain, that Niamh had been bestowed.

Chapter 14
AGATHA CONLON 1972

Eighteen months had elapsed since the two women had moved into the house at 14 Liddle Street, Coburg purchased by May. In that time, business had increased, and the girls were busy every day of the week with regular customers as well as new ones, an endless stream of new ones. Instead of advertising every week in the newspaper, they limited the advertisement to one edition per month. This afforded them more than enough customers and they often wondered how they would ever find time for a holiday or a rest.

The back garden was thriving, and much time was spent pruning and tending to the vast array of flowers, herbs, bushes and trees that they planted or were already in cultivation. Agatha was experienced in growing vegetables as her family had in Ireland, though she found the climate so vastly different. In Ireland, due to the cold and wet, they grew mostly potatoes and root vegetables, but here in Melbourne, they had the opportunity to grow tomatoes, cucumbers, lettuces and enough other types to feed the two of them all year round. They even had their own lemon tree, orange tree and limes as well as plums and nashi pears.

Agatha often thought of her mother, and knew she would have loved Australia with the warm weather and abundance of available fruit, vegetables and meat, but the biggest change was that she was not taunted and harassed for being a witch. In fact, it was quite the opposite. The Melbourne public were fascinated by the fact that they were real-live witches. The regular customers adored the two women, May in particular, and the rest of the public couldn't get enough of them.

Only yesterday, Agatha had been filling out a form to apply for a Learner's Permit so she could learn to drive a car. As she always did where asked what her occupation was, she wrote 'witch' and her employer as 'Marvellous Maybelline'. The girl behind the counter at the Road Traffic Authority read the answer and her face broke out in a large grin.

"Oh, are you Marvellous Maybelline?" she asked.

"No. My employer is," Agatha answered.

"Oh, how wonderful. My friend Irene and I want to have a reading. Oh, we must do that soon. How lovely that you work for her," the girl gushed.

Agatha thought her mother would laugh at the absurdity that she left Ireland because the people couldn't accept a witch in their area, and here in Australia, it was embraced so enthusiastically.

Agatha and May's relationship had grown close in the time they had known each other. Each enjoyed a great sense of humour and wit, with May being the most outrageous. Although both true witches, they had grown up in different families and different countries and possessed different abilities. Each was able to learn much from the other, and together, they grew their magical skills.

There weren't too many altercations between them, luckily thought Agatha. The last time May had been angry at Agatha, she used her magic to make Agatha's hair stand on end. Agatha resembled a giant toilet brush with auburn bristles. It took three days to settle her hair back to normal.

Then, there had been that time that Agatha played a trick on May and used magic to make her teeth turn yellow. May had entertained customers all day without realising and hadn't been impressed with Agatha when she looked in the mirror and saw her teeth.

Most of the time, they were the best of friends and amused themselves by playing magic tricks on others including neighbours. They temporarily turned Mr Cook's tomatoes purple on the vine just to see the look on his face when he saw them. Instead of the postman being chased by a dog, they convinced a ginger cat to chase the postman up the road. One time they caused the rain to fall in pink drops and coat everything in pink which wore off as it dried.

Most of their days were spent laughing, joking and enjoying each other's company, both aware that there was a very dark cloud hanging over them. Since the day they met Dora Grimm at the gate when she presented as a customer, an ominous presence of evil hung over them. They knew they were being watched and stalked, and at times were aware the enemy was close due to the tingling sensation.

Both Agatha and May had spied a man following them on several occasions and guessed he was connected to Dora Grimms. In a strange way, they even looked alike with blonde hair and dark eyebrows.

Safety became a more serious consideration, and they began to ensure the windows and doors were locked each night. Agatha had shown May how to create charms and tokens and explained how other magical beings could not enter the house without an invitation. The house became their strong fort where they felt safe and secure behind the fortified walls. Their weakness was when they left the property and they both knew it. Unfortunately, they could not permanently live inside their property and trips outside were necessary. After a few scares when they were aware that the blonde man was following them, they decided to only leave the property when they were together.

Of course, this was not always going to be possible.

Chapter 15

NIAMH FLYNN 2018

Niamh slept late into the morning, resisting the reality of facing the day. Emma would already be on her way down the beach with her family by the time Niamh contemplated leaving her bed. Niamh thought under the circumstances, the safety and familiarity of her bed was preferable. She pulled the doona up over her head, leaving just enough room for air to sneak in.

Eventually, the urge to use the bathroom became overwhelming and she emerged from the bed covers. The bedside clock display announced it was after 10am and she cursed the clock for being so late and ruining her thoughts of staying in bed longer.

She'd been invited to hang out at the shops with two girls she had attended school with. Maddie and Lee were her 'go-to' friends when Emma was not available, and that suited all concerned. She was relieved to have something to do and somewhere to go for the next few weeks and did enjoy the company of the two girls. Aware she was a bit reliant on Emma for entertainment and company, but also knowing that would change once they commenced university and left their childhood behind. For now, she was happy to continue being as much of a child as she possibly could.

Dressed for the day, she headed to the kitchen for a coffee and snack, noting there was no sound in the house and her mother must be out. On the kitchen counter were a few objects that caught her attention, obviously placed there for her to review. One was a large, old photo album with a dark brown leather cover and next to it, was a necklace with a note. The note read, 'Please wear this'.

Niamh picked up the necklace and studied it. On a gold chain, the golden circle of the charm pendant sparkled in the light, recently cleaned. Her mother had always had similar charms and amulets around the house to ward off evil spirits, and her aunts did as well. She had grown up with various tokens and symbols scattered around so it was no big deal. It wasn't until Emma questioned it when visiting Niamh's house once that Niamh realised that other people did not have these charms scattered all over their house and particularly at the doors, windows and entrances such as fireplaces.

This was the first time her mother had asked Niamh to wear one of her charms. She wondered why. Why now? This must have something to do with the witch conversation. Weren't charms meant to ward off witches as well, or was that only some types of charms?

She put the necklace down and made a strong coffee, sipping it as she turned back to the photo album and turned the cover over. She hadn't seen this album before, but knew immediately it must have belonged to her grandmother. There were a number of old black and white photographs of a woman and young girl with a stone cottage in the background. The stone cottage was quaint and charming, with a cottage garden in the front. A memory stirred in Niamh's mind of people dancing and folk music playing, the sounds heard when the grandmother was dying. She shivered involuntarily.

The young girl must be her grandmother when she lived in Ireland with her mother. Niamh studied the faces acknowledging that the quality of the photographs was poor and detail was difficult to see.

She turned the page and viewed a few photographs of her grandmother as a young woman. Her grandmother was quite a stunner and so familiar. Although the photographs were in black and white, her hair easily could have been dark red, like Niamh's was. Looking at her face, Niamh could see her mother and her two aunts, and herself if she was being honest. There was a strong family resemblance between the females in their family. Same long and thick hair, though in different shades throughout the family, same icy grey eyes, red eyebrows though Niamh's were more pronounced than the older generation, same chiselled bone structure and rosebud mouth.

Skipping over the rest of the pages, she saw some photographs of a good-looking man smiling at the camera in most of the photos. His hair was almost to his shoulders and appeared to be dark blonde or light brown and in some photos, he wore old fashioned overalls. There were various photos of him with her grandmother and it didn't take Einstein to work out this must be her grandfather. There were photos of him holding a baby and a few of him with her grandmother and the three girls.

She snapped the cover closed on the photo album, trying to remember if she had been told where her grandfather was or what had happened to him. Idly, she wondered why her mother had left the album in the kitchen for her to look at. She looked at the necklace charm and thought about taking it, then changed her mind and left it sitting on the kitchen counter.

Why did her mother suddenly think she needed a charm? Was this an ominous sign?

Chapter 16
AGATHA CONLON 1972

Ciaran Jordan Flynn lived three doors further east on the same street in Coburg to where the girls lived, at 20 Liddle Street. He was a twenty-six-year-old man considered a baby boomer, entering the world just after the end of World War II in Melbourne with both parents Irish and proudly so. They had immigrated after marrying to seek a better life and better weather. They found both and were happily entrenched in Melbourne life in 1972.

Ciaran was their only child, born late in life unexpectedly and doted upon, hence he was still living with them at twenty-six years of age. Handy with anything mechanical, he apprenticed to the Coburg Main Mechanics garage on Bell Street ten years earlier and was now a fully qualified vehicle mechanic.

Agatha and May decided to jointly purchase a vehicle to drive as neither had sat their driver's licence yet, and both had managed to secure their Learner's Permit. They purchased a Toyota Corolla, a small car with only two doors. To use the backseat, the passenger pushed the front seat forward and climbed through to the back. The car was bright sky blue, and the girls nick-named her 'Lola'.

Lola sat out the front of the house parked on the street waiting for the girls to sit their license and make use of her. So far, they had only managed a few driving lessons which had not gone particularly well. The driving instructor, a bespectacled middle-aged man, had very little patience and the two excitable girls were more than he could cope with. In frustration, May used magic to give him a bad case of eczema causing him to scratch non-stop and eventually, they decided to use magic to give themselves a driving license without having to do anything further. Agatha did worry that it may be obvious to other people that both girls had licenses but were completely unable to change gears.

One afternoon, Agatha spied a man inspecting Lola quite openly. This stranger walked around her, head cocked on the side as he studied every panel and tapped at her wheels. He didn't look like a Grimm or an official parking inspector, dressed in overalls and work boots, and covered in black grease. After a few minutes watching him, Agatha decided to confront the stranger.

"Excuse me, can I help you?" Agatha asked, standing inside her gate calling out to him.

He looked up with his messy, dark blonde hair blowing back in the wind and grinned at her, not embarrassed at being caught studying her car but in a genuine friendly manner. For the first time in her life, Agatha felt weak at the knees, and she smiled back at the stranger.

"Hey there, I've seen your car parked here for a few weeks now, and thought I'd look it over and offer to fix it up a little. You know, shine it up, repair a bit of rust and make it look like new," he said brightly, wiping his black greasy hands on the legs of his overalls.

"Oh ... why would you do that?" asked Agatha, feeling a bit flustered and unsure what to say.

"Not for any money," he said, looking alarmed that she may think he was after money. "I have a bit of spare time, and I love working on cars, and you're my neighbour, after all."

"After all ... yes ... I am ... we are," Agatha stammered.

"Are you Irish?" he asked, head cocked on the side again, blue eyes gazing into her soul.

"Yes. I moved here two years ago," she said shyly, and felt her face blush. She thought it was because he was looking at her so closely, so deeply, as if he could see inside her mind.

"My parents are from Ireland. I'm Ciaran and live just up there." He indicated with his hand a house further on in the street.

"I'm Agatha, and my friend who lives here is May," she said warmly.

"So, how about it?" he asked.

"How about what?" she asked, confused.

"Umm ... that I do some work on your car," Ciaran said.

"Lola."

"Huh? What's Lola?" Now he was the confused one.

Agatha laughed. "Lola is the car. That's her name. She would love some attention."

They both laughed and he arranged to take her to his garage the next day. For a few weeks, he spent time on Lola until she sparkled in the sunlight and the engine purred. Before long, he was helping the girls with their driving skills on various, interesting drives around the local area.

May adored Ciaran and couldn't believe how fortunate they were to live so close to this polite and kind man. It was difficult not to like Ciaran and they never heard him say a cross word or act in anger in any way.

Agatha was totally smitten and it was three weeks before she realised that he felt the same. It was just after he had completed the latest wax on Lola and was showing Agatha the result, when he became tongue-tied and twitchy. It took at least five minutes for him to gather the courage to ask Agatha to go out with him. May, who was peeking out the window at the time, would later swear his face was the colour of beetroot.

After the first date to a coffee shop, they became a couple and spent time together on weekends and the occasional date night during the week. They attended a local cinema as the movie, *The Godfather*, had just been released in Australia, caught the train into Melbourne to view the festive shop window at Myer when it was Christmas, travelled to Ferntree Gully to ride the Puffing Billy steam train to Emerald and dressed up in their finery for the Melbourne Cup race at Flemington.

Ciaran's parents thought Agatha was the most idyllic creature they had ever met. Who ever thought that in this far-flung country, they would find an Irish girl so perfect for their son? Agatha was cautious about telling them that she was a witch, knowing how superstitious the Irish are, and fearing their disdain resulting in Ciaran wishing nothing to do with her. Instead, she alluded to the fact that May was the witch, and she was the assistant and roommate. His parents, Meg and Jim, had been away from Ireland long enough to have left the superstitions behind in their native country and embraced the Australian culture.

Ciaran and Agatha dated for close to twelve months before Agatha thought it appropriate to confess to him that she was a true witch. She discussed the situation with May and how she felt confident the relationship was becoming more serious. May agreed that she should be honest with Ciaran and also that he should be aware they were often stalked by a blonde man and at times, a blonde woman.

Agatha chose to tell him in the large garden behind their house, where they could enjoy privacy and should Ciaran became upset with her, he could just walk off home. They sat at an outdoor wooden bench under a large tree and Agatha sought the courage for her confession.

"Ciaran, there's something that I must tell you ... about me. Something that I've kept hidden." She stole a glance at his face and saw he was grinning.

"You're not secretly a man, are you?" he asked, jovially.

She tried not to laugh at his humour, biting on her lip. "I'm ... well, I'm really a witch, a true witch. It's not just May." He was still grinning, and she frowned, puzzled at his reaction. Did he think she was joking?

He put his hand out and took her hand, drawing her close to him. "Agatha, I already know that," he said calmly. "I've known that almost from the first time I met you." He pulled her close into a hug. "Did you think I didn't' know?" he asked softly.

"Well, yes. I didn't want to scare you off," she admitted.

He released her from the hug and lifted his hand to play with a loose auburn curl on her forehead. "I love you and I want to marry you. Nothing is going to scare me off, even the fact that you could get angry with me and turn me into a bullfrog."

This time she did laugh. "Oh well, I'll make sure it is a handsome bullfrog though. There is something else."

He looked at her expectantly.

"We're being stalked by a man and a woman, at least we think it's only the two of them. The lady booked an appointment with us some time ago, and we knew as soon as she got out of her car that she was evil."

She looked closely at his face and could see she had his full attention. "You see, there are some people out there that have magical powers and want to harm people like us ... witches."

"So, what happened when she got out of her car, and you realised this?" he asked.

"May and I stood at the front gate and told her she couldn't come in. She tested us a bit with her magic, tried to get in our heads but she wasn't strong enough. Then she left but since then, we sometimes see a man following us or spying."

She could see Ciaran's face change a little and become sterner.

"Does he have blonde hair?" he asked.

"Yes. Blonde hair, dark eyebrows and probably in his thirties or so," she answered.

"I've seen a blonde man hanging around from time to time. I've always thought he must be a bit of a peeping tom and had the hots for some girl in the street." Ciaran said, shaking his head.

"He's been stalking us for two years and sometimes, we see her, the woman who came here. Her name is Dora Grimm," Agatha explained.

"Ok. Thanks for telling me. Next time I see him, I'll be telling him to bugger off."

Chapter 17

NIAMH FLYNN 2018

Are you sunburned yet?
Spending today with Maddie and Lee.

Niamh was undecided exactly when she felt she was being watched, or even if that was what was happening. It was a gradual realisation, and she was convinced it was all in her imagination. At times she was positive that there were eyes on her, but when she scanned around her periphery, there was no indication that anyone was looking her way.

She was accustomed to the occasional male glances in her direction over the past twelve months as she matured with her tall, leggy frame and dark red hair, but this felt different. This was not a feeling of admiration or curiosity, but angry and evil danger. It made her hair stand on end and shivers run up and down her spine.

Niamh felt this odd feeling after she caught the train into the city as she walked through Melbourne Central on her way to meet up with Maddie and Lee. She continued to act unaware and resume her journey, but every fibre of her being was tense and on guard, ready to defend if needed. Was she losing her mind? Why did she suddenly feel this way?

She had been catching public transport around the suburbs of Melbourne all her life and knew the system well. She always felt safe and secure. There seemed to be more people around today than there had been all summer, and she reasoned it was the Boxing Day sales still in force and people venturing out to get away from the summer heat.

Niamh was relieved when she saw the two girls waiting for her at the laneway café. They ordered iced coffee and sat at the outdoor table in the narrow laneway behind Melbourne Central catching up on all the gossip since they had last seen each other. Before long, she was laughing and joking with the girls and the thought of being watched disappeared from her mind.

It wasn't until later in the afternoon as the small group left the shoe shop where Lee had just purchased new shoes that Niamh felt the hair on the back of her neck prickle. Quick as a flash, she spun around and looking directly at her ten metres away was a young man. He immediately spun and looked away as if all was in innocence, but she had seen the startled look on his face when she had caught him.

He sported very fair blonde hair, almost whitish, spiked up a little and yet his heavy eyebrows were quite dark, light brown eyes and she guessed him to be in his early twenties. She openly watched him now and saw him moving through the crowds and heading away through the shops as if he had not been watching her at all. Perhaps she was mistaken, and it was all innocent. She shook her head, thinking she had been a bit nervy ever since her grandmother had died in front of her.

At the end of the day, she said goodbye to her friends, and they all arranged to catch up again the following Saturday at their local shopping centre. Niamh headed to the train station for her ride home and endured a crowded train where she had to stand the whole way, holding on to a pole to keep upright.

Once off the train, she hesitated before walking home as she usually would. Instead, she zig-zagged around a few streets and wandered through a park, sitting on a park bench for a few minutes to ensure there was no one following her.

Once assured that there was no one around, she wandered home, halting just inside her front gate and stared up at the house. Above the front door was an object that appeared to be fastened to the house. It was the shape of a cross and as Niamh peered at it, she could see it was made from sticks and grasses like reeds, all intertwined and plaited together. It was quite an incredible looking natural cross and she immediately knew her mother had created this and that it was a Brigid's Cross, to ward off evil and protect the health of the inhabitants. No doubt the neighbours would think them weirdos.

The very sight of it filled her with foreboding.

Chapter 18
AGATHA CONLON 1972

"Did he really say he wanted to marry you?" asked May, as Agatha told her how the confession with Ciaran had gone.

"Yes. He did," said Agatha, smiling at the memory of it.

"I'm so jealous," said May, pretending to pout. "I'm a bit worried about him confronting the stalker though. This guy may have magic, and Ciaran could end up a target too," said May.

"I wonder if the blonde man and Dora Grimm are related, like brother and sister or something. They do kind of look alike," said Agatha.

May stood and collected the phone book, returning with the large white volume which sat near the telephone in the hallway. "Let's find out how many Grimm's live in Melbourne," she said.

She turned to the G section of the huge tome and moved her finger down until she reached Grimm. "G & D Grimm, 44 Fisher Parade, Ascot Vale," she read out. "That's it. They're the only Grimm's."

"G and D. He must be her husband then," said Agatha.

"Maybe they inter-marry so they keep the magic. He could be her brother. Keep it in the family, so to speak," said May and they both stared at each other wide-eyed at the thought.

"I think we should drive past their house. You know, just to see where it is and what it is. 'Know thy enemy' is the old saying," said Agatha. "I'll ask Ciaran if he'll drive us."

May nodded, and it felt as though they were taking back a small amount of control rather than sitting back and letting themselves be stalked unfettered. They were not prepared to sit back and be victims in this saga which was not of their doing.

The next afternoon after work, Ciaran picked up the girls in his bronze-coloured Ford Fairmont and they headed to Ascot Vale, a fifteen minute drive from Coburg on the north side of the city. As they passed a sign for *Melbourne Zoo*, Ciaran asked Agatha if she had ever visited the zoo, and when she said she hadn't, he promised to take her soon.

The section of Ascot Vale they headed to was very up-market and expensive. Ciaran drove slowly down Fisher Parade, and the girls cautiously peered out the car windows.

"Someone's home," announced Agatha.

"How do you know?" asked Ciaran, glancing over at Agatha as they had not quite reached the right house yet.

"I get a tingling sensation when a witch or a magical person is anywhere near me, and I can feel it now," she answered.

"Me too," said May. "Chances are that they feel it too and know we're outside. That'll scare their socks off."

The reached number 44 and looked up at the tall brick fence with security gate, and behind the fence they could see the top of a brick house several storeys high. It was very imposing, expensive and private, designed to keep people out.

"Seen enough?" asked Ciaran and the girls agreed.

He drove slowly away down the rest of Fisher Parade and headed back to Coburg.

"That place reeks of someone with lots of money," said May.

"... and someone looking for privacy and security," added Agatha.

"Why would they care about poor little nobody's like us?" asked May. "Why stalk us?"

"Because we're witches. Obviously, having witches around threatens them in some way and they want us gone. Don't forget, we don't know exactly what they are. They're not witches, but they are not normal people either," said Agatha.

"But ... they haven't tried to harm you, have they? They are just stalking. Is that right?" asked Ciaran, concerned.

"True, but I think they're waiting for the right opportunity. What would be the purpose in just stalking for the hell of it? They can't come on to our property to do us harm so that's what ...," Agatha started to say.

"Why not?" interrupted Ciaran.

"Other witches or people of magic must be invited. It's like this rule. So, they can only get us if we're not on our property and usually, we're together. Hard to get two people at once and harder to get two people in public where you might be seen and arrested," Agatha added.

"So, you think they're serious about actually hurting you, as in killing you?" asked Ciaran.

May and Agatha looked at each other. "Yes, I think they would. If stalking us was to scare us then why keep it hidden? Why not let us see him?" said Agatha.

"I agree," said May. "I've a bad feeling about the whole thing."

Chapter 19

NIAMH FLYNN 2018

The three teenage girls sat outside on the deck in their shorts, hoping to add a little summer colour to their winter white legs. Being a red head, even a dark red/auburn one, Niamh's legs were never tanned. She had been spared from freckles, but her skin was a soft almost translucent milky white unlike Maddy and Lee with their tanned Australian legs. She still enjoyed the warm sun tingling on her legs so kept them in the bright sun for as long as she could.

Niamh's mother brought out iced water in a jug and glasses for the girls and they sat up on their beach towels to sip the refreshing liquid.

"Thank you, Mrs Flynn," responded Lee.

"Oh please, call me Lucinda." She smiled warmly at the girls, pleased to see Niamh laughing and enjoying their company and thinking how lovely to have a houseful of children, even big children like these three.

So, Maddy ... tell Niamh about your stalker," teased Lee.

"Stalker?" asked Niamh, sitting forward to pay attention. "What sort of stalker? Like a Facebook stalker?"

"No. A real one," answered Lee.

Maddy put her glass down and looked across at Niamh. "I 've seen this guy everywhere I go lately. Seriously! If I go to the supermarket … there he is. I go to the hairdresser, and I see him walk past the shop. I get on a train, and I catch him peeking at me from the other end of the carriage."

"Oh, that's creepy," said Niamh. "Who is he? Do you know him?"

"No. I don't know him, but he looks kind of cute." She giggled and Niamh looked at her frowning.

"How long has he been stalking you for?" she asked.

"Ummm … I don't know. Maybe a week or so." Maddy shrugged.

"Hey, I got a photo of him," said Lee, grabbing her phone from her towel and flicking through screens. She passed the phone over to Niamh.

Niamh stared at the small screen, and she felt a chill run up her spine. The photo was at a train station with a crowd of people on the platform. Staring straight at the camera from a distance of around twenty metres was a young man with pale blonde hair and dark eyebrows. She recognised him instantly as the young man she had felt watching her in the city the previous week. At the time, she had thought he was watching her, but now she realised that he must have been watching Maddy.

She looked up from the phone at Maddy and smiled awkwardly. "It would creep me out, some guy following me everywhere. There are psychos out there. He could be checking you out to kidnap and murder you." She finished dramatically but she saw Maddy flinch and look alarmed for a moment.

"He doesn't look like a psycho or a murderer," said Lee.

"Oh, really? What does a psycho look like?" asked Niamh sternly.

The three girls stared at each other, realising the foolishness of the comment.

Niamh looked back at the photo in front of her thoughtfully. "When was this photo taken?"

"About ninety minutes ago at the station," answered Lee.

"So, he was following you today? He could've followed you here?" said Niamh, as a statement rather than a question.

Maddy nodded. "Yeah. He probably did."

Niamh looked away uneasily. The thought that this person might know where she lived bothered her more than she could account for, and she couldn't work out why she felt that way. After all, this guy with the black caterpillar eyebrows was stalking Maddy, not her.

Chapter 20
AGATHA FLYNN 1973

Ciaran and Agatha embraced in the kitchen and May could hear little endearments even though she was trying hard not to listen.

"Oh, stop it you two," she said in mock frustration at them.

Ciaran and Agatha had been married for six months, and May thought the honeymoon would never end. They moved into May and Agatha's house as there was plenty of room, and better for a newly married young couple to live with May than Ciaran's older parents. May did concede that Ciaran was very easy to live with and such a helpful person around the house. She joked, telling him to introduce her to his friends.

Agatha and Ciaran agreed that it was difficult to comprehend that such a beautiful person as May didn't seem to attract boyfriends, and they decided everyone thought of her as a sister rather than a partner. Ciaran was sure the right person would come along and sweep her off her feet.

Agatha had made a small charm necklace and threaded it onto a silver chain, asking Ciaran to wear it around his neck. She had made it as small as she could, knowing Ciaran wasn't really a necklace kind of guy and mechanics generally don't wear any form of jewellery.

She had made the necklace with a mixture of her hair, saliva, herbs and leaves and cast protective magic over it. She hoped it would keep Ciaran safe should he run into blonde Mr Grimm.

May sensed Agatha was pregnant before Agatha had even realised. One morning, Agatha walked into the kitchen and May jumped up excitedly, announcing that she could hear the baby's heartbeat, and it was a girl. Sure enough, a few weeks later Agatha tested positive for pregnancy, and they all were happy to take May's word for it that it was a girl.

Ciaran was delighted as were his parents. They had reached middle-aged when Ciaran made an unexpected arrival into the world, so were now in their seventies and thought they would never see grandchildren.

Ciaran and Agatha agreed that their children's names must be Irish names so they chose Bethany for a girl and Sean for a boy. The third bedroom in the house was redecorated as a child's nursery and the three of them eagerly awaited the birth.

"Do you think my baby will be a true witch?" Agatha asked May.

May thought for a moment. "I don't think she is. I can't feel any magic from her. Maybe having a normal person as a father takes away the magic gene," she suggested then paused. "Naw, that doesn't make sense, does it? Chances are my father was normal and probably yours too."

"If a child is not a true witch, does that mean the gene is gone forever, or is it a recessive gene that sits hidden and needs another recessive gene to reignite the true witch gene again?" Agatha asked.

"Crikey," said May. "So, your daughter would need to marry a son from a true witch to make that a possibility."

"Come on, May. You'd better have a few sons in the future," said Agatha and they both laughed.

"Do we really want our children to be true witches anyway?" May asked. "I've never really thought about it before."

"In Ireland, I would have said no. I don't want a child that is a true witch due to the poor treatment of witches, though I think it would have happened to any child in our family even if they were not a true witch. Here in Australia, it's different. I don't think the child would be treated different or bullied as long as they were brought up with manners and the right attitude," said Agatha.

Later in the day when she was alone, Agatha thought seriously how she felt about her child not being a true witch. She reasoned that Ciaran was just a normal person and she couldn't love and adore him any more than she did. Her child could still be a witch, just not a true witch. By definition, a witch learns magic with potions, charms, herbs and spells but a true witch is born with magic powers.

Carrying her first child made Agatha more aware of how vulnerable she was, and the stalker threat was very frightening. She needed her magic more than ever to keep her and the baby safe. She barely left the property, feeling safe behind the fence, and the onus was on May to conduct the shopping. She then worried about May on her own and beseeched her to be super careful when out and about.

One afternoon on a Saturday, Ciaran spied the blonde man in the small laneway. He had used the laneway to travel down to the shops as a shortcut and was on his way back when he saw the figure of a man at the entrance to the laneway, peeking out and waiting. Ciaran stopped in his tracks and contemplated what to do. He didn't have any weapons on him, only a shopping bag with bread in it. All he could do was scare the man away, and he was also aware that this man may have a magical power which he didn't have a good understanding of.

Slowly and quietly, Ciaran crept up the laneway, keeping to the left side to keep his profile low. He could see the man was a stocky build with blonde hair starting to grey slightly at the sides, wearing khaki-coloured trousers and a brown shirt. Camouflage?

He was only ten metres behind him and was surprised the blonde man had not yet realised he was there. He deduced that the man must be intent on something in the street, and he did seem to be almost shaking in anticipation of something. Up close, Ciaran could see he had a quite large knife in his hand. Frantically, Ciaran tried to remember where May and Agatha were. He was sure Agatha was home but possibly May had walked down to the shops.

Taking a deep breath from ten metres away, Ciaran yelled loudly.

"WHAT ARE YOU DOING?"

The blonde man jumped as if stung by a bee and spun around, knife at the ready. His face turned from shock to anger within a very short time, and he walked purposefully toward Ciaran with the knife thrust in front of him. Suddenly, he stopped, and Ciaran could detect a slightly puzzled look in his eyes as he scanned Ciaran up and down, looking for something. His eyes settled on the charm necklace, and he stared at it intently.

With a glance to the side, he stepped around Ciaran and took off jogging down the laneway. Ciaran watched him, knowing there was no point in trying to stop him or subdue him while he held a knife. He was also aware that the charm necklace had just saved him from certain knifing.

He turned and walked toward home, stepping out of the laneway and almost bumping into May who was returning from the shops with a few grocery bags in hand. Two of them had been spared today ... just.

Chapter 21

NIAMH FLYNN 2018

"Meet you out at the car," called Niamh to her mother.

They had finished breakfast, and it was one of the rare days where they were planning to shop together. Niamh saved money from Christmas to spend and her mother promised to add a little extra to the total so she could buy a few extra items she had been yearning for. Niamh knew her mother was trying to be extra nice to her, hence the extra money but she decided to go along with it.

Niamh headed to the front door as her mother locked the back door and collected her handbag and keys. The car was out on the road in front of the house, so it was easier for the two of them to leave via the front door.

Her mind on the boots she was planning to purchase, Niamh wasn't paying attention to details around her. She pushed the front door open, stepped out and turned to push the door closed. Something caused her to look down at her hand, the hand that had just grasped the door handle, and she saw something on her hand, something red. She shook her hand and felt something flick on to her face. Her cheeks acknowledged the cold sensation of something landing.

A little confused, she stopped and stared at her hand and saw that it was dark red and dripping droplets on to the porch. She looked down at the ground and couldn't identify what she was seeing. Shocked into immobilisation, she stood statue-still while her mind raced in circles, trying to identify what was happening.

It was not until her mother pulled the front door open that the situation changed. Niamh saw the slight confusion on her mother's face as to why Niamh was standing just outside the door where her mother had nearly walked into her, and didn't show any sign of moving. Slowly, she saw her mother look down at the porch tiles, take in the scene and then her mother's head flew up and she let out a blood-curdling scream.

The scream snapped Niamh out of her stupor, and she yelped, throwing herself backward toward the front path where she rolled on to the grass, grazing her knee on the pavers. She sat on the grass, rubbing her injured knee while her mother jumped over the porch pavers onto the path and joined her.

"What is it?" asked her mother, horrified.

"It's a possum," answered Niamh. "Poor thing."

The two of them looked back toward the front door where a large possum had been eviscerated with its entrails hung across the door with what appeared to be masking tape, in a mock Christmas style decoration. The possum's blood was all over the door, the door handle and the step with tufts of fur scattered around the area. Niamh looked down at the soles of her runners and saw the blood and pieces of guts stuck in the tread and knew these runners were destined for the rubbish bin.

"Who would do that?" asked Niamh.

Her mother just stared at her in a strange silent manner and then the two of them spent some time cleaning up the remains of the possum and washing down the door and porch. From sheer terror when they first discovered the carnage, the two of them were calm and accepting while cleaning up and returning the property to its former self.

Niamh wondered if her mother knew more about the attack on them than she was letting on, just by the pursing of her lips, the frown on her face and a feeling that she was hiding something. What could her mother possibly know? What could she be hiding? It was ridiculous so she put that idea out of her mind. Her only possibility was the blonde stalker with the caterpillar eyebrows but why on earth would he do this to an animal and leave its entrails on her door? That was just bat shit crazy stuff.

Chapter 22

AGATHA FLYNN 1973

Baby Bethany was born at the local hospital in the usual scene of panic once everyone realises the water has broken. Once labour started, not long after Agatha's water broke, it was chaos at The Coven. Each time there was a contraction, May braced for what was going to happen next as the lights dimmed and flared, dimmed and flared and a few exploded into millions of tiny shards. One time, the wall in the kitchen cracked from the floor right up to the ceiling during a contraction. Another time May felt the whole house shake, and in a particular violent contraction, she saw lightning streak through the window and touch the table, leaving a black char.

How on earth could they take her to hospital? She could burn the place down or incite an earthquake. If ever Ciaran doubted the witch story, it was proven to him many times over during the labour. May wanted to hold off them taking her to the hospital until the last moment for obvious reasons. If May had felt confident to deliver the baby herself, she would have suggested they don't attend hospital at all.

Ciaran walked the floors of the house with Agatha, rubbing her back and soothing her. A few times in the midst of a contraction, he found himself thrown backwards as if an invisible force had picked him up and tossed him. Agatha was apologetic each time a contraction ended but May and Ciaran knew it was not intentional, and she had no control over it.

May phoned the hospital to find out how far apart the contractions needed to be to ensure Agatha was at the hospital in time. She was told four minutes as it was a first baby, however as her water had broken, they should make their way to the hospital as soon as possible. The sound of a crash indicated another contraction had just occurred and a vase had ended up in pieces on the floor. May breathed a sigh of relief that it was only a vase. She informed the hospital that they would be on their way shortly.

Ciaran brought the Ford Fairmont as close to the front gate as possible and they manoeuvred Agatha into the back seat with May tending her while Ciaran drove. Although May now had her driver's licence and could drive, it was fortunate she didn't drive this time as Ciaran found that when Agatha was having a contraction on the way to hospital, he had to suddenly veer around trees falling on the road and other cars smashing into each other. It was with relief when they arrived at the Preston and Northcote Community Hospital (PANCH) without an accident.

Bethany was born within thirty minutes of their arrival at hospital, screaming and healthy. By the time of her arrival, the delivery room was in complete disarray with everything upturned, the window smashed as well as the ceiling downlights and the doctor was close to a nervous breakdown. The two nurses had already abandoned ship and sought safety elsewhere.

From the moment the baby arrived, the room was immediately transformed into a calm and serene place with Ciaran and Agatha gushing over the baby and peace restored. May disappeared to seek a chair for the doctor to sit down, and let the nurses know it was safe to re-enter the delivery room.

Bethany had tufts of strawberry blonde hair on her cherubic face and perfect features. Agatha thought of her own mother often and wished she could have seen her grandchild. Bethany was cherished by her parents, her grandparents and May, her godmother.

May was completely besotted with her and in the months to come, could be found nursing her or peeking on her in her cradle.

"May, you are going to make the best mother in the world one day," said Ciaran, watching May soothe the crying baby.

"I can't wait to be a mother. Then I'll really be 'Marvellous Maybelline'," she joked.

Chapter 23

NIAMH FLYNN 2018

Niamh couldn't erase the image of the slaughtered possum from her mind the entire time they were shopping. She couldn't imagine that anyone could harm an animal in such a callous manner and to what purpose? Her mother had told her she thought it was a warning but a warning for what? A warning to her or to her mother, or to both?

They didn't arrive home until the afternoon and installed a Google outdoor security camera near the front door. Niamh felt a solidarity with her mother that day after finding and cleaning up the bloody mess at their doorstep in the morning, shopping and then the installation of a security camera. She was sitting in the kitchen with her mother when there was a knock at the front door.

Her mother looked at Niamh with a serious expression. "I invited my sisters here today because it's time we all talk before someone gets hurt. You saw what happened this morning. Will you please stay and listen?"

Niamh looked at her for a few minutes and then agreed. After the horrible event of the morning she was in the right frame of mind to listen to what they had to say.

Her mother invited the two aunts in and after a greeting, they sat in lounge chairs while her mother made them coffee.

"Bella, Beth, I want you to know that last night someone gutted an animal, possum we think, and spread its intestines and blood all over our front door for us to find this morning," her mother said calmly.

There was a gasp of shock and horror from the two aunts.

"We didn't see anyone but have a camera out there now," she told them. "I ... umm ... have also kept a secret from you both," she said.

The two aunts looked at her mother with a worried look. What on earth was she talking about? "Niamh is a true witch and I've always known. That's why I kept her away from mum."

The two aunts looked at each other with raised eyebrows and wide-eyes while Niamh looked at her mother waiting for more information. This was news to her too.

"Niamh, although you don't really understand it yet, you are a true witch, and what was left at the door this morning, was a warning."

"A warning for what?" asked Niamh, looking at her mother and then the two aunts.

"There are people in the world that wish to harm witches," her mother answered.

"I don't understand any of it," said Niamh, frustrated. "If I'm a witch, how would anyone even know? Why would they want to warn me? Warn me about what?"

There was silence as the three sisters looked at each other. Finally, her mother spoke.

"The three of us ... we're not true witches. We have spent our whole lives ... ashamed really, that we're not true witches like our mother was."

"Are you sure she's a true witch?" asked Arabella, peering at Niamh as though seeing her for the first time.

"Yes. She is. I knew from the moment she was born, and mum saw her once when she was a young girl, and she knew it too," said her mother.

The two aunts looked at each other and there was a slight nod between them, an acknowledgement that they understood and accepted this to be true.

"We always felt like imposters because we're only normal people and not a true witch. Our mother ... your grandmother ... she was difficult ... she was a true witch. I think she was disappointed in all three of us because we didn't inherit the gene that made us a true witch," said Bethany.

"What is a true witch?" asked Niamh.

Another silence as the sisters tried to determine how to answer.

"Well, we three are witches but we are like ... cultivated witches. We grew up in the witch world and know how to make remedies and spells and how to treat people for ailments, but we have no natural abilities. A true witch is born with natural ability, with magic, and it is recognisable to other witches and people with abilities," said Arabella.

Niamh looked at her mother. "And you think that I'm a true witch and have inherited some witch gene? Why do you think this? Have you always known this? Why have you never said anything to me?"

Her mother sighed and looked out the window, choosing her words carefully. "We didn't have a very happy childhood." She looked at her two sisters who nodded slightly in agreement. "I didn't want that for you. I thought if I kept you away from the witch world, you could lead a normal life and may never even need to know what you are."

"What about your children?" Niamh addressed her two aunts.

"Witches are only females, so we were relieved we had boys," said Bethany.

"Because we're not true witches, we assumed we wouldn't pass any witch genes on to our children so we wouldn't need to worry about it. That's why we didn't know or suspect it about you, Niamh," said Arabella.

"It wasn't until our mother was dying that we realised she must bestow upon someone, and I guess I thought ... it may turn one of us into a true witch." Bethany looked at Arabella and then at Lucinda, and her eyes welled with tears. "Did you think that too?"

They nodded.

"Is that why you took me to see her when she was dying? So, she could bestow on me?" asked Niamh looking at her mother, feeling a little anger flare.

"No," her mother responded, offended. "Not at all. It didn't even cross my mind. I had kept you away from her all these years and with her dying, I thought it was the right thing that all her children and grandchildren say goodbye."

"What is bestowing anyway?" asked Niamh.

Arabella cleared her throat. "A witch can't take the magic with her and must bestow it on someone, or so we understand. Bestowing gives the magic to someone, so if you are a true witch like your mother said, then it would make the magic stronger."

"Did she bestow on you, Niamh?" asked Bethany.

All eyes were on Niamh and almost holding their breath waiting on the answer. Niamh looked at each of them in turn and then after a few minutes of contemplating her answer, she spoke firmly, "Yes. She did."

The silence continued for another few minutes as the three sisters digested this information. Bethany suddenly stood up and turned to the other two sisters. "I'm going to get May."

Chapter 24

GEORGE GRIMM 1974

George was beginning to feel he was aging before his time. At thirty years of age, the sides of his hair were completely grey already and he would swear he saw a few grey strands in his dark eyebrows that morning.

He blamed Dora, his wife, for the early greying hair and stress in his life. He liked to think he was a simple man and liked the simple things in life, - his house, his car, his children and his leisure time. He didn't seem to get any leisure time these days as Dora was constantly on his back demanding he go and rid the world of the witches.

The witches, the witches, the witches, the witches, THE WITCHES ... HE WAS SICK OF HEARING OF THE GODDAMN WITCHES!

He wished they had never found out about the witches, but that horse had bolted. It had been years now since they became aware of the shorter red-haired witch called Marvellous Maybelline and the taller auburn-haired witch, the one that had the stronger magic. He had explained to Dora that the taller one was now a mother and rarely even left her house. It was always Marvellous Maybelline who went to the shops alone almost daily.

Dora wanted him to kill Marvellous Maybelline as a way of weakening the taller witch. Marvellous Maybelline was not very powerful so should be relatively easy to kill, provided no neighbours interrupted him as had happened on two occasions before. With Marvellous Maybelline gone, the taller witch would have to go to the shops herself and that would leave her open to attack.

Dora had it all worked out.

His mother-in-law, Hannah Grimm-Hauer from Sydney thought he was a weakling, according to Dora, and had offered on many occasions to send family members to Melbourne to sort their little problem out for them. That was how the in-laws saw the witches in Melbourne, as their little problem. It made him angry every time Dora spoke these words to him, as if he were a useless, ineffectual schoolboy who needed the big boys to come and sort out his affairs.

He was going to have to destroy the two witches just so he could have some peace and quiet in his life. He promised Dora he would assassinate Marvellous Maybelline this week and now she was reminding him every morning of his promise.

Over coffee and muffins, he determined that he would have to take the afternoons off for the rest of the week as it was afternoons when Marvellous Maybelline ventured out to the shops. He had no way of knowing which day would be suitable, as it was determined by a number of factors including the number of people on the street that day, whether Marvellous Maybelline walked past the lane where he had chosen to hide, and even what the weather was going to be.

Whatever the possible variations, he was ready this time. He would not fail and be the laughing stock of the family any longer.

Chapter 25

NIAMH FLYNN 2018

Within fifty minutes, Bethany had returned with someone who would change Niamh's life. May entered the room and embraced Niamh's mother and Arabella as they ran to her.

"Ah, my girls, my girls. How I have missed you."

All Niamh could see was a tangle of arms, bodies and various shades of red hair, then the cuddling was over, and Niamh stood to meet the newcomer. She was quite short, only reaching Niamh's shoulders in height, and petite yet rounded with large plump breasts. Niamh guessed her to be aged in her late sixties with dyed red hair and bright red lipstick. What immediately drew Niamh to her was the huge contagious smile that lit up her entire face and the warm, intelligent eyes.

"Niamh, I'd like you to meet 'Marvellous Maybelline'," her mother announced.

Maybelline opened her arms wide and enveloped Niamh, pulling her into the softness of her chest and squeezing her tightly. Niamh couldn't help but giggle like a child.

"Niamh, I'm so pleased to meet you, darling girl," she gushed, squeezing harder. "I saw you when you were a baby and I've been just dying to meet you." She squeezed harder. "Marvelous Maybelline, gosh, I haven't heard anyone call me that for years. I sound like a cheap brand of cosmetics, don't I?" She addressed Niamh, winking and grinning. "Call me May." She took Niamh by the hand and dragged her over to sit with her on the couch.

"Oh, but you are so pretty," May said, looking Niamh up and down while Niamh blushed self-consciously. "You do look a bit like your grandmother did when she was young. Oh, how I miss Agatha." She blinked back the threatening tears then looked back at Niamh. "Now, Bethany tells me that you are a true witch, bestowed and have no knowledge of witchie stuff. Does that sound right?"

Niamh nodded and smiled at this strange character who she couldn't help but like. May put her hand on Niamh's knee. "Now, don't you worry about a thing, love. May is here now."

She positioned her bulk to be comfortable and returned her hand to Niamh's knee. "Let me tell you about who I am. I'm a true witch, born overseas ... well ... Tasmania, actually, and I was a very good friend of your grandmother, Agatha. I've made a living all my life out of being a witch, you know, with crystal ball and reading Tarot cards and all that. I don't have any children, and I still am actively a witch."

She eyed Niamh speculatively. "Agatha did bestow upon you, didn't she?"

"Well, yes. She did say something like that, and she grabbed my arm, but like, I haven't changed or anything."

"Hmmmm. Has there been any changes at all, anything different to normal?" asked May.

Niamh frowned. "There's been animals outside my window at night and they're not scared of me. I can walk among them. Does that count?" Niamh's face lit up when she recalled this special behaviour.

"And ... I have wondered a few times if someone is watching me." She saw alarm on May's face and she heard rustling as the news caused restlessness from the other three women.

"Tell me more about why you think you're being watched," said May.

"Sometimes I just feel the hair on the back of my neck prickle, but I can never see anyone obviously looking at me. In the city last week, I turned suddenly and saw this young man looking straight at me. The weird thing about him is that I found out he is stalking my friend, Maddy, so maybe I was mistaken, and it wasn't me he was watching after all," Niamh explained.

"What did the young man look like?" asked May.

"Maybe early twenties, very pale blonde hair and dark heavy eyebrows."

She heard multiple intakes of breath from everyone, and she sat forward, glancing over at her mother and aunts and wondering what had been so alarming.

May squeezed her knee. "He's from the Grimm family, and he is not stalking your friend. He is after you. He's probably following her because he lost you, and he thinks your friend will eventually lead him to where you live."

"She did. She was here yesterday," said Niamh nervously.

"And someone left a death warning on your front door last night," said Arabella.

"Is that what it was, a death warning? What the hell is a death warning?" asked Niamh, voice rising.

May patted her knee to calm Niamh down, and it worked. Niamh sat back and took a deep breath.

"The Grimm family are not witches, but they have similar abilities, and they don't like competition. They like to be the ones with all the power in Melbourne, so you are a big threat, just like Agatha and I were."

"Were?" asked Niamh.

"They left us alone once ... after ... well, after a certain incident that I'll tell you about one day. I guess the younger generation are more dangerous to them. They all have blonde hair and dark eyebrows, and I think they're inbred." She chuckled quietly.

"I think the death warning left on your front door is to frighten you, which it has and to let you think they are very powerful and they know where you are," said May.

"But ... I don't have any power," said Niamh.

"Yes, love. You do and I am going to teach you how to use it."

Chapter 26

AGATHA FLYNN 1974

It was almost Christmas 1974 and the end of another year. Agatha watched Bethany let go of the chair she had been standing holding on to and hesitantly take her first steps across to grip Agatha's legs.

"Oh, clever girl," Agatha said to her and swung her up to kiss her cheek.

There would be no stopping the little girl now that she had become confident enough to attempt walking. She couldn't wait to tell Ciaran when he arrived home from work. He would be disappointed he missed the big moment. May had left for the grocery store only thirty minutes earlier so she had also missed the first walking episode.

Agatha walked through to Bethany's room to change her nappy when she suddenly felt a strange sensation wash over her. She stopped and waited to see if the sensation would become more pronounced or give an indication what was going on. As nothing further happened, she completed the task of changing the wet nappy and wondered if it was something to do with the new pregnancy that May had announced to them only a few days ago.

May had declared Agatha pregnant with another girl on the way. Agatha had not yet visited a doctor or performed a home pregnancy test, but she imagined May was probably correct and had no reason to doubt her. She touched her stomach fondly, delighted to know that she and Ciaran would be adding to their little family. She hoped everything was fine with the pregnancy and the sensation was not relating to losing the baby.

Heading back out to the kitchen area with Bethany in her arms, she glanced up at the wall clock. Four-thirty in the afternoon and the day was still bright and sunny. Something felt strange and again, she couldn't pinpoint what it was. Ciaran was due home in thirty minutes and May should be back any moment now. She stood in the middle of the kitchen as the strange sensation again washed over her. Something was wrong and she didn't feel it was her; it was one of her loved ones. In a panic, she spun around wondering who was in harm's way and what she could do to help.

Scooping up Bethany, and the bag which held spare nappies, bottles and formula, she raced out the front door and headed three houses further up the road. She could hear noises at the other end of the street but didn't want to waste time looking to see what was happening. Quickly, she banged on the front door of Jim and Meg, Ciaran's parents and as Meg opened the door and expressed surprise and delight to see them, Agatha pushed Bethany into her arms and asked if she could watch the child for possibly a few hours.

Satisfied that her daughter was safe and in good hands, Agatha raced back on to the footpath and ran back past her house and continued running to where the noises were coming from. As she ran, the sensation she had earlier became more pronounced and dread overtook her.

This was bad, really bad and someone she loved was dying. It was May, her darling May and she could feel her life ebbing away.

Ahead, she could see a group of people milling around and could hear a range of voices. Puffed from the exertion of running down the street, she pushed through the group, yelling 'excuse me' as she manoeuvred through until she reached the centre. Lying on the ground like a tossed away ragdoll and covered in blood was May. Agatha screamed out and threw herself down next to her on the ground. The air cracked as a loud thunderclap was heard above and lightning streaked across the sky followed by further thunderclaps.

"We've called an ambulance," a man told her. "Do you know her?"

Through sobs, Agatha managed to say, "Maybelline Connor, my friend."

May's eyes were closed, and she was not conscious. Agatha could see wounds down her front which were wet and bloody and she could hear her heartbeat, softer and weaker than it should be. She studied the wounds and realised none had pierced her heart, but they were seeping blood and at least one of the wounds was gushing, causing a large blood loss. Through tears, she placed her hand on May's face whispering to her.

"May, May, sweetie, its Agatha. I'm here. We're going to get you fixed up. It's ok," she whispered as soothingly as she could. She gently pushed May's hair back from her face and noted her breathing was laboured.

Looking down May's body, she located the gushing wound and placed her hand over it, blood immediately coating her hand red and leaking through her fingers. Agatha moved her hand slowly and concentrated all her magic on slowing the blood flow in this wound and healing the damaged tissue. She whispered incantations and leaned forward to kiss May on the cheek. Energy, like small bolts of lightning moved through her hands and she felt the blood flow slow. The magic did its trick, and the damaged organ began repairing unseen to the outside eyes.

The sound of sirens reached her, and she knew help was close by. Agatha looked down at the wound she had been healing and removed her hand, noting that the blood was now oozing and not gushing. She could hear May's heart still weak but more stable than it had been just moments ago. Relieved and knowing the ambulance and police were just arriving, she moved back slightly, still on her knees and looked up at the people milling around.

"Did anyone see what happened?" she asked.

A young boy of about nine years old stepped forward. "I was coming up the lane and a man was running down the lane. I could see a knife in his hand and blood all over him. Then I saw this lady lying on the ground and I thought she was dead."

A lady next to him patted the boy on the head fondly. "Good job Nicky. You got help and you saved this poor lady."

The group split apart, and two medics appeared and immediately started tending to May. Agatha sat back giving them room but not prepared to leave May's side. She was aware of the police asking questions of the people standing above her and then one of the police squatted down next to her.

"Excuse me. You are a friend of this lady, yes? he asked, his voice gentle and kind.

Agatha dragged her eyes away from May to glance at the policeman. "Yes. Her name is Maybelline Connor." She turned back to watch May, afraid if she stopped looking at her, May may stop breathing. She could see the medics had put an oxygen mask on her and was checking her blood pressure and assessing the injuries.

"What's your name, miss?" the policeman asked.

"Umm ... Agatha Flynn. May lives with my family," Agatha said absently.

Suddenly, she became aware of someone above her and Ciaran's arms pulled her to her feet. He wrapped his arms around her. "Are you ok? Oh my God. Agatha, are you ok?"

She nodded and tears fell from her bloodied face. "It's May."

"You go with the ambulance." He indicated to where the medics had lifted May on a stretcher. "I'll talk to the police and meet you at the hospital."

Chapter 27

NIAMH FLYNN 2018

"But I don't understand. How would they even know I'm a witch or who I am, or that my grandmother died? It doesn't make sense," said Niamh.

"Well, we can sense things, and they can too. They're aware of who else in Melbourne has power. They would have known the moment your grandmother died. There's a good chance they had someone nearby waiting for it to happen. Did you feel any tingling? They would have realised there was a young witch who was bestowed. They might not have known who you were, but they knew of your existence. I don't know how they haven't found you before now." May looked up at Lucinda reproachingly.

"What do they want?" asked Niamh.

"In a perfect world, they would like us all dead. They almost succeeded with me once." May looked down at her hands for a moment. "It's harder to kill someone in today's world than it was hundreds of years ago when witches were murdered all the time. If there was an opportunity where they could kill us without getting caught, damned right they'd kill us, but I think the warning they sent is to scare a young witch into being submissive and quiet."

"But ... but ... I don't have any power. How do I let them know that?" Niamh could feel the frustration building.

"You do have power. You just don't know how to use it yet and you need to learn ... quickly. No witch will ever be subservient to the Grimm family." May almost spat the last sentence out and Niamh looked at her in surprise.

May turned back to where Niamh's mother was standing. "Lucinda, I'd like to spend a few hours with Niamh every day for a few weeks. I'm going to turn her into a proper witch. Do you understand?"

Lucinda nodded her head. "I thought I was doing the right thing keeping her away from it all, but now I see that it was the wrong thing to do, and I've put her in a dangerous position," she said, her voice teary.

"I get it. You thought you were protecting her. I understand but you should have spoken to your mother and let her train Niamh. Now, it's time to get serious about it," said May firmly.

"Are we safe?" asked Niamh. "Can they come into our home and hurt us?"

She saw her aunts shaking their head to say no.

"No," said May. "They cannot enter your home without being invited. I saw Brigid's cross above your front door which is the strongest charm. You are safe inside your house."

"Just don't go inviting them in," said Arabella, trying to make a joke but no one laughed.

"What about in my backyard?" asked Niamh, addressing May. "Can they enter?"

May thought for a moment. "Well, technically they can. Have you got side gates you could put locks on? I would be locking them to make it very difficult for them to do that. If you are out there and see someone you don't recognise, immediately get inside the house. Also, put a charm on the front gate."

Niamh nodded.

May stood. "Ok. Well, I must be on my way. Got a few frogs to boil." She looked at Niamh grinning and winked. "Can you come tomorrow at 10am?"

Niamh nodded.

"Your mother will give you the address." May looked at the three sisters fondly. "I really miss your mother, you know."

May had a way about her that assured everyone that it would be fine. Niamh liked her and couldn't wait to start learning to be a witch. She still found it outrageous and unbelievable but was prepared to go along with it and see where it all led and obviously, this other family, the Grimm's thought the situation serious enough to warn her via a dead possum. She hoped the dead possum would be the last time they tried something like that. Just the thought of hurting an animal made her blood boil.

Chapter 28

GEORGE GRIMM 1974

George Grimm had been a hero in his home for at least two hours until the late news on television announced a breaking story that a young woman had been stabbed in Coburg by an unknown assailant and was rushed to the Preston and Northcote Community Hospital where she was in intensive care.

Dora had thrown a tea towel at him in disgust upon hearing the breaking story, having earlier made him his favourite meal of crumbed lamb cutlets, mashed potato and peas as a treat.

"You didn't even kill her. She's just hurt. You fool!" she had screamed at him. "What's my mother going to say about this?"

He swore under his breath and had been so positive she was either dead or about to die. He had stabbed her at least ten times and blood had spurted out everywhere. He had been covered in the spray and had to quickly get out of that neighbourhood before seen by someone other than the young boy. His car was a mess, and he still needed to spend a few hours that night, cleaning up the blood before anyone saw it.

He would never forget the look in her eyes as he stabbed her. From surprise and shock, he had seen her eyes turn to intense fear, then acceptance and finally, surrender as the light in her eyes seemed to vanquish. He knew she was dying. He could feel it. Why was she not dead?

"You could get caught now, you know. You said a young boy saw you. Did he get a good look? He might be able to point you out or get a sketch drawn of what you look like," Dora said, still fuming. "What would I do if you go to prison? Need I remind you that we have four children and another on the way?"

He looked up at his wife and her swollen belly and thought about the young boy who had seen him in the lane. It is quite dark with the overhanging branches so possibly the boy didn't get a good look at him. One thing he knew, he couldn't go back to that street, lane or area again in case he was recognised. He had spent so much time there that neighbours had seen him from time to time.

If the police talked to all the neighbours, they could piece together a sketch of him he thought. It was only one year previously that the other witch's husband had seen him in the laneway. This was all way too close for comfort.

He stood up from the table. "If the police come knocking, you'll have to say I was here with you and the kids. I'm going to burn the clothes I wore and clean out the car. There's blood all over it," he said. "Dora, don't forget, they only know our name because YOU were the one who made an appointment with them and gave YOUR REAL NAME."

With that, he turned and marched out of the house to complete his cover-up of the crime, leaving Dora stunned and mouth agape.

Chapter 29

NIAMH FLYNN 2018

After her two aunts had departed, her mother walked back into the kitchen and Niamh was waiting for her. Mother and daughter stared at each other for several minutes, waiting to see who would speak first.

"You should have at least told me about the witch world," Niamh said reproachingly. "You left me vulnerable."

Her mother looked suitably ashamed of herself. "I'm sorry, Niamh. I really am. I thought I was doing the right thing." She brought out the gold necklace charm from her pocket. "Will you wear this now? Please."

Niamh looked at the charm spinning in her mother's hand and reached out to take it. She knew she was going to need all the help she could get against a whole family of powerful people. Silently, she placed the necklace around her neck and fastened the clasp. Her fingers continued twiddling the charm and she excused herself to go to her room.

> *Magic family called Grimm stalking me. Killed a possum on my doorstep. Wish you were here. Whole world gone mad.*

Niamh sat at her desk and sent a text message to Emma. Her mind imagined Emma in her swimming outfit, relaxing on the beach with her family. Niamh sighed, wishing she was with her friend to tell her about this strange turn of events that had happened in the past week. What would Emma say? She'd probably think it was cool. Niamh didn't think it was cool at all.

She turned on the computer screen and saw she had several friend requests on Facebook, Instagram and Tiktok. Suspiciously, she scanned the profiles of these people and realised she didn't know any of them, and they had no other friends in common. She deleted the requests and blocked the new people following her on the other social media platforms.

Realising that these people stalking her, would have searched for her online as well, she went through the settings on all her applications and enforced stricter privacy rules. A search revealed her name mentioned in relation to a sports event at her school last year but there were no photographs or detail about her. She felt she was being paranoid but needed to take some control and tightening online security was one step closer to taking control.

These people knew where she lived, and she felt like a sitting duck. How dare this family think they could frighten her or stalk her friends. Her anger simmered away under the surface as she contemplated the current situation. Was her mother safe? If it were true that her mother was not a true witch, was she in any danger? It was true that she was often at odds with her mother, and they grated on each other regularly, but she despaired at the thought that her mother could potentially be harmed in any way.

How could she even prevent anything from happening? She knew nothing about these people, and they apparently knew things about her. They held all the power and she hated the imbalance of power. In a burst of frustration, she pushed back firmly on her chair sliding back one metre. At the same time, a pile of books crashed on to the floor beside her. She looked down at the books puzzled, wondering how they had fallen. She hadn't even touched them. Shaking her head, she picked up the books and placed them back on her desk.

Tomorrow, May would help her realise her witch powers and she knew tomorrow couldn't come soon enough. How ridiculous to have some sort of powers and yet have no idea how to use them or what they could do. At least she was safe in her house, or that was what she had been led to believe. No one could enter the house with the Brigid's Cross above the door and other charms at all entrances, not without an invitation.

She didn't want to find another dead animal tortured and spread across the doorway in a *Jack the Ripper* style. What could she do to prevent someone from entering the property at all?

She had an idea.

Chapter 30

AGATHA FLYNN 1974

When Ciaran arrived at the hospital, he carried a bag containing a set of clean clothes for Agatha. They embraced in the hospital waiting room and Agatha explained that they had wheeled May off to surgery and it was expected to take a few more hours before they heard any news. Agatha headed off to the bathroom to clean up and change clothes.

Looking down at the dress she was wearing, it was covered in large blood stains and when she looked in the mirror, she barely recognised herself. Blood and tears had streaked her face, and she looked a mess. Not wanting to frighten any visitors to the hospital, she filled the basin with warm water and washed herself down before changing into the clean dress Ciaran had brought for her.

"What did you tell the police?" Agatha asked Ciaran when she reappeared in the waiting room.

"I didn't give any details about the Grimm family. I just said that we had been aware for a few years that May had been stalked by a blonde man and gave them the details of when I caught him in the laneway last year with the knife. Do you think we should tell the police about the Grimm's?" he asked.

"No. We can't do that. It's too ... complicated. If we start talking about magic and the Grimm family wanting to kill us because we are witches, I think the police would think we're all mad." Agatha said. "You've said the right thing."

"How was May when you got to hospital?" he asked.

"She was holding her own. I heard one of the medics say she had a punctured lung and lots of stab wounds in her lower body. Thank goodness they didn't get her heart." Agatha started quietly weeping again and Ciaran put his arm around her in comfort.

"Oh, May. I don't want to lose her," Agatha wept. "How are we going to stop them from doing this again and it might be worse next time?"

Ciaran thought for a moment. "I don't believe this blonde man will be back. He would be totally deranged to appear in our street again. Too many people have seen him now."

Agatha nodded at the logic. "They might send someone else. How do we protect ourselves and our children?"

It was close to five hours before a doctor appeared in the waiting room looking for them.

"How's May?" asked Agatha, clutching Ciaran's hand tightly.

"She's in recovery now. We had to perform surgery to repair her liver and there was a fair amount of internal bleeding. She has a punctured lung, but a few wounds missed vital organs, lucky for her. There is damage to her reproductive organs, fallopian tubes, uterus, ovaries and so forth. There's a good chance they will cause scarring as they heal." The doctor pulled a face and lowered his voice.

"She may need a fertility expert in the future if she wants to have children."

"Oh. She might not be able to have babies?" asked Agatha.

The doctor shrugged. "We don't know. Maybe not. She's lucky to be alive and has lost a lot of blood. She'll be here in hospital for some time."

"Thank you doctor. Can we see her?" Ciaran asked.

The doctor agreed but explained she was not yet awake. The two of them washed their hands and donned masks before entering the Intensive Care area where May lay on a hospital bed, hooked up to various monitors. She looked so pale and small, and Agatha couldn't help but break into tears again at the sight of her.

She held May's hand and talked to her, telling her that she would be fine. May showed no sign of hearing her and the beeping from the machines monitoring May brought some confidence to Agatha that she was in the best place she could be.

When they were ready to leave for the night, Agatha leaned forward and kissed May on the cheek, whispering in her ear. "Don't worry. The Grimm family will never touch you again."

Chapter 31

NIAMH FLYNN 2018

Niamh stepped out It was after 11pm when Niamh quietly opened the back door and ventured out on to the back deck. She had remained in her bedroom waiting for her mother to retire for the night and it seemed to take forever, before she heard the familiar sounds of her mother preparing for bed.

into the cool night air and closed the door quietly behind her. Looking up, she was rewarded with a brilliant view of the moon, almost full and which added a slight glow to the darkness. She closed her eyes and breathed in deeply, the night, the dark, the world. So many sensations tickled at her as she stood with her eyes closed. The sound of cicadas echoed in her ears as if serenading her, the moisture in the air from the night rehydrating the dry grass from the summer day, the heart beats from the animals hidden in the undergrowth and yet, not afraid of her. Had she always been able to feel this or was this a new awareness of life around her?

After several minutes of standing with her eyes closed and breathing in the night life, she opened her eyes and smiled. The night was her friend and welcomed her, wondering where she had been while it had waited for her emergence. This was her domain and for the first time in her life, she felt every inch a witch. She knew in that moment that one day, when she knew how to be a witch, she would be the most powerful at night.

Niamh walked around her backyard noting that the neighbours had all retired to bed for the night and there was minimal amount of electric light. She couldn't detect any other humans in the vicinity or any Grimm's. Silently, she removed all her clothes and left them lying discarded over the lounge chair on the back deck. Wearing clothes suddenly felt so awkward, claustrophobic and unnecessary.

Stepping through the side gate to the front yard, she walked naked and gracefully across the grass to the front gate. The gate was an old-fashioned wire gate about one metre tall, and it sat in the middle of a wire fence about the same height. On the inside of the wire fence was a garden bed which stretched across the front of the property, leaving a gap in the middle for the gate and concrete path that ran up to the front door of the house.

Niamh stood at the gate, then carefully unlatched the gate and stepped out. With her body just on the outside of the property, she squatted down and urinated. The stream only lasting a few seconds before she cut it off, saving as much precious liquid as she could for further fortification of the border. Moving across to either side of the gate, she systemically squatted and left a small urine puddle every metre.

Satisfied with protecting the front boundary, she moved to the side gate and urinated at that point and then at the steps to the front porch. By the time she had reached the backyard, the well was dry, but she knew she had the entire night to replenish so she could also protect the back borders before morning.

She saw a pair of rabbits appear from behind the side shrubbery and stop, watching her. She smiled at them in greeting. No one was going to attack her animal friends tonight while she was on watch. She almost wished someone would appear as she felt an overwhelming urge to attack and seriously harm someone, an enemy, the enemy.

Maybe this was going to be her life's work, removing the Grimm family from the possibility of harming any witches. She smiled in anticipation. She was ready for this challenge and felt a power and strength deep within her core that she never knew existed.

By morning she had completed fortifying the property and felt confident that no one would be able to cross the lines without invitation. She quietly dressed and headed back to her bed to catch a few hours sleep before she was due to meet May. Her last waking thought was that she must clear the video footage on the security camera of her naked and peeing all over the front yard before her mother saw it.

Chapter 32

JUSTIN GRIMM 2018

"Time is of the essence," his mother growled to him.

Justin had just finished explaining why he had not ventured out to North Ringwood to frighten that red-head witch last night, but his mother was not impressed with his excuses. The truth was that he was so pleased with himself over the possum guts he had hung all over her door the night before that he thought he would take the night off and sleep.

He hated being the youngest and the shit kicker of the family. His older brothers and sisters, as well as his cousins could sit back and issue instructions and opinions on the situation while he had to lose a whole night's sleep and hang about outside the house of this red-head girl.

He didn't even know her name, only that her surname was Flynn. He'd seen that on the mail left in their mailbox one night. He thought his family should be proud of him and praise him for the inhuman number of hours he had put in to finding this girl, where she lived and scaring the bejesus out of her. After all, they had not known anything when they had first become aware of her.

He'd spent so much time hunting around shopping centres, train stations, cinemas and city laneways, with nothing to go on other than she was a red-head and a late teenager. His family said that he would instinctively know when he was near her, and he had no idea what they were talking about as he had yet to experience anything relatable.

The old witch had died apparently but he had never met or seen the old witch, so it didn't mean much to him. His parents knew her and knew she was dying so they had sent one of his siblings to monitor the situation. At the time of her death, all the dogs in the neighbourhood had begun howling and had howled for ten minutes. His brother, Beaton, had been sitting on a park bench in the gardens of the aged care home at the time the howling commenced and immediately known what it meant. He watched as the three sisters left an hour later with the red-head teenager and a few boys. He knew immediately that the teenage girl was the one bestowed. He could feel it, a skin prickling sensation all over his body, a strange fear curling in his stomach, and his family knew none of the three sisters were true witches.

A family meeting ensued and discussions into the night and the house had been filled with people. His mother, his four siblings, their partners and children, and his grandmother had all sat around the long dining table at his place and talked about the latest developments. They all agreed that the primary focus was to find out where the red-head teenager lived and as much information about her as possible. The only clues they had were that the three sisters lived in the outer eastern suburbs of Melbourne, somewhere near Box Hill to Ringwood, which was on the Lilydale train line.

This important and yet, boring and low-end task, had been given to him as he was the youngest in the family, at twenty years of age and had yet to prove himself in any way. He didn't mind at first and looked forward to using his talents to track down this strange young witch, similar in age to himself.

Once they knew who she was and where she lived, there would be more family discussions to determine what to do with her. They would make a decision on her future before she became a strong witch and was untouchable. Beaton reported that most likely, she was unaware of even being a witch and didn't appear very strong at the time of the old witch's death.

There was some support in parts of the family that they should expedite the process and kill the young witch. With the old witch dead, and the three sisters not being true witches, it only left this young witch and Marvellous Maybelline, the other old witch. Maybelline was due to expire before too long so if the young witch was eliminated, there would be no stopping the Grimm family from owning Melbourne and it being witch-free.

The rest of the family felt that it would be enough to frighten her into not embracing her true witch status. The modern world didn't allow much wriggle room for witchy spells and magic, so there was a good chance that this young witch would just let it go, especially if threatened and intimidated enough.

Justin had been tasked with finding her, learning as much as possible about her and commencing a fear campaign against her. So far, he had located her in the city with two other girls and immediately known it was her by the skin prickling sensation. In the crowd leaving the Melbourne Central train station afterward, he had lost her in the rush and ended up following one of her friends. He had successfully stalked the friend hoping it would lead to where the young witch lived, and sure enough, a few days later the three girls had met up at the house of the young witch.

Now he had her address and surname and had been spending many hours day and night watching. The night before, he had found great enjoyment in killing and disembowelling the possum that had been waiting outside the window of the young witch, and then for extra effect, he had taped the intestines all over the front door. He just wished he could have taken a photo of his work to show the family.

They had not been as impressed as he had hoped, claiming that he had given away the fact that they knew where she was. The family hadn't made it clear to him that he was to keep it secret so despite what his family thought, he was pleased with himself.

Now, his mother was giving him a hard time for sleeping and relaxing the last day and night instead of watching the young witch. He had told them not to worry, she would just be sitting in her bedroom and not doing anything. She was probably too scared to even leave the house now. He smiled to himself, pleased with that thought.

Just to be sure, he would head over to the witch's house today for a long session of watching and maybe he would up the ante and try to find her name.

Chapter 33

AGATHA FLYNN 1975

It was six weeks before May was released from hospital, and she was under strict instructions to rest and not lift anything. The change in May was so profound that Agatha was really concerned about her mental health. The happy, chirpy young woman had disappeared and this version of May was quiet, wishing to be alone, staring into space or sitting in the garden.

Partly, Agatha knew May would be suffering from shock and in some ways, Agatha still had not recovered from the shock of seeing her best friend hurt, bloodied and near death. She could only imagine the shock that May must be feeling and the residual pain from her injuries.

The probability that she would not bear any children had sunk May into depression, and being around Bethany and knowing that Agatha was pregnant again must be very difficult for May. Agatha felt May's pain and could see it in her aura that she was surrounded by sadness and pain. May just needed some time to recover physically as well as psychologically.

Agatha also wondered if that was the end of it with the Grimm family. She agreed they were unlikely to send the blonde man back to this street again after he had been seen by so many, but she still felt it was unfinished business.

Agatha started searching for a kitten for May, but the stipulation was that it must be black. Of course, a witch must have a black cat. Everyone knew that. It took three months to locate a black kitten but she arranged for Ciaran to pick it up one night and they presented it to May. It was a young male, jet black with not a single white hair that they could see and big golden eyes.

May burst into tears and buried her face in the soft fur of the kitten. Agatha knew in that moment that finding this kitten was the best thing they could do. The kitten was lightweight enough that May could easily pick him up and carry him around and cuddle in her time of need. May named the kitten 'Warts' and they all had a giggle over the witch with 'Warts'.

Warts ended up being a big hit with the customers. May eventually reopened Marvellous Maybelline six months after the attack on her. She was smiling and talkative, but that incident had taken more from May than just the loss of ever having children. It had taken away a bit of her enthusiasm, her zest for life and appreciation for all around her.

The last six months had been filled with concerned customers phoning, sending cards or leaving flowers or gifts on the doorstep. Agatha marvelled at what generous and caring people the Australians were and appreciated how loved May was.

May never spoke of the attack in any detail and hadn't mentioned the Grimm family either. Agatha knew that in time, she may wish to talk about it but she could take her time. Agatha was the one that couldn't stop thinking of the Grimm family.

Chapter 34

NIAMH FLYNN 2018

May's house was an older style weatherboard house on a huge block in Coburg, eight kilometres north of Melbourne. As soon as Niamh walked through her gate, she was assailed with the sound of birds chirping and could smell a variety of herbs and flowers. All around her were an array of colourful plants and flowers, a suburban oasis. It took her breath away and she marvelled that there could be this oasis in the middle of Coburg.

As she mounted the steps to the front door she saw a plaque on the wall with the inscription, 'The Coven', and a brass plaque informed her that 'Marvellous Maybelline' lived here. She giggled as she remembered May saying it sounded like a brand of cosmetics and Niamh pictured May as a large magenta coloured lipstick.

She rang the doorbell and could hear May approaching the door, talking to herself.

"Niamh, darling. Were you followed?" May asked, grabbing Niamh by the arm and dragging her into the house before peeking out. It felt like an episode in a spy movie.

"No. My mother dropped me off and I can't sense anyone near me," she responded.

"You can sense it?" asked May, looking at Niamh in surprise.

"I can now. Something changed last night, and I am more aware now," answered Niamh.

May led her down a hallway with a high ceiling and fretwork high above, and down to a drawing room at the other end of the house with large windows to view the jungle of a backyard. Niamh gasped at the sight of all the green. It felt like she had walked into another world, an exciting, friendly and slightly eccentric world.

Looking around, Niamh could see the kitchen at the other end of this long room and immediately, her gaze fell on a black cauldron sitting on the old low wood stove, bubbling away with steam rising from the gentle simmer.

"Oh, a cauldron. Oh, I love it," Niamh gushed, walking over to the cauldron and inspecting it. As she walked closer, she could smell the delicious smell of vegetables cooking and realised May was cooking soup in the cauldron. She thought it was the most beautiful thing she had ever seen. Every witch must have a cauldron, she decided.

Her gaze swept over the rest of the room, noting the trinkets, charms, garlic and other herbs hanging upside down from the ceiling, the ancient looking straw broomstick in the corner. It was designed to be the kitchen of a witch in everyone's imagination. It was perfect.

"I bring my customers into this room," said May conspiratorially. "They expect to see charms, trinkets, broomstick, and all the various ingredients of potions. It makes them feel they are getting value for their money." May chuckled.

"Let's sit at the table," suggested May, leading Niamh over to the small wooden table. "Would you like coffee?"

Niamh looked around at the odd, antiquated kitchen and wondered how she was going to make coffee. There were no obvious signs of a kettle or any modern appliance. Did May produce a cup of coffee via magic? May read her mind and suddenly opened a cupboard with a theatrical "Ta Da." Niamh couldn't help but laugh. Hidden on a shelf in the cupboard sat a new Nespresso machine. It looked so out of place in this odd little kitchen and hence, hidden in a cupboard.

Before long they were sitting sipping their large mugs of Nespresso Stormio coffee with an overhead fan giving them a slight breeze.

"Did you know your grandmother lived here, in this house?" May asked her.

"No," said Niamh.

"She lived here along with Ciaran, your grandfather and two of their girls. They then moved three houses up before your mother was born." May's eyes glazed over as she recounted the memory. "Now, tell me about you becoming more aware." May gave Niamh her full attention.

"Well, I snuck outside late last night when my mother went to bed. I ... don't know, I just stood outside in the dark and closed my eyes and breathed in the night. Then, everything changed, and I suddenly felt like a witch. I could hear and smell things that normally I wouldn't be able to, and I was aware of everything around me. I fortified the boundary of the property."

"How did you do that?" May asked.

Niamh looked at May straight-faced. "I pissed along the border."

May's eyes widened and then a grin broke across her face. "Oh, my girl. I'm so proud of you. Welcome to becoming a true witch. We are going to have such fun."

Chapter 35

AGATHA FLYNN 1979

"May, I'm worried. I can feel something bad's going to happen. I don't know where or what, but I feel a dread in my heart. I can't seem to shake it," said Agatha softly.

May put down her coffee cup and stared at Agatha. "Maybe, it's because you have such a perfect life, that your mind tells you it is too perfect and can't last."

Agatha shook her head and sat down opposite May at the table. She looked down at one year old Lucinda crawling around under the table. "I couldn't' bear anything to happen to my girls."

"Nothing is going to happen to the girls," said May, firmly.

Agatha's negativity was making May nervous. She couldn't feel anything amiss, and she glanced around at the doorway to see a charm hanging above the door.

"Are you worried about the Grimm people?" she asked Agatha.

"I don't know. I feel like it's ... like a premonition or something," said Agatha.

May felt a chill go through her. She looked down at Lucinda, such a pretty, cheeky little girl so close to walking now, and over to the other side of the kitchen where six year old Bethany and four year old Arabella were playing with dolls. Surely, nothing could happen to them.

Agatha and her family had lived in this house for two years now after Ciaran's father died and his mother decided to move to an aged care facility. They were only three doors up the street from May's house and yet, May missed them terribly. She was so used to having people underfoot and children laughing or crying, that she hated the silence in her own home now. Luckily, she had Warts to keep her company and entertain her.

Neither of them had heard anything or seen anything to indicate the Grimm family were still after them but they also knew to keep aware and be safe. May knew she would always be looking over her shoulder after being attacked as she walked home from the shops. She never walked on that side of the street anymore and she constantly monitored where she was and who was around her. Life was never the same for May since that fateful day.

"Did you have a premonition before my attack?" May asked.

"Not before but I'm sure I knew the moment it happened. I remember a strange sensation and knowing something was wrong. That's why I took Bethany up to Jim and Meg immediately and came looking for you," Agatha remembered.

"I don't think I've ever had a premonition, but you've always been stronger than me," said May. "Can we get the girls to wear charms?"

"Bethany and Arabella, probably but Lucinda could prove more difficult. You know what little ones are like." They both looked down at Lucinda crawling around and trying to eat May's shoes.

"Maybe if you take her out of the house, pop a necklace on her. She'll be too distracted with looking around to bother too much with it," suggested May.

It never crossed Agatha or May's mind to check that Ciaran still wore his charm.

Chapter 36

NIAMH FLYNN 2018

See if you can boil the water," May told Niamh.

Niamh looked at the cup of water sitting on the kitchen wooden counter.

"Huh? What do you mean, boil the water?" she asked, confused.

"Well, look at this cup of water and concentrate. Push your mind to force the water to boil. That's how it works. You focus all your mind power and push for something to happen," said May.

Niamh looked at the cup dubiously. Just a white cup three quarter filled with tap water, sitting there innocently. How on earth could she possibly make it boil? It seemed like a task too far removed from anything she knew. Ok. If May said she could do it, then she would give it a try.

She sat forward in her chair and focused all her attention on the white cup. She noticed the cup didn't have a handle and was a type of tumbler for drinking cool drinks rather than a mug for drinking something hot. She stared, focused and told the water to boil in her mind. She repeated the request a few times silently then urged and pushed, demanding the water to boil.

Nothing happened.

Her mental requests became more urgent, more demanding as the minutes ticked by. She refused to give up and tell May she couldn't do it.

BOIL, BOIL, BOIL, BOIL, BOIL, BOIL!

Her mind yelled to the water in the cup, then taking a deep breath and summoning all her inner strength, she pushed as hard as she could while demanding the water to BOIL.

BANG!

The cup flew straight up and hit the ceiling and stayed there. Niamh and May stared at the white apparition of the cup sitting up there, sucked on to the ceiling and waited for it to fall back down but it stayed glued to the roof. They looked at each other in shock, then May couldn't help herself and started giggling. That set Niamh off and within minutes, the two of them were laughing so hard, Niamh nearly fell off her chair.

"Oh, I'm so sorry, May," she managed to say between giggles. Niamh climbed up on to the kitchen counter and stood, reaching up to disconnect the cup from its nesting place, but it wouldn't budge. She wriggled the cup but it was firmly stuck to the ceiling. She looked back down at May.

"It won't budge and it's really hot. I think it's made from plastic and melted on to the ceiling. I'm really sorry, May," Niamh said, apologetically.

May giggled again. "No. It's ok. Not your fault. I should have thought about not using a plastic cup."

Niamh climbed down and sat at the table again. "Why do you think it went up to the ceiling and didn't just boil?" she asked.

"It's all about control. You learn how to control the different levels of power. In this case, you didn't just push magic at the water, you blew the smithereens out of the cup."

They both looked up at the guilty party now part of the ceiling permanently as if it had always been there, a white nipple poking out of the white ceiling. Then they looked at each other again and burst into laughter.

"Right," said Niamh. "What can I blow up next?"

Chapter 37
JUSTIN GRIMM 2018

Justin drove to North Ringwood still annoyed that his mother had given him a hard time about sleeping the night before. Sometimes he took the train and walked the rest of the way but today he wanted to be able to get there quickly and return home quickly, He parked a few streets away from the young witch's house as he always did and walked around the quiet neighbourhood to her cul-de-sac.

The sun had just set, and it was dark enough to be considered night though he could still see outlines of objects. He had spent so much time watching the young witch at night that he had developed a good sense of sight in the dark and familiarity with the surrounds. As he walked toward her house, he realised that it had been thirty-six hours since he had last been there.

He could see lights on in the house from behind the shutters so he knew they were home, and he smiled, thinking of what mischief he could cause overnight. Last time he had disembowelled the possum and that was going to be hard to beat. What could he do this time to scare her? They had a wire front fence which would be a good place to hang the carcasses of a few animals. Maybe a rabbit or two and a cat or dog. He almost salivated at the thought. Surely, that would impress his mother and the rest of the family.

He had almost reached her fence and glanced around the street to ensure no one was around to view him sneak onto her property. The street was deserted and at this time of night, people would be inside eating dinner or bathing the children. He reached the gate and put his hand out to push it open when he stopped dead in his tracks. He inhaled cautiously; his fists clenched tightly out in front of him. The sweet and strong odour of urine assailed him, and he stumbled backwards as if stung by a bee. Was he imagining it? Cautiously, he stepped forward again and sniffed the air, nostrils dilated. Again, he was driven back and his whole body trembled and shivered. He could also see a hand-made charm had been placed on the gate.

He had never experienced witch's urine and never even knew it was a problem for him, but he had no doubt in his mind what that odour was and what was happening to him. Was there some sort of magic in a witch's urine? He had no idea but all of a sudden, he was the one who was terrified. He walked along the outer wire fence and could detect that the urine trail was along the entire stretch and he knew that she had outsmarted him.

There was no way he could now get inside the property. He was completely exiled to the outside. He stood in the dark, concentrating on breathing to calm himself. What was his mother going to say now? Maybe he should be the one angry as they had never warned him against witch's urine.

Reluctantly, he headed back to his car to report to his family the latest development.

This young witch was proving more difficult than he had anticipated. He thought dealing with her and frightening her was going to be a quick and easy task and would then stand him in good stead with his family. Now he had failed and would be seen as a dud. There had to be a way.

He sat in his car and drummed his fingers on the steering wheel, contemplating the situation. He didn't want to go back and report his failure like a dog with his tail between his legs. What could he do to retrieve the situation and gain control back?

Then it dawned on him. He knew where her friend, Madeline McCraw lived as he had stalked her for a few days until she led him to the young witch. He would go and pay her friend a visit, and although not as good as scaring the young witch herself, it was next best and at least he would not be going home with nothing.

He started up the car and headed to the other side of North Ringwood.

Chapter 38

NIAMH FLYNN 2018

Niamh and May relocated to May's backyard, sitting under a lovely old Oak tree. May thought it may be safer to be outside in case Niamh managed to blow up the entire house. In various locations around them lay the remnants of experiments with magic. A pot plant lay on its side on the ground with the succulent that had once proudly sprouted in such an aesthetically pleasing manner now fried to a crisp. The bird bath lay empty having boiled dry and the branch that they had snapped off the tree lay charred on the ground as if the victim of a bushfire.

May laughed. "Well ... you're certainly destructive." She looked around at the aftermath. "Maybe you'd better practice."

Niamh knew she needed a ton of practice but thought it best not to practice inside her mother's house.

"May, tell me about my grandmother. I never knew her," said Niamh.

May paused and sat quietly for a few minutes staring out at the jungle of a garden. "Well, I met Agatha when she'd only been in Australia for a few months. She came over from Ireland on her own after her mother died," May recited.

"How did you meet?" asked Niamh.

"With witches, we can generally tell if there is another witch in the same area. It's hard to explain, but for a few months I felt this magnetic pull, and one day your grandmother was at the shops nearby and followed her magnetic pull. She found my house and I was waiting at the gate for her, and we recognised the other was a witch. We were immediately friends," May reminisced.

"What was she like? I'm trying to understand why my mother kept me away from her," said Niamh.

May gave a sad smile. "I loved her. She was fun and beautiful, but everything changed when your grandfather died. I'll tell you all about it one day. Agatha became depressed, and the three girls suffered. Your mother blamed the witch life for their upbringing,"

"What was wrong with that life?" asked Niamh.

"Nothing's wrong with it, but it's different to normal people's lives. It can be dangerous and maybe your mother was being protective," suggested May.

"What do you mean by dangerous?"

May paused and sat back thinking. A shadow passed over her face. "Years ago, there was danger from village people who tortured and burned witches. These days there's danger from other people who have some magical ability, because they recognise it in us."

"You mean the Grimm's?" asked Niamh.

"Yes, though there are others. The Grimm family are the ones who are in Melbourne but I'm sure there would be similar families or groups in other cities and countries," replied May.

"Why do they hate us?"

"It's a territorial thing, like dogs I suppose. They don't want to share the city they live in and want to be the only ones who are powerful in the area. Who knows how long it's been like this, but it seems to be an inherited hatred."

"But they have lived here with you and my grandmother in the same city?"

May glanced at her and wondered how much to tell her. She couldn't tell Niamh everything just yet. It wasn't the right time.

"I was attacked years ago ... stabbed and ... nearly died. We suspected it was a Grimm who did it. Your grandmother saved my life," May said in a quiet voice.

Niamh stared at her, shocked. "Oh my god. They seriously tried to kill you?"

May nodded. Niamh could sense her reluctance to talk about it. She was silent for a few minutes wishing she could ask more questions.

"I wish, now ... that I could have known my grandmother before she died. There are so many things I'd like to ask her," said Niamh wistfully.

May sat up straight. "It's her funeral this Friday, isn't it?"

"Yes. It is," answered Niamh.

May thought for a moment. "The Grimm's will be there or send someone."

"To the funeral?"

"They'll be watching. Now that Agatha's gone, they will want to be sure of who's left in the family and where the threats lay," May said thoughtfully.

"Hmmm, interesting," said Niamh. "Forewarned is forearmed."

Chapter 39
GEORGE GRIMM 1980

"Do you realise it's been ten years since we first became aware of the two witches in town and we're no further advanced than we were back then?" said Dora, always looking for a reason to criticise her husband.

"We certainly are further advanced," he responded. "We now know that the shorter one is not from Ireland like you thought. So, she was already here in Melbourne, and we never even realised. Is that failure ours?"

Dora bristled at the insinuation that she had been at fault in any way. "She's much weaker than the taller witch. She must be weak if you managed to attack her, and you couldn't even finish the job."

"If they hadn't advertised in The Age newspaper, then we'd never have even known they existed. Do you ever wonder if there are more in Melbourne that do not advertise?" he asked her logically.

She was silent for a few minutes as she thought of what he had just said. "Our problem is that our families have gone for so long without having to really use our magic that we are the ones who have become weak. We need to practice and use our skills to become stronger and get back to the way we used to be. Our family has hunted the witches for centuries and if it hadn't been for the Grimm family, we'd be over-run with witches. We're pathetic. I'm ashamed of what we are."

"That's ridiculous," said George, dismissing her.

"It's true!" she demanded. "Can't you see it? The rest of the family look down on us because we can't manage our own affairs in Melbourne. Did you know my mother offered to send someone down to sort out what we are unable to?"

George looked at her sharply. No. He had not been aware of that offer. "What do you want to do, Dora?" he asked.

"Well ... I think it's time to clean up Melbourne properly. My mother said that Gerhard, you know ... my cousin, is prepared to come down and hunt the witches," she responded.

"That's not as easy as it sounds. For one thing, any man with blonde hair is going to be a suspect. It's only been twelve months since I nearly killed the small witch so anyone hanging around that fits that description will be reported. Also, their house is guarded so he couldn't step foot on their property. They barely left their house a year ago so I can't imagine that has changed. What I'm saying is that it will be almost impossible to achieve," he finished.

"We've already discussed all this," Dora said, and he stared at her, realising that there had been complex discussions on this topic that he had been unaware of. "Gerhard said he could shave his head and wear different outfits so he may appear as an old man one day and a businessman another day. He also has an alibi for twelve months ago, having not even been in the state."

"So, what's the plan?" asked George, feeling a bit left out and humiliated.

"He is going to check the situation out and assess how hard it will be to kill the witches, and at the very least, he is going to eliminate the husband," Dora answered, unable to contain the smirk that sprang to the surface.

"But he's just normal!" said George, shocked.

Dora was still smirking, but it was gradually turning into a large grin. "Collateral damage. Getting rid of him will weaken the tall one and she's the strongest. We already know the small witch will be weakened by her ... umm ... attempted murder the year earlier. The whole family needs to go."

George looked away, stunned that they would go after a normal person. He was not aware that their family had ever gone after normal people. He couldn't think of anything to say to his wife as the plan was already decided upon and he was obsolete.

Chapter 40

NIAMH FLYNN 2018

The funeral for Agatha Caitlin Flynn was simple and only attended by May, the three sisters and their children. May thought back to the huge number of customers they used to have who would have attended back when they were young. May still had a number of regular customers though she no longer saw new people, whereas Agatha had not been part of 'Marvellous Maybelline' since Ciaran died.

The funeral director was a middle-aged woman dressed subtly and professionally. She delivered a quietly spoken summary of Agatha's life along with a slide show of photographs of Agatha on a large screen.

Niamh thought it depressing that there was not one meaningful or major achievement in her grandmother's life that could be reported. Mentioned was the date she was born, where she came from, her move to Australia and the birth of her daughters. Niamh resolved that one day at her own funeral, there would be something more tangible to report on and that her life would have more purpose. She understood that the funeral director couldn't report that Agatha had been a true witch and give an account of her magic ability and perhaps, there had been plenty of achievements that were unknown.

She looked at the large shiny wooden coffin sitting at the front of the room topped with flowers, and thought back to how her grandmother had looked just before she died. The sunken face and sallow skin and the piercing eyes that had looked up at her. Knowing what she now knew about being a witch, she wished she could have known her. Niamh was sure there had been a lot of interesting and noteworthy events in her life.

Part of the funeral service was tea and biscuits in an adjoining room which Niamh also thought was lame. At her funeral one day, she wanted champagne and lamingtons, not tea and biscuits. The family talked in quiet voices and Niamh learned that her grandmother had amassed a large amount of money over the years and willed it to the three sisters. Also, she had managed to repurchase the old cottage in Ennis, Ireland where she had grown up and it was currently rented out. Niamh remembered seeing old photographs of the stone cottage in the photo album that had been left on the kitchen bench.

Niamh was chatting with her older cousin, Marcus when she felt a shiver run up her backbone and she could have sworn her hair was standing on end. She froze, looked across the room to locate May and saw that she was also frozen in mid-sentence and staring back at Niamh. No one else in the room seemed to be aware that there was a Grimm nearby. Niamh realised that not being true witches meant her mother and two aunts were oblivious to other witches or people of magic. If they had been targets of the Grimm's, they would have been sitting ducks.

Silently, Niamh headed for the door where she could peek out unseen. She saw the Grimm family immediately standing in the carpark. There appeared to be around eight of them and they had arrived in two vehicles parked next to each other. The pale blonde hair they all possessed made it obvious to her who they were. The prickling sensation continued up and down her spine and she glanced back at May who was still chatting with the family, but her attention was on Niamh.

She remembered seeing an old film once where there were a whole village of blonde children called *Village of the Damned*. Seeing this family was so reminiscent of that horror film and Niamh felt a chill. She hoped they didn't have glowing eyes like the children in *Village of the Damned*.

The family headed to the left, led by an older woman who appeared to be the matriarch of the family. She was the only one who no longer had blonde hair. It had greyed to a silver blonde colour. They ascended the few steps to the verandah and entered the main door into the foyer area. Niamh was glad that the service was over and her family were now further away in the refreshments room or the Grimm's would have walked straight into where the service was.

Niamh stepped outside and disappeared from sight for three minutes, appearing again at the door as if nothing had happened. May had been about to venture outside looking for her when she reappeared.

"Where did you go?" asked May.

"I put an Apple AirTag on each of the two cars so I can find out where they live," said Niamh.

May didn't know much about technology but she understood an Apple AirTag to be some sort of tracking device.

The Grimm's remained, speaking to a staff member in the foyer area for another fifteen minutes and then departed. Niamh knew that the short visit was intended to scare her and her family and indicate that the Grimm's were aware of the death of her grandmother and the funeral arrangements.

Niamh smiled to herself. The Grimm family had no idea what they were getting into.

Chapter 41

GERHARD GRIMM 1980

Gerhard Grimm sat smugly in Dora's house sipping tea and feeling important. He was a thirty-five year old bachelor, good-looking and he knew it. His family had been pushing him to marry for years and selected various possibilities in the small pond of cousins and nieces, but he wasn't ready yet. He felt there was something big in the world waiting for him, a super task that would stamp his name in the history books.

This Melbourne job was not his big break, but it was more exciting than sitting in Penrith studying figures for the corporate world. It offered him a change of scenery, an opportunity to impress his seldom seen Melbourne family, and a way to hone his magic skills. He was ready for the task at hand, and he would succeed where George had failed.

George sat in his lounge chair trying to be polite to Gerhard, but Gerhard could see he was sullen and seemed a little embarrassed, and so he should be! Two young girls had got the better of him after all. Gerhard would try not to look too pleased with himself when he removed the witches from existence and made George look even more useless.

Dora and Gerhard had been close cousins when they were children and she doted on him now, bringing him his tea and refreshments. He'd stay at her place while he was in Melbourne and be spoiled rotten. Why not? Back in Penrith, he was basically on his own with this roommate rarely home and was forced to fetch his own food and drink and perform his own housework.

Dora had given him the address of the witches and tomorrow morning he would make a start, driving past and identifying the house, the street and familiarise himself with the shops. Dora had supplied a mud map complete with text that showed where one of the witches was almost killed by George last year, and where there was a laneway. Also marked was the garage where the husband of the other witch worked. Gerhard would need to know all about the husband's routine and abilities to be able to make an assessment.

He was eager to make this assessment and identify the best way for the witches to die. He hoped it would be possible to kill them up close and personal. He knew about a witch bestowing their magic to another witch prior to dying and he had a theory that if he killed a witch and looked in their eyes before they died, he could take their magic like a bestowment. Everyone knew that witches were more powerful than members of his family. He had always been told this information, but they lacked the cutting throat edge that made him so dangerous.

If he could take the magic from two witches when they died, then he would have to be the most powerful Grimm in existence, or at least in Australia. Then he could go on to perform this huge history worthy job in the world knowing he was at his absolute best.

Dora brought out a bucket and towel and placed scissors and clippers on the side table next to him. Ah, yes. He had agreed to shave his head to hide the fact that he had blonde hair while hanging out in the witch's neighbourhood.

"Is it ok if the kids watch? They asked me earlier," Dora asked Gerhard.

"Sure," Gerhard answered grinning.

Dora opened the lounge door and called out, and suddenly six children entered the room ranging in age from fifteen years down to four years. They had been giggling among themselves but stopped and were dead-silent when they spied Gerhard. He knew that children were usually in awe of him, so this reaction was not unexpected.

Dora indicated to each child. "This is Grady, Aaron, Shera, Annastacia, Hardy and little Tarren."

Gerhard studied each child, as if he were a lord looking to purchase a fine horse. He could see Shera was a beauty and would be a knockout when she grew up. He wondered if he hung around in Melbourne, how long he would have to wait for Shera to be old enough for him. Also, the youngest child, Tarren was a stunning looking child, even at four years of age.

Gerhard turned back to Dora. "You've done well, Dora."

She smiled proudly and picked up the towel, placing it around his neck and shoulders to catch the falling hair. Then picking up scissors, she lobbed off the longer part of his locks so it would be easier for the clippers to shave the rest. The golden locks fell to the floor around him and the children sat on the floor in front, mesmerised by this large scary family member who was going to end up bald.

Fifteen minutes later, Gerard ran his hand over his reasonably smooth head and felt sexual excitement at the soft flesh of his bald head. He asked for a mirror and gazed at his reflection, turning his head from side to side, noting how prominent his bushy dark eyebrows were.

"You know, I think I look better without hair," he said to his audience.

Chapter 42

NIAMH FLYNN 2018

Niamh answered her phone cheerily, knowing it was Lee calling and assumed Maddy and Lee wanted to arrange another shopping trip or get together. Briefly, she wondered how she would fit a shopping trip in with her visits to May each day but resolved to work it out.

"Lee, how's it going?" Niamh said.

She could hear sobbing on the other end of the line, and Lee trying to talk.

"What's wrong? Lee, what's going on?" she asked in a panic.

"It's ... it's ... Maddy." The words came out between sobs. "She's in ... hospital."

"Why? What's happened?" cried Niamh, sitting up, heart pounding.

"She's ... she was beaten up."

"WHAT? Beaten up. When? Who?" Niamh was standing now with the shock.

"I'm not sure. I haven't ... spoken with her yet but her mother told me she thinks it was that guy who was stalking her," Lee sobbed.

"OH MY GOD! How bad? How bad is she?" asked Niamh. She could feel a sob caught in the back of her own throat.

"Pretty bad," admitted Lee.

"Oh my God, I can't believe it," said Niamh. "Can we see her?"

"Her mother said we'd be better to wait until she's home which should be in the next couple of days," said Lee and gave another sob.

"Is she going to be ok? Is anything broken?" asked Niamh.

"Broken nose, black eyes, bruises all over, three broken ribs and a broken jaw," repeated Lee remembering what Maddy's mother had told her. "Oh, and some internal bruising and bleeding."

"Oh, poor Maddy. Do you know where it happened? Sorry to be asking you all this," Niamh said apologetically.

"It's ok. He came to her front door and beat her up inside her own house," said Lee.

"Bastard! Poor Maddy. Thanks for letting me know. Please keep me up to date if you learn anything and I'd really like to go visit when she gets home and is up to it," said Niamh.

After her call, she sat thinking and feeling incredibly guilty about what had happened to Maddy. This was the Grimm guy, the one she called caterpillar eyebrows. She was sure of it and wondered what would make him turn back to stalk Maddy when he knew where Niamh lived now?

Anger? To beat Maddy up to such extent reeked of a sheer anger and a desire to hurt and scare Niamh. She felt confident that was the reason Maddy had suffered this attack, to further terrify Niamh. Suddenly, it dawned on her that he could not enter her property anymore because she had fortified it with her own urine and the charm. Could that be it?

She sought her mother and found her in the kitchen, making vegetable soup, or at least that was what Niamh thought she was making. She asked her mother to look at her phone app to see what had happened on the security camera at the front door in the past twenty-four hours. The two of them scrolled through various footage including them returning from the funeral the day before.

Just on sunset when darkness had almost fallen across the screen, they could see someone at the front gate. Luckily, the infrared showed the person up well against the darkness around. The figure clearly had light hair and dark eyebrows and was about to open the front gate when the person stopped dead in their tracks, arm still stretched out.

Slowly, the figure backed up and they could almost see the horrified look on his face. Then he moved out of sight to the right, back into view and then disappeared to the left. Niamh knew he was seeking an entry to the property along the fence line but encountered her pungent smell wherever he went. Finally, he disappeared off the camera and there was no further sight of him.

Niamh told her mother the reason why caterpillar eyebrows was unable to enter the property and what he had subsequently done to Maddy. Her mother was suitably horrified.

Chapter 43

AGATHA FLYNN 1980

At 11.20am on Thursday 6th March 1980 life changed for Agatha and her three young daughters, and the world would never be the same again. Bethany was at school at the time, Arabella should have been in school that day in her first year, but she had stayed home with a slight fever. Lucinda was due to be fed an early lunch and put down to nap.

The two girls at home watched as their mother suddenly stopped in her tracks in the middle of the lounge room, screamed a blood curdling scream which blew out several of the windows, and fell to the floor screaming. The two girls were whimpering, terrified and unsure what to do. Arabella sat down next to her mother and tried to comfort her but with no response to stroking her mother's back, she burst into tears. This was followed by Lucinda who also burst out crying in unison.

After several minutes, their mother rose to her feet, sobbing and reached for the phone.

"May, May, I need you," she sobbed into the phone receiver.

Within minutes, May was in the house and pushing their mother to sit down. Once accomplished, May took the two girls into the bedroom with a plate of dry biscuits she had found in the pantry.

"Ok, Arabella, Lucinda, you need to sit here on this floor rug and quietly eat your biscuits. I'll be back to see you very soon. Stay here and don't move from this rug. Understand?"

The two girls nodded.

May headed back to Agatha who was sitting on a dining chair with her head and arms on the table. She looked like a broken rag doll and May was almost afraid to find out what had caused this distress. She sat next to Agatha and put her arm around her knowing this was going to be bad, but unsure how bad.

"Agatha, what is it?" May asked.

Agatha looked at her, with salty tears that had smothered her entire face and red bloodshot eyes. May was shocked at her appearance and drew in her breath.

"Ciaran. He's gone." Agatha started sobbing again and buried her face in her arms, low on the table.

"Agatha. Agatha," May spoke firmly, pulling her back up to a sitting position. "What do you mean he's gone? Gone where?"

"He's dead. He's dead. They killed him." With that she fell back to the position with head down and May stared at the tangle of auburn hair which was all she could see of her friend.

Ten minutes later, a firm knocking at the door shook May and she stood to go answer, aware that Agatha was in no position to respond.

"Who is it?" she demanded before opening the door.

"We're from Coburg Police Station, Constable Mark Sweeney and Senior Constable Abigail Clarke," came the voice from the other side of the door.

May opened the door and was confronted by the two police officers in uniform.

"Are you Agatha Flynn?" the male policeman asked.

"No. I'm a friend. Please come through." May ushered them into the house and through to the dining room where Agatha had not moved from her position.

The two police officers stared uneasily at Agatha, no doubt wondering why she was so upset when she had not yet been told. They glanced at May looking for guidance.

"Agatha is a witch, just as I am. She called me and just told me that her husband is gone. That is all I know. Is this true? Has something happened to Ciaran?" May asked and tears ran down her face as well.

"Yes. I'm afraid there's been an accident at the garage." The male policeman coughed slightly. "I'm sorry to tell you that Mr Flynn was under a car which was on a hoist when the hoist collapsed ... and the car fell on him. He was unable to be revived and died at the scene."

Agatha let out an anguished cry and May fell into the chair next to her. Numbly, she put her hand out and rubbed Agatha's back.

"Hoist collapsed? How is this possible?" asked May.

"We don't have any details yet. This will be fully investigated by the workplace accident team."

"Where is he?" asked May.

"He's been taken to PANCH ... the hospital at this stage. Do you think you should call a doctor for Mrs Flynn?" asked the female police officer, looking at the still sagged over figure of Agatha.

"Maybe later. I need to be with her now. Thank you for coming around and letting us know," said May, trying to dismiss them.

The two police officers looked again at Agatha. "We're really sorry for your loss, Mrs Flynn."

Agatha didn't answer as May led them out the door, thanking them again.

When she returned to the dining room, Agatha was sitting up waiting for her, swollen eyes and dishevelled.

"May, will you stay with the girls? Please? I have to go out for a little while. There's something I must do." She stared at May beseechingly.

"Agatha, don't you go and do anything stupid. You have three beautiful little girls relying on you," said May starting to be concerned.

"Please, May. I must go. Will you pick up Bethany from school at 3.30? It will be ok. I'll be ok but I have to do something. I need to go see Ciaran first," Agatha pleaded.

May looked at her friend who had just lost the love of her life. How could she say no?

"Of course, I will. The girls are fine with me but please, Agatha, please be careful. Please don't do anything bad. Are you going after the Grimm's? You don't know it was them. It could have been a genuine accident" she said.

"It was them," came the curt reply from Agatha. "They couldn't touch him direct because of the charm around his neck, but they could use magic to make something happen around him."

"Maybe something could happen around them," she said quietly, staring up at May.

Chapter 44

NIAMH FLYNN 2018

Niamh was keen to tell May all the news the following day regarding caterpillar eyebrows at the gate and the attack on Maddy. Although sympathetic for Niamh's friend, Niamh felt May was holding back on information. She could tell as May was not quite maintaining eye contact.

"Tell me what you're thinking of doing?" May asked.

Niamh looked around the room and hesitated. Should she show May how angry she was? "These people ... this Grimm family, they cannot just do whatever they fucking like to us. Hurt my friend and beat her up? Why? Because he was pissed off that I had prevented him from entering my property and killing another animal? They have to be stopped." She looked at May to judge her reaction. "I'm going to stop them."

May sighed. De je vu. She patted Niamh's hand affectionately. "Oh honey, I know you feel like that but you're not strong enough yet. Your magical ability is incredible. It really is and you have progressed so fast in such a short time, but I don't think you can take them all on yet ... the Grimm's. Not yet,"

"But I have to. I feel it. I know it," Niamh said quietly to May.

The two of them were in May's drawing room at the table. May sighed and leaned back in her chair.

"Ok. I'll tell you the story as I know it and maybe it'll help," said May.

Niamh nodded, knowing there was a story somewhere.

"The Grimm family first found the two of us via our advertisement in the paper for Marvellous Maybelline. Dora Grimm made an appointment and when she arrived, we realised she was magical and banned her from the property. Next thing we knew, there was a blonde man that looked like her hanging around the street and following us to the shops. Sometimes it was Dora but mostly, it was this man." May hesitated and Niamh saw her shiver slightly.

"This man was the one who attacked me when I was walking home from the shop one day. I had a lot of serious stab wounds, and I should be dead, but your grandmother sensed I was in trouble and arrived just in time to prevent me dying of blood loss."

May heard Niamh's intake of breath and saw her wide-eyed listening to every word.

"I was in hospital for six weeks and could never have children as there was too much damage to my organs." May sighed and took a few minutes before she continued.

"We didn't hear from the Grimm's again for years and we thought maybe they would leave us alone after the failed attempt on my life. By then, Agatha ... your grandmother had the three girls with her husband, Ciaran and were living three doors up from here." May took a deep breath.

"One day, a car fell on Ciaran at work ... and he was killed. Your grandmother knew it was not an accident, and that the Grimm's had used magic to kill him. I can't tell you what a horrible day that was." May's eyes filled with tears at the memory. "Your grandmother was inconsolable and broken-hearted. She was also angry and wanted revenge. She left the girls with me, and I didn't see her for a few days."

Niamh was almost holding her breath, hanging on every word.

"She ... she told me she was going to use magic to kill them by affecting something around them, just like they did with Ciaran. An eye for an eye. She went to their home in Ascot Vale and watched them for a few days. I don't think she even ate anything or slept for those days. She saw Dora and her husband, who was our stalker, six children and another man who looked like them but had a bald head. We believe he shaved his head as a disguise so no one would realise he had blonde hair as well. Anyhow, your grandmother was positive he was the one who had killed your grandfather. She saw that he had a car parked out on the street as the Grimm garage wouldn't fit the extra car so she waited until he got into his car one night when it was dark, and she used magic to lock the doors so he couldn't get out. Then she walked up to the driver's window and stood smiling at him."

Niamh shivered as she tried to picture this scene at night with no light but streetlights, an inner suburban street, a car parked in front of a house and a bald man sitting inside. A young woman with auburn hair standing outside the car window smiling at her husband's assassin.

"She used magic to start a fire inside the car and ... watched him burn."

Niamh visibly shivered but strangely, she felt an excitement. Her grandmother stood and watched her enemy burn.

"She said he was screaming and beating at the window with his fists and she just smiled at him. She watched him until he no longer moved and was just a charred corpse. Then, she turned to face the house, still on the street outside, and used magic to lock the doors and then caused the house to catch fire."

"Oh my God," said Niamh, mouth agape.

"She told me later that she saw the husband and older children upstairs trying to open a verandah door which wouldn't open, and she could see Dora and smaller children at a window near the front door. Dora saw her and was begging for their lives and promising they would never touch a witch again." May paused and took a sip of water. She could see Niamh was invested in the story and on the edge of her seat.

"You have to remember Agatha ... your grandmother, she was overwhelmed with grief and the need for vengeance. Even so, she still had some empathy for a mother with young children. The fire was fierce and finally, after much consideration, she used magic to open the front door, allowing Dora and four children to escape the flames."

"What happened to the father and the other older children?" asked Niamh.

"They burned in the fire," said May.

Niamh sat back stunned. She couldn't believe it. Her mother had never told her any of this.

"Does my mother know about this?" asked Niamh.

"Yes. She would know," confirmed May.

"From the day your grandfather, Ciaran died, your grandmother was never the same again. I didn't know her anymore. There was no joy in her life and no fun. She was still a good mother, made sure her daughters had everything they needed but there was no love. It was like that final act of vengeance had taken its toll on her and taken away her spirit. I felt so sorry for the three girls and tried to spend as much time as I could with them. She just spent lots of time brewing potions and growing herbs and flowers."

Niamh nodded, wondering how such a traumatic event or series of events would affect someone. She thought it likely that in today's language, her grandmother may have suffered from post-traumatic shock disorder (PTSD) and was untreated. She was looking forward to asking her mother some questions about what she had just learned.

"So, do you see why I am suggesting you are not yet strong enough and to wait before seeking any revenge?" said May.

Niamh nodded. She did.

Chapter 45

JUSTIN GRIMM 2018

No matter how hard he tried, it was never satisfactory for the rest of the family. He was positive they would be pleased with the possum guts scattered over the young witch's front door but they were not. He assured himself they would be delighted that he had beaten one of her friends to a pulp in order to rattle the young witch, but they were not. WHAT DID THEY WANT FROM HIM?

To make matters more uncomfortable at home, his grandmother, Dora was staying tonight, and she was a crazy old bitch. She took turns staying at each of her children's houses for a week or two at a time. Her house had burned down years ago and she never rebuilt so she had lived in temporary quarters all that time.

Justin's father, Tarren was the youngest child of Dora and George Grimm. Dora was forever prattling on about George and two of her children dying in a fire that one of the witches had deliberately lit, and a family member had perished as well. They all heard the same story so many times that they barely listened these days. It was many years ago and Justin wished she would just get over it and move on.

This night differed because his father was home where he usually wasn't until very late. Justin guessed he was home early because his mother was staying with them, and he felt a duty to entertain her. His father was an aloof member of the family and seldom attended family functions or meetings, preferring to disappear to some hotel and drink himself into a stupor then stagger home in the early hours of the morning. Everyone knew what he got up to and ignored it.

Tonight, he was hanging around the dining room, waiting for dinner which smelled delicious, along with his brother, Beaton and sister, Monica. His other brother, Anton was absent for some unknown reason. He was the youngest so always copped the taunts and teasing and tonight was no exception. Beaton especially, was always on his case about the young witch and how inadequate he was.

His mother and grandmother appeared from the kitchen, and they all sat, intent on the roast beef, potatoes and roast vegetables in front of them. The door opened and his father appeared unexpectedly, kissed his mother and wife and sat at the head of the table. He nodded at each of his children who were present but didn't say anything.

Half-way through the meal, Beaton upped the ante intent on obtaining a laugh from the entire family at Justin's expense.

"So, Justin, I heard we're serving witch's piss for sauce on the beef tonight. How does that suit you?" said Beaton, smirking at his own joke.

Justin almost spat his mouthful of potato scallopini out on to the table and quickly found a serviette to dab at his lips. Monica looked at Justin and then Beaton.

"What's that about?" she asked.

Beaton laughed. "The young witch outsmarted our little brother. She pissed all over the place so he can't step foot on the property." Beaton laughed loudly.

"Please Beaton. We are eating dinner. We do not wish to talk about such things," said his mother.

"Sorry mum. What are you going to do now? Shouldn't you have just ended her by now? What's the hold-up?" asked Beaton.

Tarren stopped eating and looked at his sons, intently. Having not been party to family meetings for some time, he was not aware of the plans currently in action. His eyes were intense as he stared from one to the other, trying to determine what the conversation was about.

"Did you know I beat up her friend?" Justin said, proud of his achievement.

"A small, normal girl much younger than you. I hardly call that worthwhile. In fact, I think that is rather cowardly," responded Beaton.

Justin swallowed his potatoes, and his face showed the anger building inside him.

"What young witch are you talking about?" asked his father, his voice sounding tense.

"The one at North Ringwood. Oh, Tarren, if you came to family events more often, you would know what's going on," scolded his wife, Marion. "The old witch died, and she bestowed upon the young witch."

"The old witch? You mean the one called Agatha?" he asked.

"Yes," she replied.

The grandmother, Dora raised her head sharply at the name and looked around the table, her eyes settling on Tarren.

"You do know she's the one who killed your father, your brothers and my cousin?" she asked, her voice becoming high pitched.

"Yes. I'm aware of that. Who's the young witch? Is it one of her daughters?" he asked quietly.

Marion, his wife looked at his face as she thought his tone to be strange.

"Does it matter?" Marion asked bluntly. "She's too young to be a daughter. I believe it's a granddaughter."

"I don't know her name, but I saw the mail in the letterbox and her mother's name is Lucinda Flynn," said Justin.

Tarren's eyes bulged, his face turned white, and he appeared to be holding his breath. Everyone at the table stopped eating and looked at him with concern wondering if he was having a medical episode. He turned to look at Justin and his face turned from white to red with anger in seconds.

"What are you trying to do?" he asked, his voice raised.

Justin's mouth fell open in surprise. "I ... umm ... I was told to scare her at first, but now I believe the family wants her dead."

Tarren stood up so quickly that his plate and cutlery banged as they were pushed forward on the table. Everyone jumped in shock, wondering what on earth was wrong with him. Without touching Justin, he used magic to throw Justin up against the wall behind where he'd been sitting, the chair landing sideways on the floor with a thud. Justin's body hit the wall with a loud thump, and everyone jumped to their feet in shock.

"You do not touch the witches, do you understand?" he said slowly, emphasising each word to his son.

"But ..." Justin began.

"No buts. No one touches the witches. NO ONE!"

He let go of the magic and Justin slid to the floor in a heap, shaking his head confused at what had just happened. Tarren looked slowly around at each person in the room, ensuring everyone heard what he said and understood. His eyes stopped on his mother who stared at him wide-eyed.

"You agreed that there would be no more hostilities between the witches and us, nearly forty years ago. Have you forgotten? Do you want them seeking revenge like last time?" he asked her, his voice incredulous.

His mother stared at him, her eyes narrowing. "No. I've not forgotten. Maybe now is the right time for us to seek revenge."

Tarren was speechless as he stared at her for a few more minutes, then he turned to leave the room, slamming his chair against the table.

Everyone stole glances at each other, the unspoken consensus being that Tarren's brain was affected by too much alcohol which explained his strange behaviour. It didn't change their plans for the witches.

Chapter 46
NIAMH FLYNN 2018

Niamh eyes fell on the family photo album still sitting on the kitchen bench and she gently pulled it over and sat on a stool. Her mother was humming as she stirred something on the stove top which smelled very much like Spaghetti Bolognese.

Niamh turned the pages and stopped on a photo of a young Agatha. She looked around twenty-five years old and was smiling at the camera. The photo was in colour though the old-fashioned poor-quality photos from the 1970's. Niamh put her hand out and gently traced a line down Agatha's face with her finger. It was an affectionate gesture, and Niamh was remembering the sound of music and visions of people dancing she had experienced when her grandmother had held her wrist. Was that Ireland?

Her mother turned in time to see Niamh staring at the photo intently.

"I always loved that photo of her. She looks so carefree and gay," her mother said.

"Yes. She does," Niamh looked up at her mother. "May told me the story today about what happened to my grandfather, Ciaran."

"Oh," said her mother, waiting to see if May had told her the rest of the story.

"... and about herself being stabbed."

Her mother pulled a sad face.

"... and about the revenge Agatha sought on the Grimm family."

Her mother looked at her for a few minutes without speaking, then turned to the stove top. "I'd better turn the spaghetti down," she said.

"Let me do that for you," said Niamh as she used magic to turn the induction stove down to level two.

Her mother saw the digital numbers change in front of her, and she giggled in surprise. "Wow, May has been teaching you well. Damn, I wish I could do that."

"Why have you never told me the story about my grandmother, my grandfather, May or any of it? Don't you think I should know?" Niamh asked. "May is so close to you all and I don't even know her."

Her mother nodded, accepting the question, the complaint and the seriousness of the situation.

"Again, Niamh. I'm sorry. I just couldn't tell you one bit without telling you all of it. I accept it was wrong, and I made a mistake," she said.

"May said my grandfather, Ciaran was a lovely man. I guess you were too young to remember, him" Niamh said.

"I was only two years old when he died so I don't remember him, sadly. I always understood he was a wonderful man," her mother said.

"It seems a black mark against his name that his own granddaughter didn't even know of his existence or name. I don't want any more secrets, mum. No more. I want to know who I am and where I have come from. That's only fair, isn't it?" Niamh asked.

"Well ... yes, of course," her mother said but Niamh could see she was becoming uncomfortable with the questioning.

Even now, after the cupboard door has been opened and the skeletons laid bare, her mother couldn't help but keep secrets. Niamh could see it on her face. Angrily, Niamh stood up tucking the photo album under her arm to take to her room.

"You wonder why we have a distant relationship. I've heard you tell people you don't know how to handle me. Let me tell you something that's not a secret. I DON'T LIKE TO BE LIED TO. I don't like to be kept in the dark, and don't you DARE tell me that you are being honest now. I can see you're not being honest. You're still holding back secrets from me. When you can open up and be honest with me, perhaps we think about having a good relationship."

With that, Niamh turned to walk out of the room. She paused, stuck her hand in the air with the middle finger sticking up and gave her mother the bird, at the same time she used magic to set the Spaghetti Bolognese on fire. She knew it was childish as that was her dinner tonight as well, but she just couldn't help but show her anger.

She grinned as she heard her mother gasp and rush back to the stove top, as Niamh left the room.

Chapter 47

TARREN GRIMM 1999

Tarren Grimm had been restless for a few weeks since his mother recently filled him in on details of the disaster that has struck his family twenty years earlier. Of course, he had already been aware of that fateful night, his mother having mentioned it countless times to her children over the years, but he was only four years old at the time and the exact nature of the catastrophe had escaped him. Her knew his father and two older brothers perished when the house burned in a fire, his mother and her younger children having escaped, but until recently, he hadn't known it was the witch who had caused the fire.

At twenty-four years of age, he questioned his mother this time when she casually interjected the catastrophe into a conversation. He was blown away when she told him that this witch had single-mindedly, visited on this particular night and burned his second cousin in a car and then used magic to set the house alight after ensuring the doors were locked. This seemed so outrageous and such a callous and inhumane thing to do that he was tortured with the thought of it.

Was his mother telling the truth? Did this really happen? He couldn't sleep, his mind imagining the fateful night, reliving it over and over in his mind. He did have vague memories of it as a four year old, seeing the flames so hot and fierce, and escaping into the cool night, but he didn't remember anything else, such as why this had happened. Now, as an adult, he was struggling with the detail of it and why the witch had been able to get away with killing members of his family without recourse.

His mother told him that she promised to leave the witches alone, and that was the reason she was allowed to escape the flames with the younger children. She kept her word and there had never been another incident or even a mention of the witches for twenty years. Now, all her children had grown up and Tarren, as the youngest, was now twenty-four years old.

Suddenly, she was talking about the witches again, and Tarren wondered if she was also mentioning it to his siblings. He had not yet spoken to them about his mother's latest ramblings of that terrible night, but he thought he should do so soon. Maybe it was tormenting them as much as it was tormenting him.

Tarren arose from the bed, trying to be as quiet as possible so as not to awaken Marion, his wife, and made his way to the study. He had spent a bit of time at night in the study lately, pacing and staring out the window at the night sky. He'd married Marion when he was only eighteen years old after his mother showed him a photograph of his attractive cousin. Arrangements were in place, and he didn't actually meet Marion until the day of the wedding.

He couldn't say that he regretted his choice or the partner he chose, as Marion was pretty enough, and a good wife and mother. He could not say they were friends in any way or had a close relationship, and he felt jealous of the characters in movies where it was apparent that they were so in love and suited to each other. He had four children with Marion including six year old twins, and he was aware that he should be counting his blessings and grateful that he had more than many other people.

Why did he feel so restless then? Was it really this tale of the witch who burned his family that kept him awake at night? If he were being honest with himself, he had been seeking his study at night for longer than he cared to remember. It was just that now he felt he had a good reason to be pacing at night, and tormented. He had a topic to focus on and become obsessed with.

Maybe it was time that someone ... him ... seek revenge on the witch who had destroyed his family.

Chapter 48
NIAMH FLYNN 2018

I'm home early. Brother got too sunburned. Can we catch up?

Niamh immediately left the house to walk to her friend, Emma's house. It felt like months since she had last seen Emma, but it was really only ten days or so. She was looking forward to discussing recent events with her and gaining Emma's opinion.

The girls hugged and excitedly caught up on pleasantries. They were sitting inside Emma's bedroom at the far end of the house to where her parents congregated.

"You've been getting my texts about being a witch and all that?" Niamh asked her.

"Yeah. What's all that about?" asked Emma.

"Ok. So, it turns out my grandmother was a witch from Ireland and had three daughters who are not witches. Then when the three daughters had children, one of them was a witch, which would be me," Niamh flourished her hands in the air, to indicate herself.

"A witch?" Emma repeated, with eyebrow raised.

Niamh nodded. "There's a family in Melbourne who hunt witches and they tried to kill my grandmother's witch friend, May, and stabbed her, but she survived, and then they killed my grandfather. He wasn't a witch, as witches can only be females, but I guess they were trying to get at my grandmother. Anyway, she lost the plot and went out and burned four of their family to death."

Niamh stopped and looked at Emma. She could see she had lost her in the story and Emma was looking at her with a disbelieving look on her face as if Niamh had lost her mind.

"Are you ok? Is this from a movie or something?" asked Emma.

Niamh smiled to herself, as she understood exactly what Emma was feeling. She hadn't believed it either when she had first become aware of the situation.

"Em, let me show you," Niamh said as she looked around the room. Her eyes fell on a pink teddy bear sitting up on top of a dresser. It had been Emma's childhood comfort teddy bear and looked a little moth eaten.

"Look at your pink teddy," instructed Niamh, and Emma turned her head to look.

Pink teddy bear suddenly stood up from his seating position leaning against the wall and moved to the edge of the dresser where he wriggled back and forth as if twerking. Niamh giggled as Emma sat up suddenly on her bed. Pink teddy bear returned to his seated position and the old childhood jewellery box which had been next to pink teddy bear, opened with a musical melody filling the room and the small ballerina twirling. The lid to the jewellery box closed softly and Niamh looked up at the ceiling.

"Emma, look up," Niamh said, and Emma looked up at the white ceiling.

The light fixture turned on and off a few times, then the ceiling looked to be filled with the night sky with hundreds of stars twinkling, then just as quickly, the night sky disappeared and what appeared to be fire lit up the ceiling. It only lasted a few seconds and then the ceiling returned to normal.

Emma looked at Niamh, her face showing a puzzled look.

"Don't believe me yet?" asked Niamh, giggling. "Go look in the mirror."

Emma swung her feet on to the floor and padded over to her mirror on the dressing table. She looked at her reflection and saw her hair had turned from brunette to bright red. She gasped and her hands automatically reached up to touch the red locks. A few seconds later, she looked normal again. Emma turned back to look at Niamh.

"Oh my God, you did that? What else can you do?" she asked and sat back on the bed next to Niamh, mouth agape.

"I'm still learning. I'm kind of like a witch on L plates." She laughed. "May is this old witch, the one that was stabbed. She's teaching me how to do magic. I've been seeing her each day to learn more. I'm going there after I leave here. I'll ask if you can come one day and check it out. You'd like May. She's so lovely. Anyway, I wanted to tell you about this family that hunt witches. They are called the Grimm family, and they have harmed my family in the past."

Niamh looked at Emma and could see she had Emma's total concentration.

"One of them was stalking Maddy and then found out where I live and started stalking me. He killed a possum and stretched its guts all over my front door for mum and I to find the next morning. He went back to Maddy's house and beat her up. She was badly hurt and in hospital but's home now."

Emma drew in a large breath in shock and stared at Niamh as she tried to keep up.

"I'm waiting for Maddy's mother to tell me it's ok to visit. Maybe you could come too."

Emma nodded, concerned.

"Maddy knows she had a stalker but not that the guy was really after me. I don't want to tell her, ok?" she asked, and Emma nodded.

"Why is this guy after you and how do you know it's a guy?" asked Emma, finding her voice again.

"Well, I have seen him and he's blonde with dark eyebrows ... caterpillar eyebrows. He's a Grimm and sounds like the Grimm family either want to scare me and threaten me or kill me. Not sure which it is yet," said Niamh, shaking her head.

Emma stared at her friend. Was this serious? Why was Niamh taking this so lightly if it were true?

"Be careful, Niamh," Emma said. "If this guy has already harmed Maddy, then he could harm you too."

"No. I have stronger magic than him. I'm sure of it. He should be more worried about what I will do to him," Niamh said as she looked at her friend with fierce eyes. "I just haven't caught up with him yet."

Chapter 49
TARREN GRIMM 1999

After weeks spent haunted by the tale spun by his mother of a witch causing the fire that killed his father and brothers, Tarren decided that it was time for him to identify the facts once and for all.

He didn't want his mother to discover his quest so without her knowledge, he searched the newspapers for the 8th March 1980 and discovered several reports of the fire.

According to the media, a man was torched in a rented car out the front of the house at the same time as the house was set alight. The deceased man in the car was Gerhard Oban Grimm visiting from Penrith, New South Wales. A father and two sons were killed in the house fire, George Sherman Grimm (31), Grady (15) and Aaron (13). The mother and four children were able to escape the flames. The cause of the fire and arsonist have not been identified.

Now he knew the basics of the events, and it matched up to his mother's story, he needed to find out where the witches lived. The only way he could think of doing this was to make an appointment with Marvellous Maybelline just as his mother had twenty-nine years earlier. He didn't plan to turn up to the appointment, but at least he would have her address. He phoned and the voice that answered was bright and friendly, a female voice with a sweet tone.

"Good morning, this is May from Marvellous Maybelline, how may I help you?" the sweet voice answered.

Tarren had been rehearsing this call in his mind, yet now that it was real, he found himself stammering a little.

"Umm ... hello. I would like to make an appointment to see Marvellous Maybelline. I saw the advertisement in The Age," he managed to say.

"Sure. Can you tell me what you wish an appointment for so I can ensure that I will be able to assist?" the sweet voice asked.

"Yes, umm ... err ... I've never been to a ... witch before, and I have trouble sleeping. Toss and turn all night and end up pacing the floor. I thought ... there may be something you can give me to help me." It was the best and most truthful scenario he could come up with.

"Hmmm, there are a number of herbal potions that can help people to sleep. Why don't you come and see me, and we'll work out what's causing you to lose sleep. I'm sure I'll have something to help you. When would you like an appointment? This week, I have some time left on Thursday afternoon, Friday morning, or Saturday afternoon," the witch offered.

"Ok. Thursday sounds good. As late in the day as possible and I'll just leave work early," he countered.

"4.30pm is the latest one I have available on Thursday. Does that suit you?" she asked.

"Umm ... yes. That's perfect. My name is ... Robert Dubois."

"Great. The address is 14 Liddle Street, Coburg. See you then, Robert," she said sweetly.

"14 Liddle Street, Coburg," he repeated, writing the address down on his notepad. "Thank you. See you."

Tarren hung up and looked down at the notepad with the address. He had managed to get her address so easily and within just a few minutes. He felt a bit rattled that she had such a sweet and friendly voice, but he also had heard that there were two witches, and this was not the one who had burned his family. This one was May and the other one was Agatha. All he had to do was find May and she would lead him to Agatha.

He searched for the address in Coburg using his computer and a search engine. The street name, Liddle Street, came up with a number of articles from twenty five years ago. He clicked on the article that had appeared in The Age on Saturday 14th December 1974 and read.

COBURG WOMAN STABBED IN FRENZIED ATTACK

On Friday afternoon, the self-appointed witch known as Marvellous Maybelline was stabbed in a frenzied attack walking home from the shops on Liddle Street in Coburg. She suffered many stab wounds and is in critical condition at P.A.N.C.H. Friends and neighbours have told this journalist that a blonde man with dark eyebrows had been seen in the street and appeared to be stalking Marvellous Maybelline. Anyone with information is urged to contact police.

Tarren sat back stunned and stared into space. A man with blonde hair and dark eyebrows in 1974 in Melbourne could only be his father, George. There were no other Grimm family members in Melbourne at that time. Just his parents and their children with himself, not even born yet.

Obviously, Marvellous Maybelline had survived as he had just spoken to her on the phone. News of this attack changed the scenery in his mind. There had been shots fired for some time, judging by this article as this had occurred six years before his family had been burned. Is this why his family had been burned? Was this revenge? He needed to know.

Chapter 50
NIAMH FLYNN 2018

Maddy's mother opened the door to Emma and Niamh and ushered them in. Lee had phoned a few hours earlier and informed Niamh that they could all visit Maddy together at 11am. It had been almost one week since the attack on Maddy and she'd been home from hospital for a few days. Her mother thought she was now ready to talk to people.

Mrs McCraw led the girls through to the back of the house where there was a built-in porch used as a sunroom. It housed a lounge and a number of chairs with a television and Maddy had often escaped to this room away from her parents to watch her favourite television shows.

Lee was already present, sitting on a chair and Maddy sat on the lounge chair, legs tucked under a thin blanket. Although Niamh and Emma had discussed the fact that Maddy's face would be battered and bruised and to expect it, the reality was still a shock. Niamh sucked in her breath at the first sight of her friend, and Emma started quietly crying. Maddy looked up at the two of them, knowing how they were going to react, as many had in the past few days when first seeing her. She tried to smile but the swollen and broken lips made it difficult.

"Oh, Maddy," said Emma. "You poor thing."

Niamh had brought a bunch of colourful flowers from her mother's abundant garden, and she handed them to Maddy.

"Sorry, Maddy. This is a horrible thing to have happened," said Niamh.

Maddy put the flowers to her nose and breathed in deeply, inhaling the perfume. "Oh, they're beautiful. Thank you," she said. Her words were slightly muffled as she was trying not to open her mouth very far due to the swollen lips.

"Here, let me take those and put them in a vase," said Maddy's mother and left the room with the flowers.

Niamh studied Maddy's face in sympathy. As well as the swollen lips with healing cuts, one eye was black, and half closed with swelling from her eyebrow pushing downward. There were dark bruise patches across her forehead and jaw and white tape across the bridge of her nose.

"I look terrible, don't I?" Maddy said quietly, more as a statement than a question.

"You do, Maddy. I'm not going to lie to you," said Emma, putting her hand on top of Maddy's hand in tenderness.

"I'd like to get my hands on that dude," said Niamh fiercely. "You are sure that it is the same guy that was following you? That blonde guy with caterpillar eyebrows?" she asked.

Maddy nodded. "Yes. It was him. I was home alone and there was a knock on the door. I opened the door and he just barged in, nearly knocking me over." Her eyes stared off into space at the memory. "He just ... bashed and kicked me like a crazy man. I fell to the floor and he kept kicking me." She gave a sob. "I thought I was going to die."

Lee leaned forward and put her arm around Maddy gently. "We're here for you."

At that moment, her mother walked in with the vase of flowers and placed them on a low bookshelf. She smiled at the obvious care and tenderness her friends were showing Maddy and left the room.

"Why would he do this? I don't understand why this random guy would stalk you for weeks and then beat you up. It just doesn't make any sense," said Lee.

"He didn't ... try to sexually ...?" Emma began to ask.

"No. Nothing like that," Maddy cut in.

"He sounds like he was angry," said Niamh. Her guilt factor had risen so much higher after seeing how badly Maddy had been beaten. Emma glanced at Niamh, realising how she was feeling.

"So, what are your injuries?" asked Emma.

"Well ... I have a broken tooth which is very sensitive, but I can't have it fixed until my lips are better. Broken nose, fractured jaw, broken ribs, internal bruising and my wrist has a cracked bone." She lifted her right hand which was in a cast.

"He could've killed you," said Lee.

"Do the police know who he is, or where he lives?" asked Niamh.

"No. They have the photo that Lee took of him at the train station a few weeks back and I think they got some of his DNA from me," Maddy shrugged.

Emma and Niamh spent another hour with Maddy and then said their goodbyes with a promise to see her the following week. Niamh was more determined than ever that she was going to put an end to the Grimm family.

Chapter 51

TARREN GRIMM 1999

The first act was a drive-by of 14 Liddle Street, Coburg on the Thursday afternoon. Tarren had toyed with various scenarios of how he would be able to find out information on the witches. He couldn't just park his car on the street and sit for countless hours watching Marvellous Maybelline's house or he would soon be under suspicion. He hadn't reached a solution yet but was eager to at least drive past and familiarise himself with the house in question.

He had arranged an appointment with Marvellous Maybelline at 4.30pm and it was close to that time now. Of course, he would not be attending the appointment, having made the appointment purely to gain her address.

The day was overcast, and it had rained earlier so the ground was still wet. He turned his Holden Commodore into Liddle Street and drove slowly, checking the house numbers. The houses were all simple, neat and tidy, a working-class neighbourhood. Within seconds, he was out the front of number 14 and stopped momentarily, gazing up at the neat, white weatherboard house with a full and colourful garden. The fence was quite tall and secure, constructed from metal but he could still see through to the house and garden.

He drove slowly forward, contemplating how he could find out any further information than this, when across the road at number 19, he saw the back of a caravan and heard the acceleration of a car. He pulled over his car, parking it on the side of the street and jogged over to number 19 where he could see a man in a red Ford Falcon trying to reverse a caravan out of his driveway. The man had no idea how to reverse a caravan and was turning the steering wheel too far to one side, then too far the other way, causing the caravan to swing from side to side and almost hit the fence, the bushes and very close to the gate.

Tarren called out to him. "Hey, can I help you with that?"

The frustrated man stepped out of the car and walked over to Tarren, shaking his head. "Never backed a caravan before. Bloody tricky, isn't it? Can you back a trailer?" the man asked.

"Well, I've backed a boat and trailer a ton of times so happy to give it a go," said Tarren.

"Thanks mate. We're off to Torquay for two weeks leaving tomorrow. If I damage the caravan, the missus will have my guts for garters," he said, and they both laughed.

Tarren sat in the driver's seat and adjusted the side mirrors, then slowly backed the car, turning the wheel the opposite direction to where he wanted the caravan to manoeuvre. By moving the wheel back and forth, he was able to smoothly back the caravan out of the driveway without touching anything on the sides and out on to the street. He pulled up in front of the house at number 19.

"Aw, thanks man. You're a life saver," said the man. "I'm Bill Johnson." He offered his hand to Tarren and Tarren took it, giving it the good old Australian handshake.

"No worries, Bill. Have a good holiday," Tarren said and jogged back to his car.

A plan was forming in Tarren's mind and meeting Bill Johnson was obviously meant to be. Tomorrow, the Johnson family would have left for their two week holiday at Torquay and their home would be empty. All he had to do was arrive at 19 Liddle Street tomorrow in work clothes, and if anyone asked, he was hired by Bill Johnson to conduct minor gardening in the front yard while the family were away.

From number 19, he could clearly see the gate for number 14 across the road and had a clear view of the street. Movement caught his eye, and in his rear-view mirror, he could see someone had opened the front door of the number 14 house. He glanced at his watch and saw that it was 5pm, way past his appointment time. Marvellous Maybelline would have realised that her appointment was a 'no show' by now.

He hoped he didn't look overtly suspicious as he sat in his car watching someone moving in the front of number 14 in his rear-view mirror. Looking around the car interior, he quickly opened the Melways, a book of Melbourne maps and pretended to be looking up street directions. Holding the book up, he was able to snatch glances in the rear-view mirror.

He saw a woman leave the property and close the gate behind her. The woman was quite petite, with bright red hair in a bob cut and a dress of various colours. This had to be Marvellous Maybelline that he had spoken to on the phone and the one who was attacked. She walked casually toward his car and Tarren felt his heart almost stop in fright. Surely not. Had she detected him already?

His mind started racing, looking for excuses or what he should do if confronted. At one stage she stopped in her tracks and stared at the back of his car for a few minutes. He held his breath and turned another page of the Melways, feigning interest in the Eastern Freeway. Then she turned left just behind his car and entered a gate at number 20.

With his driver's window down just a small amount, he could vaguely hear female voices and then Marvellous Maybelline entered the house, and the front door was closed. Interesting, he thought. Number 20 was right across the road from number 19 where he would be gardening tomorrow. Two houses to watch.

Roll on tomorrow.

Chapter 52
NIAMH FLYNN 2018

"I'm dying to find out what happened with those tracking device things you put on the two Grimm cars. Did they work?" asked May, inviting Niamh into her house for daily witch school.

"Yes. They worked. One went to a house in Templestowe and one in Doncaster. I have their addresses," answered Niamh.

"So, have you driven past or checked it out?" asked May.

"No. I can't. I don't have a car. Hell, I don't even have a driver's licence yet and I can't ask my mother as I don't want to let on anything about the Grimm's if I don't have to," Niamh responded.

"You're old enough to have a licence, aren't you?" asked May.

"Yes, I am, but I have to amass 120 supervised driving hours including 20 at night before I can sit my licence and my mother never seems to have time, or isn't around," said Niamh.

"Hmmm," said May pursing her lips in thought.

"I ... well ... I can't bring myself to deliberately venture close to where the Grimm family are ... due to ... what happened to me, but I can certainly help you get your hours up," said May.

"Really?" asked Niamh, brightening.

May grinned, "Come with me," she ordered and walked out of the back door.

Niamh followed thinking that they were on their way for a drive now in May's small silver Mazda which was parked in the driveway in front of the old garage. She was surprised when May walked to the side door of the garage, unlocked the bolt, opened the door and walked in. Niamh followed May into the dark garage and was pleasantly surprised to see a small car parked in the garage. It was a bright sky blue, and Niamh could see it had two doors and was quite old.

"Oh," said Niamh in surprise.

May placed her hand on the bonnet of the car and almost caressed the panel fondly. "This is Lola," she announced.

"Lola," repeated Niamh.

"She was your grandmother and my car and we learned to drive in her. Your grandfather cleaned her up beautifully," May said, smiling at the memory.

"But that was a long time ago. She looks like new," exclaimed Niamh looking at the shiny paint work and gleaming wheels.

"I have kept her clean and in good working order. Every month I come out here and start her up and give her a shine."

"You wash her?" asked Niamh, trying to imagine May physically washing and cleaning a car.

"No. Silly. Why have magic if you can't use it?" May laughed, and Niamh laughed too.

"Lola is a Toyota Corolla built in 1970," said May proudly.

"1970? Oh my God, she's nearly fifty years old. That's amazing," said Niamh, noticing that Lola still had registration plates on.

"She's still registered and roadworthy, and you can use her when you get your licence, if you want to," May offered.

Niamh stared at May, open eyed and stunned. "Really? Oh, wow. She's so cool." Niamh stepped forward, touching Lola's door. "Oh, I'd love to use her. Thank you."

"Jump in," instructed May, and Niamh stepped around to the driver's side, opened the door and sat in the seat. May climbed into the passenger seat. Looking around, Niamh found it hard to believe that this car was nearly fifty years old as everything from the outside paint to the inside seats and carpets looked like new.

"I'll get my mechanic to take her for a spin to make sure she's ok, update the insurance with your name and park her out the front ready to go," said May.

"Oh, thank you so much, May. I don't know what to say."

Chapter 53

JUSTIN GRIMM 2018

Justin swore under his breath when he realised that his brother, Beaton, was present for dinner again, as was Beaton's wife, Alannah and their two whiny children. Great! Slobbering children while you're trying to eat a delicious roast dinner. Just what he needed. To make the night even worse, his grandmother, Dora, was present again.

At least his father didn't appear to be home which was preferable after he'd lost his cool at dinner last time and used magic to throw Justin up against a wall. Justin still didn't understand what had happened to cause this complete and sudden blow up. One minute they had all been discussing the witch and how she had urinated on the boundary to keep him off the property and next minute, his father was losing his shit and demanding they leave her alone. A witch? Leave a witch alone? He sure had lost his marbles.

Paying more attention to his father's activities than he had previously, he'd noticed a few things that he should be concerned about, but he really didn't give a shit, if he was being honest. As he was the only child still living at home, he saw things with his parents that his siblings would not be aware of. He knew his father didn't sleep in the bedroom with his mother. He'd slept in his office on a sofa for many years now, and if Justin ever headed to the kitchen for a snack at night, he could see the office light on.

Lately, he had noticed that his father was packing items in boxes, and they were stored in the office. He'd seen them one afternoon when his father left the office door open by accident. Justin was certain his father was separating from his mother and moving out. Good riddance. He was planning to move out of home anyway. The family had lately shown him photos of a distant cousin of his in Sydney named Natasha who had turned eighteen years old, and though she wasn't the prettiest girl he'd ever seen, she was adequate and had reasonable magic skills. He had tentatively sent out a marriage proposal and was just waiting on the affirmative reply.

Once everyone was seated at the dining table and the two children were quiet for at least five minutes, Justin decided it would be a good time to update everyone on the latest witch situation, given his father was not present.

"So, I drove out to North Ringwood today," he said, scanning the table for any interest. All eyes were on him.

"And?" said his mother.

"I saw the mother and the young witch leaving so I decided to follow them, discreetly of course," he added, grinning at his stealth. "They drove to a street in Coburg called Liddle Street and the mother dropped the young witch off at a house there."

He heard his grandmother gasp, and all eyes turned to look at her.

"That's the house. That's the house where the witches lived. 14 Liddle Street. I know it well," she said with a mouthful of carrots.

“The old witch, Agatha is dead, so does that mean the other old witch still lives there?” asked Beaton.

“Looks that way,” said his grandmother.

“Hang on ... so ... the young witch going to the old witch’s house means that she might be learning more about magic and witchcraft,” said Justin.

Everyone looked suitably concerned at this information and they all agreed that this was the most likely scenario.

“Ok,” said Beaton, putting his hand up to stop the chatter that was becoming more animated around the table. “Two things here. One is that we can’t allow the young witch to become too educated in witchcraft and secondly, we can’t allow the old witch to teach her anything. It’s time we got serious. Both need to be taken care of ... now. I’ll help Justin and we’ll sort it out once and for all.”

Inwardly, Justin groaned at the thought of Beaton helping him with the witches as he knew Beaton would take all the credit and be a smartass to boot, but at the same time he knew he couldn’t handle two of them. Heck, he hadn’t even handled one of them yet.

“Just get it done and do it sooner than later,” said his mother.

Chapter 54
LUCINDA FLYNN 2018

The three sisters met at Bethany's house to discuss the possible investments regarding their mother's inheritance. Bethany lived in a lovely home at Warranwood, east of Melbourne and only ten minutes from where Lucinda and Arabella lived.

"How's Niamh doing with May?" asked Bethany.

"Oh, she's doing really well. They get on so well together and Niamh adores her, as we all do. She's already able to do so much with magic. She was angry with me a few nights ago so burned what I was cooking while it was on low," said Lucinda, and laughed weakly at the story.

"Funny isn't it, how none of us three turned out a true witch and yet, Niamh, a granddaughter, did," said Arabella.

Lucinda looked away quickly to compose herself. "Sure is ... funny," she said.

"Ok. Let's get on with it. I never realised our mother had hoarded so much money over time. Where did it all come from?" asked Bethany.

"I asked May this question," said Arabella. "... and she said that the house at 20 Liddle Street was left to our father when his parents died and then left to our mother when dad died."

They all nodded thoughtfully knowing that their grandparents had owned that house originally. Only Bethany had a very slight memory of older grandparents, but it was very vague.

"She also said that both her and our mother, had a few generous and rich customers who willed their estates to the two of them. Imagine that!" said Arabella. "They must have been very grateful customers."

"They wouldn't have earned a lot as witches," said Lucinda. "They would have done ok in the early days when our mother was part of the outfit, but never a fortune, surely?"

"So, we have the house at 20 Liddle Street to decide what to do with it, and also the old cottage in Ennis, Ireland," said Bethany.

"Hmmm ... the cottage in Ireland is currently rented out so should we just leave it for now, and we can earn a little bit of income from the rental?" asked Arabella.

"Yes. I hate the thought of selling it considering it was in our family for hundreds of years, and our mother must have gone to a lot of trouble to repurchase it. I know it was sold before she came to Australia," said Lucinda and they all agreed.

"What do we do about Liddle Street?" asked Arabella.

Lucinda waited to see what her sisters would say before she spoke. She knew her sisters were doing well in life and didn't have any money problems, so they were not desperate to sell the property. They had also been left around forty thousand dollars each in their mother's will.

"Well, I feel the same with the Liddle Street house ... you know ... that it was our family home and we shouldn't sell it," said Lucinda.

"Do you think we should rent it out?" asked Bethany.

"Well ... I would like to rent it," she said. Her sisters looked at her in surprise. She had lived in the same house in North Ringwood for the past eighteen years and they knew she lived rent-free thanks to Niamh's unknown father.

"Niamh is going to university soon and it won't be long before she leaves home. I can't stay there on my own. Well ... I don't think I would be kicked out or anything, but I wouldn't feel right staying there without Niamh. I can't afford to buy the both of you out of the Liddle Street house but I could pay rent for it," Lucinda said.

Bethany and Arabella looked at each other and they both agreed that it was fine with them. They would arrange a solicitor to draw up a lease agreement and Lucinda could move in whenever she wished to.

Lucinda was excited at the move to her childhood home and the fact that she would be so close to May who was getting older. She couldn't wait to tell Niamh the news.

Chapter 55

NIAMH FLYNN 2018

Niamh clapped her hands together excitedly. "Ooh, we're going to a school?"

Only weeks ago, she would have baulked at the thought of performing at a school where there were children. She would have thought it a lame and bogan thing to do and not cool at all. More than anything, her attitude to visiting the school made her realise how much she had changed in the past month, since she had discovered she was a witch. She had even been present with a few visits from May's customers.

She had morphed from a silly and belligerent schoolgirl to young woman eager to learn more of the world, and she thanked May for this rapid transformation. She found it inexcusable that her mother had known May all her life and yet, kept her a secret from Niamh. May was older now and so much time had been wasted. Niamh intended to make it up now, and treasure May as she should have been treasured her entire life.

May had a basket of goodies ready to go and Niamh fingered through them trying to work out what they would be doing with a classroom of school children. She found the crystal ball, a wand, a folded up black witch hat, a cloak and some materials including coloured wool, beads, string, reeds, flowers and bark. May explained that she had been invited every year for the past twenty years to entertain the children and part of the activity was that she taught them how to make a charm necklace. The other equipment were props and theatrics for the day.

May disappeared and emerged holding a dress and suggested Niamh may wish to wear it to the school. It had belonged to her grandmother who was a similar size and height as Niamh. Niamh thought the dress was stunning with gold and red brocade and a long skirt. She squealed in delight as she took the dress and disappeared to try it on. It turned out her grandmother was a little shorter and thinner than Niamh but the dress still looked superb.

They climbed into Lola with Niamh driving, as they had done every day lately to gain enough hours of practice for Niamh to qualify for her licence. As she backed out on to the road, Niamh hesitated and looked around the street cautiously.

"What's wrong?" asked May.

"I'm not sure. I felt a tingle like someone may be nearby, but I can't see anyone," she replied.

They drove to the local primary school and could hear the excited squeals from the children as they were spotted walking down the hallway to the classroom. Niamh carried the basket of goodies and May was carrying the quaint straw broomstick.

The middle-aged teacher greeted them warmly and introduced them to the children as 'Marvellous Maybelline and her assistant, Niamh'. There were twenty children who appeared to be around six years old and they cheered and clapped as the two witches set up at the front of the classroom.

"Good morning boys and girls. I am Marvellous Maybelline, and this is Niamh and today, we are going to show you some magic and how to make charms," said

May in her theatrical voice with lots of waving arms around. The children were spellbound and stared wide-eyed as May waved her hands over the crystal ball and added an 'Abracadabra' and a 'Hocus Pocus' and the crystal ball turned smoky inside. The children all let out sounds of surprise and excitement. May invited the children to form a line and one by one look into the smoky crystal ball and tell everyone what they saw. Every child saw something different, and the responses were from various animals including a frog, bird, fish, cat, lizard, dog and horse.

May used the wand and cloak to conduct basic magic tricks though in May's case, they were magic and not tricks. She swiped the cloak across a chair and suddenly, there was a large green frog sitting on the chair. She waved the cloak across again and the frog had disappeared.

Niamh passed props to May and was having the time of her life. One child put her hand up and asked Niamh what she could do. May looked at her and nodded to go ahead. Niamh looked around and saw the broomstick leaning against the whiteboard. She put her hand out and the broomstick flew across the room to her hand. Then she waved the broomstick in the air and told the children to look up. There were excited tones as the children could see a pink and purple haze above them with sparkling stars floating around.

They finished off the activity by showing the children how to make charms by plaiting the coloured wool to create a band and rolling bark, reeds and flowers together with a few strands of hair from the child's head. This was tied in a tight little bundle with string and May walked around and put a spell on each little charm to protect the child. The children proudly wore their charms around their neck and the teacher thanked them for the wonderful demonstration.

The two of them left the classroom feeling elated that they had entertained the children and given them happy thoughts about witches for the future. As they were walking down the hallway, Niamh suddenly stopped. She could sense someone nearby. May couldn't but she knew she was not as powerful as Niamh.

Niamh turned about-face and walked the other way down the hallway with May following. They walked past the door to the classroom where they had just spent the past hour and continued down the hall until they came to the opposite side of the hall two doors down. Niamh stopped and looked at May, then they peeked through the window next to the door to the classroom. There was a classroom of children of perhaps nine years old, all quietly writing with their heads down.

One child toward the back of the room held Niamh's focus and she stared at the pale blonde hair of the child, a little girl. Slowly, the child lifted her head and stared straight at Niamh through the window. May gasped as she saw the dark eyebrows and recognised it as a Grimm child. Niamh didn't feel any fear looking at this Grimm child and if anything, she felt a smug arrogance knowing she was stronger than this child. She gave a smug smile to the child, one that they child would remember and be nervous about and then the two of them left.

Niamh wondered where this child lived to be at a school local to May's area of Coburg. As they were getting in Lola, Niamh again felt a presence and looking around could not see anyone.

Chapter 56
LUCINDA FLYNN 2018

Lucinda taped the boxes together ready to start packing her belongings for their move to 20 Liddle Street. She had been dreading telling Niamh the news as she felt Niamh's attitude could be so volatile at any given time, and she wasn't sure how she would feel about the move. Surprisingly, Niamh was very excited and thought it was a great idea to be near May and to live in a home that had been in her family for so long.

Niamh had never been aware that her father allowed them to live rent-free in the North Ringwood house and Lucinda planned to never tell her. The topic of the house and who owned it had never arisen in discussions, and it was rare that Niamh even asked any questions about her father. It had been ten years or so since the last time she had even asked about him.

Lucinda hadn't been able to speak to him on the phone as she found the concept of doing so, too difficult. Even eighteen years after their passionate affair, she still felt light-headed at the thought of him and became teary if daydreaming for too long. She had his work phone number so chose to phone at night when she knew he wouldn't be at the office and leave a message. She rehearsed the message all day and she even found leaving the message a difficult task.

It's Lucinda. I don't know if you are aware, but my mother passed away recently, and Niamh and I have decided to move into her old house. I would like to thank you for allowing us to live here all these years. It has helped enormously, and I don't know how we would have managed otherwise. I will let you know once we have moved so you can make plans for this house. Thank you.

After she hung up, she realised there were tears rolling down her cheeks and wiped them away with the back of her hand. This move would be a new life and a new beginning for them. It was liberating in many ways as it was severing the tie she had with Niamh's father and stepping out on her own at thirty-eight years of age. Luckily, the Liddle Street house was furnished as she didn't own her own furniture other than a few minor things they had bought over the years. She had managed to survive over the past nearly twenty years with part-time jobs and brewing organic and herbal remedies for May's customers. Money had always been tight, but they had made do and Niamh had not gone without.

When she drove over to pick up Niamh from May's house that afternoon, she brought along a key to the house at 20 Liddle Street as Niamh was keen to investigate the house. They walked up the three houses further on from May's house and let themselves in to the white weatherboard home. Niamh loved the place and chose a bedroom with a view of the back garden. As Agatha had lived there for so long, she had kept a vast array of herbs, flowers and bushes in the garden which meant that Lucinda would have all she needed to continue to make her concoctions for May. Niamh had also become very interested in plants recently. Lucinda was pleased to see that Niamh loved the house and felt positive for their future.

As they were leaving, Niamh stopped on the footpath and looked around slowly. Lucinda noticed and asked what was wrong.

"Lately, I keep getting a strange sensation as if there is someone magical around somewhere, watching me but I can never see anyone," she said.

Lucinda stared at her and her concern grew. Was it possible the Grimm's would come after Niamh? After everything she had done to try to protect her from the witch life and the magic life, was it possible?

She would speak to May about it to determine if she was also detecting someone nearby.

Chapter 57
NIAMH FLYNN 2018

Niamh couldn't believe she finally had her driver's licence. She couldn't stop running her hands over the small plastic card with her serious looking photograph on it. She thought this day would never come but she finally had enough hours of practice in her logbook and had passed the driving test.

"I just can't thank you enough May," she gushed as she dropped May off back at her house. "This would never have happened if it wasn't for you, and Lola. You're the best thing that's ever happened to me."

May blushed with the compliment but couldn't stop beaming. Niamh's excitement was contagious.

"I'm off to tell my mother, and then I'll go take Emma for a ride in Lola," said Niamh, with the rest of her day planned.

"Have fun, love. See you tomorrow," said May as she toddled back to her house, limping with slight arthritis.

Niamh hummed as she drove from Coburg back to North Ringwood, feeling that the day could not be any more perfect. Emma didn't have her licence yet, so she was looking forward to the two of them going for a drive and enjoying the freedom to go wherever they wished. Maybe they could drive past the Grimm houses in Templestowe and Doncaster for a quick look.

There was an unknown black BMW parked in front of her front gate when she arrived home. Unperturbed, she parked Lola behind it and giggled to herself as she stepped out of Lola, and just for good measure, snapped a photo with her iPhone of the two cars nose to tail and sent it to Emma. She typed 'chalk and cheese' referring to the vast difference between the modern BMW and the 50 year old Lola.

All of a sudden, she felt a strange sensation, stronger than she had ever sensed before. Shivers ran up and down her spine and she felt every hair on her body standing on end. The sensation was so strong that it made her feel nauseous. What the hell was going on?

Quickly, she tossed her iPhone in her handbag and looked at the BMW. Who owned this? Someone was here at her house, someone with magical abilities. How was this possible? Panic rose in her like nothing she had ever experienced.

HER MOTHER!

Something must have happened to her mother!

Someone was here and they must have hurt her mother! Could it be the same one who had assaulted Maddy? Was he harming her mother?

She turned and bolted for the front door, throwing the gate open on the way. How could someone get in uninvited? It was not possible.

She could feel a scream rising in her throat, unbidden and uncontrolled. In her panic, she could feel a loss of control with magic shooting around her body and she knew bolts of electricity were sparking out as she could feel the hair on her arms singe, could smell the burning. In a fluid motion, she turned the door handle and flung the door back where it hit the wall with a loud bang and vibrated. She sprinted into the kitchen area, panic in full flight, scream already half escaped from her lungs and electrical sparks shooting out around her.

"FUCK!" came a shocked male voice.

In the kitchen, straight in front of her on the other side of the kitchen bench stood her mother and a man she had never seen before. They were both staring at her with mouths open in shock at her dramatic entrance. No one spoke and the air was smoky and smelled of singed hair. She stared at the vision of these two people standing side by side in the kitchen and she knew he was a Grimm. He was tall with the trademark blonde hair, silvering at the sides and the dark eyebrows. His honey brown eyes stared at her as if he couldn't believe what he was seeing. She could feel his magical abilities.

She frantically tried to assess the situation in front of her. Was this Grimm hurting her mother? Had he kidnapped her, or was in the process of kidnapping her? Why was he in their kitchen? What the hell was going on?

It took a few minutes for everyone to inhale and realise that the world had not just ended. Her mother was the first to speak and diffuse the situation.

"Good God, Niamh. You scared me half to death!"

Niamh stared at her, dumbfounded. "Umm ... you're the one standing with a Grimm in our kitchen," she said tersely.

Her mother blinked a few times and looked at the strange man as if she had forgotten he was a Grimm. Niamh waited for a response, a reason why this man from the enemy clan was standing in their kitchen, obviously invited. She took a few deep breaths to gain better control of herself but was still on guard. The man had not stopped staring at her and his expression was one that she couldn't place.

"Maybe we should all sit down," suggested her mother.

"I'll stand," said Niamh, emphatically and not prepared to give an inch until she had an explanation.

Her mother looked at the man again, and this time, he turned to look at her as well. A mutual expression crossed between them and Niamh raised her eyebrows wondering what on earth was going on. As if an agreement had been reached, her mother turned back to look at her.

"This is Tarren ... Tarren Grimm. He's your father."

Chapter 58

TARREN GRIMM 1999

Luckily for Tarren, the weather improved on Friday and the sun was attempting to peek out from the clouds. He arrived at 19 Liddle Street and parked in the driveway of number 19, wearing his old work jeans, Blundstone boots, a baseball cap, t-shirt and checked shirt, all clothes that would be considered suitable for gardening work. Making his way around to a shed behind the house, he found a wheelbarrow, gardening gloves, secateurs and shovel which was enough to give the appearance that he really was gardening. Positioning himself at the front of the property, he had a clear view of both number 14 and number 20.

The morning past uneventfully and reluctantly, he had amassed a collection of weeds and pruning in the wheelbarrow. He was beginning to draw the conclusion that this gardening stake-out was a bad idea and it was a waste of time when the front door opened at number 20. He held his breath and watched as a young woman walked down the path and through the gate on to the foot path. She stopped in front of the gate and glanced up and down the street.

Tarren realised he was standing like a statue staring at her, so he quickly placed his equipment down on the ground and glanced back at her. She was only twenty metres away from him and he could see that she looked around twenty years of age, with red hair and wearing a purple dress. Even from where he stood, he could see she was stunning, and he felt the situation was surreal, that he was looking at a goddess rather than a witch.

The sun suddenly appeared from behind clouds, and he could see that her hair had a golden tinge to it. Bright red with a golden overlay, like copper. She carried a small bag over her shoulder and began walking down Liddle Street. Tarren quickly looked about him, straightened his clothing, removed his cap, ran his hands through his hair and followed.

He kept a good distance behind her, but his eyes never left this red gold girl, and he noted that her hair came halfway down her back, thick and luxurious. I imagined running his hands through that red gold hair. Who was this girl? He could not sense anything magical about her so she couldn't be one of the witches. She obviously was unable to sense him either, so he was beginning to think she had nothing to do with Marvellous Maybelline and perhaps was just a friendly neighbour.

Why was he following her then?

He couldn't explain it. It was a magnetic pull that dragged him along behind her, wanting to know more about her, wanting to know her. He didn't want her to turn around now and see him, see him smiling like an idiot with no excuse as to why he was there. He wanted to know where she was going and why.

They passed number 14 where Marvellous Maybelline lived, and he saw the red gold girl glance in as if ready to wave if she saw anyone. They kept walking and at the end of the street, she turned toward the shops, and he discreetly followed.

One of the shops was a small shop, once a milk bar or general store, now a small privately owned supermarket and delicatessen. She entered the shop, and he waited a few minutes before following her in. He could see her immediately, placing an order with the older man behind the counter.

"Two chicken and salad sandwiches, one egg and lettuce sandwich and a flat white coffee take away, please Mr Handley," she said. Her voice was sweet and musical as he had guessed it would be.

Tarren walked up behind her until he was almost touching her and using his magic, he breathed her in. Her perfumed body scent assaulted his senses, and he almost felt giddy at the sensation it gave him. He had never experienced this before, such a drawing in of someone's body scent and persona. She became aware of him behind her and stepped aside apologetically.

"Oh, I'm sorry," she said.

"It's ok. I was just reading the board," he said, looking her full in the eyes for the first time. He saw grey eyes, an unusual light grey with dark, long lashes and he felt her eyes were drawing him further in. Her skin looked so smooth, unlined and creamy that he longed to run his finger down her cheek to feel if her skin was real.

She smiled shyly, and he forced his eyes back to the board on the back wall with a list of takeaway available. Mr Handley patiently waited for his order with Mrs Handley had commenced preparing the sandwiches for the red gold girl.

"Can I please order a coffee, one sugar and ... umm ... a beef and salad sandwich?" he asked, aware that the red gold girl was listening though pretending not to.

He paid for his order and stepped back, placing himself next to the red gold girl. He turned to her, frantically trying to think of something to say.

"So, are the sandwiches good here? I haven't been here before," he came up with, lamely.

She looked up at him, and he noticed she was shy and couldn't hold his gaze but kept glancing away.

"Oh yes. I'm often down here ordering sandwiches," she said.

"Three sandwiches for you. You must be hungry," Tarren said in jest.

She laughed. "Oh, one is for my mother and the other for my god mother."

"I'm doing gardening in the area, and sure built up an appetite with the manual work," he said, then blushed thinking that he sounded like a silly schoolboy trying to impress a girl.

"Are you a gardener?" she asked.

"No, but I help out here and there," he answered, looking away lest she see the untruth.

"Here, Luce. Your order's ready," said Mr Handley, placing her coffee on the counter and the sandwiches in a bag for ease of carrying.

"Luce?" he asked.

She blushed. "Lucinda."

"What a lovely name," he said, and he meant it. Looking at this beautiful girl, the name Lucinda fitted perfectly, and he couldn't imagine her wearing any other name.

Mr Handley placed his coffee and sandwich on the counter, and he thanked him, carrying his lunch out of the shop at the same time as Lucinda, opening the door for her.

They both stood out the front of the shop, lunch in hand and stared at each other. He didn't want to walk away and never see her again, and he didn't want to go back to spying on her house. Suddenly, spying on the witches seemed a trivial matter and seeing Lucinda again seemed to the most important thing in his life.

"Is that coffee for you?" he asked her.

Puzzled, she looked down at the takeaway cup in her hand. "Yes, it is."

He gestured over to a park bench under a shady tree ten metres away. "Would you like to sit with me and have lunch?"

She looked over at the park bench and back at him. "Yes, I would."

Chapter 59
LUCINDA FLYNN 1999

Lucinda walked away from the group of shops on her way home, bag in hand with the two uneaten sandwiches inside. She glanced over her shoulder more than once to see Tarren standing in front of the park bench watching her walk away. Just before she turned the corner of the street, she looked back again, and he was still watching. Why was it so hard to turn that corner and lose sight of him?

They had agreed to meet at the same park bench tomorrow and have lunch together. She had only just left, and she already couldn't wait to see him again. How bizarre this was. She had been to that shop hundreds of times in her life, and in just one day, her world had turned upside down. She could feel the butterflies in her stomach just thinking of him.

A chance meeting with a stranger in a shop ordering lunch. Who would ever have imagined that could happen?

She thought back to when she had turned in the shop aware that she was in the way of someone wanting to place an order and seen him for the first time. Those eyes that looked at her and penetrated her soul. Brown eyes but not a brown she had ever seen. Not brown like a dirty river but flecked with gold, giving the eyes a glowing dark amber look to them. Dark eyebrows but not overwhelming dark, framing a strong, masculine face with medium blonde hair, worn a little long and touching his shoulder. He was tall and she found at her own height of 178cm, she had to tilt her head to look up at his face. He had to be close to 200cm tall.

Neither of them wanted this chance meeting to end so they sat for forty minutes and ate lunch together. The conversation flowed on everyday innocent topics such as where they lived. He said Templestowe, how old he was, twenty four years and what the other occupation he had other than gardening, managing a family business in real estate, selling, buying and investing.

She told him she lived at home with her mother, and that her two sisters had moved away and married. The oldest one, Bethany with her first child, a boy named Marcus. He seemed interested in everything she spoke of and asked polite questions. He'd asked what was her occupation, and she explained that her godmother was Marvellous Maybelline, and she assisted May with making potions and herbal remedies for people. Tarren admitted he had heard of Marvellous Maybelline before, perhaps from someone at work.

He asked after her father, and she confided that there had been a workplace accident, and her father had been killed when she was two years old. He then asked when that had occurred, and she told him March1980. Tarren confided that he lost his father around the same time. It was something personal that they had in common.

How could a man be so perfect? She hummed as she walked home, picturing his face and remembering the tone of his voice. She wouldn't tell May or her mother about this encounter as they were both very protective and her mother had been acting strangely before she left for lunch. She had seemed irritable and told her to be careful as she could detect someone with magical abilities was somewhere in the area. When Lucinda had left the property, she had stopped on the street and looked up and down. There had been no sign of any strange cars or people, so she thought her mother was being over-sensitive.

No. She would keep Tarren a secret, her little secret. She hoped they could continue seeing each other. What if he asked her out? Would she go? What would she tell her mother? Her sisters had managed to date guys and get married so why shouldn't she?

She'd wait and see how tomorrow's lunch date panned out and then decide whether she would tell her mother and May. Who knew? The lunch date might not turn out very well and she may decide Tarren is a bad match and not wish to see him again, but she doubted that.

Lucinda went to sleep dreaming of his golden-brown eyes and deep voice.

Chapter 60

TARREN GRIMM 1999

Tarren arrived home, showered and ate dinner, barely glancing at his wife, Marion. After meeting Lucinda, he felt like a stranger in his own home, kissing his children in greeting but avoiding Marion. He then spent an hour searching the newspaper entries on his computer for anything on the death of Lucinda's father. It seemed very coincidental that her father had died the same month as his own father. Something didn't add up and he needed to find an answer.

He found the death notice for Ciaran Flynn and realised the date was two days before the death of his family members. The death notice said he was survived by a wife, Agatha and three daughters, Bethany, Arabella and Lucinda. Sitting back in his office chair, he stared into space and his mind raced with possible scenarios. If Agatha was responsible for the fire, then why would she do it two days after the loss of her husband. It seemed very suspicious and there had to be more to it than what had been presented to him.

"I'm off to Hardy's place," he called out to Marion as he left the house.

His brother lived in Doncaster, a ten minute drive from his home in Templestowe. He knew his mother was staying with Hardy and his family, as she did with him and each of his siblings on a regular basis, usually a few weeks at a time.

Hardy's wife, Imogen, answered his knock, inviting him in where he found his mother sitting watching television with Hardy and his children. Tarren asked to speak with his mother in private and the two of them headed into the dining room where he shut the door, noticing the puzzled look on Hardy's face.

"A few weeks ago, you mentioned how that witch, Agatha, had set fire to the house and killed my father and brothers, and also a car with your cousin," he said, watching her face.

"Yes. That's right," she answered, eyebrows raised waiting for what he wanted to say.

She had sat on one of the dining chairs and he sat on a chair turned to face her.

"Why do you think the witch killed members of our family?" he asked, innocently.

"Well, she's a witch. She hates our family, and we've always been at war with the witches," his mother said.

"You don't think it was anything to do with the death of her husband two days beforehand?" he asked, sounding innocent and puzzled.

She stared at him, and he knew she was trying to decide how to answer. He patiently waited, curious to hear whether she would admit to the truth or not. She had always been an outspoken and loud person with an over-bearing personality, and he often thought it must be a family trait, as his wife and sisters were the same.

She hadn't answered so Tarren continued with the questions. "I read in the papers that Ciaran Flynn, the husband of Agatha, was killed in a workplace accident. Do you know anything about that? What was your cousin doing in Melbourne at the time?"

His mother exhaled loudly and pulled a face as if perturbed that he would be questioning this with her. "Gerhard was staying with us and was going to kill the two witches. The family in Sydney arranged it."

"Yes," Tarren said quietly. "… and?"

"And … he used magic to drop the car onto the witch's husband. The idea was that it would weaken her," she said.

"I see. So, her friend was attacked and stabbed. Was that my father who did that?" Tarren asked.

His mother looked angry. "Yes. He should've killed her, but he messed up."

"Then her husband was killed by your cousin. No wonder she was so furious. She sought revenge and burned the house and car …"

"Yes, but she killed innocent children as well," said his mother.

"I imagine anger and grief would have played a part in that. Was the plan originally to kill Agatha's children as well?" Tarren asked.

His mother looked guiltily at him, and he knew it had been the plan.

"Did you promise Agatha that terrible night that your family would leave her alone if she spared you and the rest of us?" he asked.

"Yes. I begged her to let us out and eventually, she did but it was too late for George, Aaron and Grady." He could see tears well in her eyes and he felt guilty for pushing her, but he needed the truth.

"Ok. Sorry to upset you. I wanted to know the truth," he said, giving her hand a squeeze.

"That was twenty years ago and maybe it's time that she pays for what she did."

"You promised to leave her alone and I think that promise should be honoured. There are too many of us that would be at risk if she decided to harm us all. Think of the children," Tarren said as he kissed her goodbye and left.

"I am thinking of the children," she said as he walked away.

Chapter 61
LUCINDA FLYNN 1999

Lucinda could barely contain her excitement at meeting Tarren for lunch the following day. She had not mentioned a word to her mother or May but May in particular, had noticed a glow about her that had not previously been there.

As she walked toward the park bench, her heart was racing. What if he didn't show? What if it had been a dream and he didn't exist? What if she had imagined the connection they had shared?

When she turned the corner of the street and saw him sitting on the park bench, her heart sang. He watched her as she walked the twenty metres to where he was sitting, self-conscious of every step she took.

She had made an extra effort to look nice today, a subtle amount of lipstick on her rosebud lips, a small amount of mascara on her already dark lashes. Her hair was brushed and loose as it had been the day before and she wore another bohemian style dress with a headband to match. Her smile lit up the skies as she approached him, and she was so aware of his magnetism and appeal.

He was dressed differently too, not in his gardening outfit but in office clothes, dark trousers with a white shirt open slightly at the neck. She thought he looked even better looking today than he had yesterday.

As she approached, he stood and put his hands out, taking her hands and holding them.

"Glad you chose to come, Lucinda," he said, staring in her eyes as if looking for something.

"Everyone calls me Luce," she said.

"No. You will always be Lucinda to me," he said solemnly, cherishing her name.

"Do you feel like taking a little walk?" he asked, and she agreed.

They walked along Bell Street and down another side street, both wanting to keep well clear of Liddle Street. For forty-five minutes they walked, often holding hands and talked as if they would never run out of topics to talk about or things to say to each other. She told him how she had grown up in a strict household where her mother was grief stricken over her father and the three girls longed to be free. She told him of May and how they all adored her for her empathy, caring and bubbly personality.

When he asked her what she wanted in life, what her goals were, she stopped walking and looked at him. In truth, it wasn't something she had given much thought to.

"I just want to be happy," she said. "In anything I do, or wherever I end up, I would like to be happy and content with my life." It was true and she felt that once she left her mother's house, she would achieve this happiness.

They reached Bell Street again and another group of shops where they could see a takeaway store. Fifteen minutes later, they were sitting on a brick fence eating chips from a takeaway cup and giggling at how unhealthy it was.

Tarren admitted to her that he had not lived a happy childhood either, and there had just been his mother and three other siblings, with Tarren the youngest. He said they had moved around a lot when he was younger and never had one place to call home. His mother was domineering and despite coming from a rich family, he felt poor and rudderless. She noticed as he talked that his eyes looked glassy as if tears were threatening to overflow but they didn't. She felt sympathy for him as he talked and put her hand out, squeezing his hand.

He turned toward her, eyes searching her eyes and a hunger which went well beyond the chips. Their eyes locked and as he moved closer to her, she felt that magnetic pull of wanting to swallow him whole and possess him. She lifted her head slightly, accepting that he wanted to kiss her and wanting to kiss him back.

Their lips touched, just barely at first as if the sheer touch would be enough and then within seconds, he moved his lips and the kiss became deeper, more intense and honest. His right hand came up to caress her cheek as he kissed her, and she felt her entire body tingle with a feeling she had never felt before. He pulled back slightly, so their lips were apart, and he could look into her eyes. His hand continued gently caressing her face as she looked into those gold flecked brown eyes and her heart melted further.

"Do I taste like chips?" she asked him.

He laughed and the spell was broken as it had to be, sitting on a brick fence on a busy street. They both leaned back to finish their greasy chips and glance at each other, as if wishing to enjoy the secret they both now shared.

"Can I take you driving tomorrow?" he asked. "I'll show you some of the houses around Melbourne that I'm selling."

"Sure," she said. "I'm free after 3pm."

"Meet at the park bench?" he asked, and she agreed.

The two of them stood and headed back to the shops they had met at on this day, dropping their empty chip cups in the bin on the way.

Chapter 62

LUCINDA FLYNN 1999

Lucinda stared up at the ceiling above her bed and could still feel her heart fluttering. It was dark and quiet, and the only time during her time at home when she was free to dream of Tarren and remember the times they spent together.

It had been one whole week of knowing him and yet, she felt she had always known him. How did this even happen? She had been so lonely and naïve just over one week ago, going about her daily chores and activities, clueless that someone like him was out there on her horizon. Now, her world had changed, expanded and she felt the change that can only come with awareness, with the knowledge of a love greater than her imagination.

They had been going for drives and walks every day for the past week, and neither could bear the thought of a single day without seeing each other. The relationship was all consuming and even when she was not with him, she spent every waking moment thinking about him. She counted down each day until they could meet. Luckily, her mother assumed she was with May, and May assumed she had gone home with her mother.

Three days ago, they had stopped off at a house his business owned in North Ringwood which was fully furnished and would be either rented out or sold shortly. As Tarren opened the front door to the empty house, they both knew the reason why they had visited this property and headed straight to the bedroom.

An hour had been spent getting to know each other's body and despite being nervous and naïve, Tarren had been gentle and tender with Lucinda and she had responded to the urges. They had visited this house every day for three days and she felt she was learning and growing sexually. Her body ached for him, and she inwardly giggled at the thought that she was becoming a sex maniac.

On the fourth day, as they lay together enjoying each other's company after making love, Lucinda had turned to him. "You know, I don't even have a phone number for you. Do you think it's time we shared phone numbers?"

She felt him stiffen and draw in breath and she wondered if she had said something wrong. Slowly, she ran a finger down his bare chest and nestled her head against his shoulder. "I hope one day you can meet my family, and I could meet yours."

He had mentioned his siblings a few times who were all married with children, and his mother who stayed for a few weeks with each of her children. She knew her own mother wouldn't be the most welcoming person in the world, but she had managed not to scare away Bethany and Arabella's partners. Why would it be any different for her? Suddenly, a thought struck her. Was it possible he didn't want a future with her?

"Tarren?" she asked gently, wondering why he had not answered her.

He shifted in the bed and turned his head, so he was looking at her. His eyes searched her eyes, and she wondered what he was thinking. Then he leaned forward and touched his forehead to her forehead tenderly and held the connection for a few minutes. It was such a sweet and affectionate gesture without kissing, and Lucinda closed her eyes and enjoyed the sensation of touching him.

"I can't give you my home number," he said, and his voice took on a different tone, one she was not familiar with. She opened her eyes and waited for him to continue.

He took a few breaths and looked away, and she realised he was building himself up to say something. Suddenly, he sat up in bed and swung his legs over the side. She wriggled her body over to the side where he was, pulling the sheet with her.

"Tarren, are you ok? What's wrong?"

He was staring at the floor in front of him and rocking slightly as she could feel the slight movement. He glanced back at her and she could see torment in his eyes. Now she was becoming afraid of what was wrong. Was he about to say he no longer wished to see her? She felt a dread stab at her heart and knew she would be devastated if he no longer wanted to see her.

"Lucinda ..." he said slowly.

She sat up in bed, fearful of what she was about to hear.

"I'm already married."

Chapter 63

TARREN GRIMM 1999

Tarren let the hot shower water blast over him almost hoping it would burn his skin, as a punishment for his sins, for what he had done, for what he continued to do, for what he couldn't help doing. He would never forget the hurt look on Lucinda's face when he had told her he was already married. Her beautiful grey eyes had immediately filled with tears that spilled over and slid down her cheeks as if the dam had burst and there was no stopping it. He saw the light in her eyes flicker, a shadow pass over her face and he would swear he saw her heart break, but she never said a word. She lay silently, waiting for him to explain as the tears slid down her face.

He had leaned forward and touched foreheads again, wanting some sort of touch as a show of affection and love. He didn't even know how to explain anything to her.

"I never loved my wife," he said, and he knew what a dumbass thing that was to say, so he tried to correct it. "My mother arranged my marriage with someone she knew, and I agreed to do it." It was true, but it didn't sound true. It sounded like an excuse he was making up so he could play up on his wife. "I was eighteen years old, and I thought it would be exciting to get married and make my mother happy."

Lucinda still hadn't said anything and was staring up at him with tears spilling down her face.

"The truth is ... I'm very unhappy and when I saw you, I thought you were the most perfect girl I'd ever seen. I ..."

"Do you have children?" she cut him off.

He looked away. "Yes. Four."

"FOUR?" she asked, shocked.

He nodded. "Twin girl and boy, and two boys."

Lucinda moved and he saw she was moving down the bed slowly, looking for her clothes.

"Please, Lucinda," he said quietly to her. "I know it was wrong, but I'm in love with you. I really am. Totally. I can't tell you how much."

She had reached the foot of the bed and was leaning down to pick up underwear off the floor. The thought of her walking away from their relationship that day was unthinkable and unbearable.

"Lucinda. I'm sorry. Please talk to me. I want you. I love you. I want us to be together." She still would not looking at him and had started dressing again. What could he say to make it ok? There was nothing he could say that would make it ok because it was not ok. He knew it and he seemed to have no control over it. She was still dressing, silently and trying not to sob.

He could kick himself at how he had handled it. Of course, he had to tell her the truth but what could he have said that would have made it any better. She didn't even know about him being a Grimm yet and that he had been stalking her with a view to potentially harming her family. Somehow, he didn't think that was going to go down very well when he did tell her.

"Ok," he said resigned. "I'll take you home if that's what you want. Please, Lucinda. Can we meet again tomorrow and talk? Please?"

She still wasn't looking at him, so he gathered his clothing and dressed. She disappeared into the bathroom and was only gone a few minutes. When she emerged, she had washed her face and straightened up. She wouldn't look him in the eye but at least, she was looking toward him when she spoke.

"Ok. I'm ready to go now," she said, the voice sounding brighter than he knew she felt.

They had driven back to Coburg in silence but when he stopped at the shops where they always met, he leaned across and took her arm.

"Lucinda, please believe me that I'm totally in love with you. I want to be with you, and I know you want to be with me too. Please think about us tonight. I will be here at the shops tomorrow and every day until you will talk to me."

He let her arm go and she immediately opened the car door and stepped out. It was the first time he had ever seen her walk away from him without looking back.

It felt like the end.

Chapter 64
TARREN GRIMM 1999

Tarren glanced at his wristwatch for the tenth time in the past five minutes and the time had barely moved. He was sitting on the park bench where they had first lunched together seven weeks ago and once again, he ordered a beef and salad sandwich and a coffee. He was forced to admit the sandwiches from this shop was really tasty with extra thick slices of roast beef.

He had been there for lunch every day for six weeks now, between 12.30 and 1.30 every afternoon, mostly sitting on this park bench except for the two times it had been raining so he had sat in his parked car. Lucinda had not turned up, not even once, but he still couldn't give up hoping that she would. He was starting to think that six weeks without a sign of her was probably a pretty good indication that it was all over. Next week, he would face the facts and try to move on with his life.

His home life was difficult as he couldn't look at his wife, Marion, now that he had experienced Lucinda and Marion knew something was wrong. She had tried to ask him a few times and he had shrugged it off, unable to look at her and given her some bad-tempered response. The hope that Lucinda would appear one lunch time kept him sane, and he worried how he would react next week if he gave up on the solitude lunch appointments.

"Tarren."

He swung his head around, thinking he was hearing things and there she stood at the other end of the park bench. She was a vision in a purple and red velvet dress with her red gold hair cascading down her front. She wasn't smiling but had a slightly sad and melancholy look about her. He jumped to his feet, careful not to knock the coffee and half eaten sandwich off.

"Lucinda," he said. "You look so beautiful."

It was all he could think of to say, and he saw a slight smile momentarily appear on her lips.

"May I sit with you?" she asked, and he gestured with his hand to the bench, and sat down again. She sat leaving a gap between the two of them with his coffee and sandwich in between.

"Can I get you some lunch?" he asked, and she shook her head negatively.

He looked at her, heart thumping, hoping she was here for the right reason, that she wanted to continue seeing him again, but also terrified that she was telling him to go away forever.

"I've missed you," he said.

Again, that slight smile but it didn't last. She looked away and he could see she was determined to stay strong and not cry.

"I've missed you too," she said quietly. "I can't have a relationship with a married man."

He nodded. "I know, but I want you more than anything in the world. I will walk away from my marriage to be with you."

"But you have children," she countered.

"Yes. I do but I can still see them and live apart from them."

"I'd be a home wrecker. I don't know if I can be a home wrecker," she said.

"There's more I haven't told you." He paused and drew in breath, wishing he didn't have to disclose this to her, but knowing that he must. "Another thing I haven't told you ... is what my surname is." He looked across at her and she turned to face him. He could see the puzzled look on her face as she tried to analyse what his surname had to do with anything.

"It's Grimm," he said.

There was about a two second pause in time where nothing happened and then he saw her eyes widen in shock as the name registered with her. He saw her eyes scan up to his hair and his eyebrows and then back to his eyes. Then he could see her eyes change, the wide-eyed look became more slanted and almost squinted as her anger flared.

"What are you doing? What have you done?" she asked angrily. "Is this a set up?"

She was making movements as if to stand up and he put his hand out to take her arm gently.

"No. I'll tell you the truth. I was investigating what happened to my father and brothers as I had always heard bizarre stories from my mother. Don't forget, I was only four years old when my family died."

He looked across at her and she was still, looking back at him and listening, though her body was tensed to flee.

"I only had Marvellous Maybelline's name and Agatha, the taller witch."

It was the first time he had used the word 'witch' in front of her and he saw her twitch slightly.

"I found out where Marvellous Maybelline lived and watched for a while, saw you on your way to the shop and followed."

He heard her exclamation of surprise, and he looked suitably ashamed. He knew it was vital that he was honest at this point of the story, or she would never trust him.

"I wasn't expecting to fall in love. I thought I was just researching the story so I could understand what had happened. I did learn about May being stabbed by my father and that my mother's cousin caused the death of your father. I do realise that my family were the instigators and harmed your family first. There have been terrible events on both sides, and I want to make sure nothing like this ever happens again."

He finished with an emphasis on the word 'again' and saw that she was deep in thought, still looking at him.

"Against all odds Lucinda, I fell in love with you."

She sat back and sighed, and he felt hope. She hadn't got up screaming and ran away. Could it still work out?

"I had decided not to see you anymore," she said. "It doesn't mean I don't think about you all the time because I do, but I can't be a home wrecker." She paused for a moment, and he felt he was almost holding his breath. "I came looking for you today, hoping you would be here because I needed to tell you something."

He was almost on the edge of his seat hanging on her every word. "What?" he asked.

"I'm pregnant," she said.

Chapter 65

LUCINDA FLYNN 1999

Lucinda collected the mail in the letterbox, sifting through the three envelopes to read the sender. She looked up as the silver car entered the court where she lived, recognising the vehicle immediately. She sighed and waited for the car to pull up at her front gate.

Tarren stepped out of the car and her breath caught in her throat as it always did when she saw him, especially when the sun caught the gold in his hair. He walked up to her and without a word, the two of them leaned forward and touched foreheads to each other and held. It had been their greeting almost from the start. It was a coming together where two becomes one. Tarren used this time to look down at her expanding belly as he always did. Gently, he lifted his hand and placed it on her belly.

"Tarren, you can't keep coming around here," she said, pretending to be cross. "Even if you are my landlord."

The house she lived in was the one Tarren's company owned in North Ringwood, the fully furnished house where the two of them had met each day with their lovemaking trysts and the place their baby had been conceived. He had proposed she live there rent-free as his way of helping out with the baby. She eventually agreed knowing she could not stay with her mother and unable to afford a house on her own. One condition had been that he could not expect to visit or arrive unannounced and that they were not a couple. He had reluctantly agreed but had been arriving once a week to check how she was and how the baby was. She didn't invite him in, and he didn't ask.

"I just want to make sure you are doing ok, and the little one," he said, smiling down at her belly.

"We are. You know the baby can't know you or my mother. I don't want the witch or magic life for this little one at all. Look at all the pain being magical has caused our families. This little one has it on both sides," she said, knowing what she said would hurt him.

His face fell at the thought of not seeing his baby. "I don't think you're going to have a choice," he said.

"What do you mean?"

"I can feel the baby. It's magical," he said, his face showing surprise and a little delight.

"You're just saying that. It is not," she said firmly.

"It is, and ... it can feel me too."

Her first thought was that it was a Grimm baby and would be born with dark eyebrows and blonde hair. What would her mother say? Tarren could see the look on her face and guessed what might be causing it.

"I might be wrong, but I think it's a girl and I think it's a witch," he said, trying to read her thoughts.

"No. No it won't be a witch. It can't be a witch," she said, worry in her voice. You can't come here anymore Tarren. I'm sorry. You can't. I can't let this baby be a Grimm or a witch. Do you understand? Will this baby be hated by both sides of the family? Hated by the witches for being a Grimm and hated by the Grimm's for being a witch?"

"Please don't shut me out," he said, and she could see the pleading on his face. "You know what I want, what I still want."

She did, and she had made it clear that while his children were young, she would not allow him to leave his marriage. It was better in her mind that he never got to know this baby than for her to take away the father of four little children.

"I'm sorry, Tarren," she said, and she turned reluctantly and walked back into the house. She forced herself not to turn and look back at him but once she was inside the house, she peeked out a window blind and saw him standing still staring up at the house.

She burst into tears.

Chapter 66

NIAMH FLYNN 2000

Niamh Bridget Flynn was born at 11.50pm on 12 March 2000 in an electrical storm. Lucinda had chosen to face labour and birth alone, though her sisters would happily have been present if allowed. Lucinda had kept everything to do with her pregnancy and the father quiet. Her sisters, mother and May only knew that Lucinda had experienced a short and passionate affair with a married man, fallen pregnant and he was supporting her by allowing her to live rent-free. Lucinda was not prepared for them to know any more details. For any of them to be present during labour and birth, left open the possibility of her saying something in the throes of labour pains that she didn't want them to know, and what if the baby was born with dark eyebrows and blonde hair?

During contractions, Lucinda was aware of a few strange things happening in the delivery suite around her, including trolleys upending suddenly, doors slamming, and lights flickering on and off. The midwife was sure it was the storm causing the disturbances, but Lucinda had doubts.

The relief was immense when told the baby was a girl with tufts of dark reddish hair. Within hours, Bethany and Arabella visited and were enamoured with the baby. The next morning, her mother visited along with May, though neither held the baby. They were only able to see her through the window of the nursery. Lucinda saw the two of them pass a look and she wondered if they were suspicious that she was a witch, but there was no way they could know she was half Grimm, Lucinda hoped.

Lucinda made the decision to keep Niamh away from May and her mother as much as was possible, as she knew it would only be a matter of time before they became aware that she was a witch, and it was the last thing Lucinda wanted. She was adamant that his baby would not be a Grimm or a witch. This child would be brought up as a normal child and if she was meant to be a witch, she could choose for herself one day.

In the afternoon, Lucinda made her way down to the nursery where Niamh had been placed while Lucinda enjoyed a shower. There were six other babies in cots in the nursery so she walked around viewing each newborn when she became aware of someone standing at the nursery window.

She turned and saw the familiar handsome face and blonde hair of Tarren standing quietly staring at her. Without a word, she walked over to the inside of the nursery window and placed her hand up on the glass in a greeting. He placed his hand on the opposite side of the glass against hers and they looked into each other's eyes. Time stood still as the two of them met in another world, and quietly, they both leaned forward until their foreheads were touching via the glass. They held this position for minutes and then silently, they both pulled back.

Tarren looked past her at the seven cots in the nursery and without being told, his eyes went straight to Niamh's cot which was the second from the right side of the room. Lucinda wondered if he could feel her like he could when she was pregnant. He looked back at Lucinda, his eyes pleading to be allowed to see the baby.

She nodded slightly and walked over, wheeling the cot over to the nursery window so he could see her. He stared down at Niamh sleeping peacefully, her little rosebud mouth twitching every now and again as if dreaming. Lucinda stared down at her daughter proudly and wished things could be different. She wondered how it would have been if they could have been together for this special moment, sharing this little bundle of joy.

After a few minutes, she looked up at Tarren and could see a tear rolling down his cheek. She felt a sob catch in her own throat and looked away quickly. She indicated to him that he could go now, and wheeled Niamh away and back to her room. She didn't turn back to look at him.

That had been the last time she was in close proximity to Tarren. Over the coming months and years, occasionally she saw him from a distance and knew he was watching her and Niamh but knew better than to approach them.

It was the way it had to be.

Chapter 67

NIAMH FLYNN 2018

Niamh eyes glared at her mother and then the strange man in her kitchen, then back to her mother. She couldn't decide where her eyes should rest. Did she just mishear what her mother said? Had her mother lost her feeble mind? This man was a Grimm, not the father of a witch.

Then it dawned on her, he must be using magic to influence her mother and make her believe they knew each other. This must be a ploy to get at Niamh from inside her own family, using her mother.

"Have you lost your mind? This man is a Grimm! What's he doing in our house?" Niamh asked, outrage dripping from her voice.

"Niamh," said her mother, calmly. "This is actually his house, and he has allowed us to live here for the past eighteen years."

Niamh shook her head. No. She didn't believe that. "My father, eh? Where has he been my whole life? Why suddenly appear now?"

"Niamh," spoke the man, his voice calm and smooth. "I would've given anything to be part of your life. Lucinda ... your mother, thought it best that you be raised as a normal child and not a witch or a Grimm."

"A Grimm? A GRIMM?" Niamh's voice was getting louder. She glared at her mother angrily. "I'm not a GRIMM!"

Her mother pulled a face. "No, but Tarren is your father, Niamh."

"But this doesn't make sense. There is a Grimm guy who has been stalking me and disembowelling animals on our doorstep, and he beat up my friend, Maddy and put her in hospital. I believe he wants to kill me. How the hell can I be a Grimm if the Grimm's are trying to kill me?" she said in frustration.

The man shook his head angrily. "I've just found out that the family has done these things. My son, Justin was the guilty one. I've reprimanded him and told the family they are to immediately halt anything they had planned to do."

"So, you're saying my own half-brother is trying to kill me?" she mocked. "Does he know, do any of them know that I am supposedly your child?"

"Ummm ... no," he answered. "To them, you're a witch."

"When did you tell your family to leave me alone?" Niamh asked.

"Last week," he answered.

"Well, they didn't listen because there is still someone following me around. I've sensed them a number of times including today," she responded.

She saw his eyes widen and a frown crease his forehead. He stared at her for a few minutes and deciding she was being honest, turned back to Niamh's mother.

"Lucinda, I must go and make sure this issue is over."

The two of them stared into each other's eyes for what seemed like an eternity, then both leaned forward and touched their foreheads together. It was the strangest thing Niamh had ever seen, and she wondered if she was the one who had lost their mind. The two of them pulled apart, still gazing into each other's eyes. He kissed the top of her forehead and then left, walking past Niamh who stepped back as though not wanting him to invade her space in any way. Closing the door, he was gone. Niamh looked at her mother who was standing in the same spot staring at the closed front door.

"I think you'd better tell me how this happened," Niamh said.

Chapter 68

LUCINDA FLYNN 2018

Lucinda gazed at her daughter, knowing it was time to tell her the truth of her existence after eighteen years of avoidance and untruths. She nodded and pointed to the lounge chairs where they both retired.

She had never rehearsed this and had no idea where to even start with this story. She could see Niamh sitting with her legs crossed, patiently waiting for her to begin. She also noticed that the drink coasters on the coffee table in front of them were spinning all by themselves as Niamh tried to control her emotions.

"Ok. Ok. It's time you heard the truth," her mother started.

Niamh cut her off with a raised voice. "Oh, you think so?"

"Ok. Calm down, Niamh. I've said before that everything I did, I thought I was doing it for the best."

"Don't you think you'd seriously have to reconsider what you think is the best, considering your record so far?"

Lucinda let the barb go without answer. She could understand why Niamh was so angry and she wished it wasn't this way.

"I was a naïve girl of twenty years living with my mother and I met a man at the shops. He was so handsome, friendly, talkative and polite. We had lunch together sitting on a park bench and then we arranged to meet in the same place for lunch the next day. We talked as if we were soul mates and laughed at the same things."

She wiped a tear away that had strayed down her cheek. "Don't forget, you are a witch and can sense when a Grimm is around, but I am just a normal person and had no idea." She pulled a tissue out of her pocket to dab at her eyes.

"Before long, we were going for drives and walks and eventually, we became ... lovers. We talked about living together forever and having a wonderful life. I was so completely in love with him, and I knew he was with me."

Lucinda looked over at Niamh and saw she was listening with no expression on her face.

"Did your mother or May know about him?" asked Niamh, knowing that they would have flipped their lid if they'd known.

"No. I kept it a secret at the time, not even knowing he was a Grimm. It was just my private life, and I didn't want to share it." Another dab with the tissue.

"One day, he told me he was married with four children but would leave them for me. That was the end. I would never have started the relationship if I had known he was married with children. I'll never be a home wrecker. Then he admitted that there was an ulterior motive for when we met. He said that he was a Grimm and my mother ... your grandmother, was the one who burned his father and two brothers to death. He'd been very young when it happened and didn't know much about it, so he'd began to investigate the story and we met. He said he had fallen in love with me though it was never his intention. I know this all sounds too incredible to be true, but it is. I broke up with him and then a few weeks later I found out I was pregnant with you. I met with him and told him about the pregnancy. He wanted to leave his family and be with us, but I refused. Eventually, he offered a house for us to live in as a way of supporting us, but I told him he was not allowed to have anything to do with us, and you, in particular."

Niamh just stared at her without any emotion showing on her face.

"It's true, Niamh. I don't know what to say. I've not seen Tarren since the day you were born. He came to the hospital to see you and he was upset. I only contacted him again recently to tell him that we're moving house and don't need his charity anymore. Suddenly, this afternoon, he turned up at our house to talk to me. He said he left his wife one week ago."

"One week ago?" asked Niamh. "What has that got to do with you?"

Lucinda looked down, working up the courage to tell Niamh the truth, then she looked directly at her. "I always told him that I would never consider being with him while his children were young. He says his children are grown-up, and he has left his wife. He wants us to be together now."

Niamh blinked a few times. What happened to the earlier thought of this being the best day of her life. Hadn't that turned to shit?

"You're going to be together now? Together with him? Together with a Grimm?" she asked, voice raised.

"Together with your father," she said. Niamh stared at her mother and could see the determination in her eyes.

"I've got to go out," said Niamh and headed for the door.

Chapter 69
TARREN GRIMM 2018

Tarren parked his car outside the house on the street and looked up at the house. He had lived here his entire married life and yet, looking at the building now, it felt like a prison. It had always felt like a prison, but it was one he was determined to break out of.

He had called a family meeting but the rest of the family would not arrive until 7pm which was still three hours away. Time enough for him to organise the boxes he had been packing in the past week and send them into storage with a view to staying at a hotel for the time being. He knew he couldn't just move in with Lucinda at this stage, and she had plans to relocate anyway. There was still a lot to plan and organise but for the first time in twenty years, he felt optimistic about his future.

Marion was home but other than acknowledging her, he barely spoke a word to her. He headed to his office to prepare for moving out that very night. After a few trips to the car with boxes, he walked around the house, looking at each room to determine if there was anything he should take with him. Eventually, he took one photo album that contained photos of own children. He felt that one day, Niamh may be interested in knowing more about the family.

Just over three hours later, the family were gathered in the dining room. He'd seen them arrive from the window of his office. His four children along with partners and children, had parked out on the street and headed in for the family meeting. He waited twenty minutes to allow them to settle, greet each other and be ready for him.

He knew they all thought of him as a useless drunk and the truth was that he had partaken of too much alcohol over the past twenty years. The alcohol had been a crutch to drown his sorrows, soften the edges and give him something to enjoy in life. He looked over at the liquor cabinet now and was tempted to down a shot of whisky, but he decided he needed his wits about him tonight.

With a deep breath, he headed down to the dining room and spent a few minutes greeting his offspring. He could tell by their expressions that they were wondering why the meeting had been called, and by him who never attended family meetings. He assumed the position at the head of the table and sat down with everyone following suit. The room was near silent with the exception of a few children and a baby making a few distracting noises.

"I called you all here tonight, so you hear my news straight from me and there is no confusion over what's happening."

Every eye was on him as he looked around the table.

"I'm moving out of this house, tonight. I will be seeking a divorce from your mother."

All eyes turned to Marion and her eyes dropped to the table, not from emotion or sadness, but from what the Grimm family would consider a failure to manage her marriage adequately.

"I will be staying temporarily in a hotel until I sort out my affairs. You have my mobile phone number if you need to contact me."

He could hear some slight murmuring, and he knew a few were asking why he was leaving. Divorce and separation were unheard of in the Grimm household.

"There's something else I would like to make very clear to you all, and I would like it to filter down to all members of our family. The young witch, known as Niamh Flynn, is not to be touched, harmed or stalked in any way."

Now, he really had their attention, particularly as he knew her name and other than the surname, Flynn, none of them did.

"Why?" asked Justin, the one that had been tasked with all the stalking.

Tarren looked around at all the puzzled faces staring at him, all so similar in appearance, as with his own appearance. Should he conjure up a semi-valid reason, but he couldn't think of a reason that would be enough for them to leave her alone. He didn't know how they would respond to the truth but to emphasise how imperative it is that she be safe, he felt he had no choice.

"She is my daughter."

The room erupted in movement and noise, and murmurs of 'What?' and 'How?' and exclamations of disbelief. Marion was staring at him with mouth open and horror on her face. Tarren waited for the noise to abate before he continued.

"Niamh Flynn is my daughter with Lucinda Flynn and is a witch. No one is to touch her, or you'll have me to deal with." The last sentence was spoken with a ferocity that they had never seen in him before. "I'm leaving now and as I said, you have my mobile number if you wish to reach me."

He looked around the room at his wife and his children and grandchildren, then with regret, he left the room. He walked out of the house and out to his car on the street. Puzzled, he stood and looked around him at all the cars with flat tyres, not just one tyre but all four tyres on each car, and the rubbish strewn all over the road from the kerbside bins which were placed for rubbish collection in the morning.

He knew Niamh had been there tonight and he rang an Uber.

Chapter 70

NIAMH FLYNN 2018

Niamh climbed into Lola and left the court where she lived in North Ringwood not sure where she was going. She just knew she had to leave and be on her own for a while. All her previous plans of going to see Emma and the two of them going for a drive had fallen in a heap with what had just occurred with Tarren Grimm. She couldn't bring herself to say that he was her father, and she couldn't really believe it at all. How was this possible?

A Grimm? She was a witch, sworn enemy of the Grimm family. How could she be witch and a Grimm? She likened it to finding out you were half angel and half demon at the same time. There was a major clash with this breeding, and she couldn't accept it.

Did May know? Did her aunts know? Had her grandmother known? Was she the only one who didn't know? She felt tainted as if nothing would ever cleanse her and at that moment, she hated her mother and she hated herself.

She couldn't face Emma now although she knew that tomorrow, she would need to sit down and talk to Emma about everything. Knowing Emma, she would think it was cool. Emma thought everything to do with Niamh's weird family was cool. Emma was so calm and sensible that she always made Niamh feel she was over-reacting and needed to be more accepting. That was exactly what she needed to hear but not right now. Not tonight.

Should she go and talk to May? She needed to know if May had also betrayed her, and she hoped that was not the case. She knew she was close to crying and if she found out May had known all along and not told her, she didn't know if she could contain herself. She drove toward Coburg and in her emotional state, she had very little control over magic. The windscreen wipers furiously flicked back and forward across the windscreen despite there being no rain, and Niamh had not turned them on. Traffic lights changed green, amber, red, green, amber, red in rapid succession as she approached. Cars automatically moved out of her way with startled drivers staring at her as she drove past.

Finally, she reached 14 Liddle Street in Coburg and parked Lola on the street. She hesitated before stepping out, took a few deep breaths and by the time she stepped out, May was standing on the front step, watching her and waiting, glass of red wine in hand. She watched Niamh walking slowly through the gate and up to where May was standing.

"Are you alright, love?" May asked in a worried voice, looking at Niamh's face.

"No," said Niamh and burst into tears.

May put her arm around Niamh and Niamh sunk into her large chest. "Come on inside. I'll fix you a nice glass of red wine. Fixes everything. Trust me."

Within thirty minutes, Niamh was comfortable on a cosy sofa with a toasted cheese sandwich and a glass of red wine. She had filled May in on the afternoon's events and May was genuinely shocked.

"Did you know, May? Did you know my father was one of the Grimm's?" asked Niamh.

"Hell no! I certainly did not, but it explains a few things. I remember back when we first found out Lucinda ... your mother was pregnant. She refused to say who the father was, just that there'd been an affair with a married man, and it was over. No wonder she was so secretive. Agatha would've had a fit." May gave a whistling sound to indicate Agatha's ire.

"Do you think my grandmother suspected?" Niamh asked.

"She would've said something to me. We saw you in hospital when you were a newborn and we both suspected you were a witch but no, not that your father was a Grimm."

"When my grandmother was dying and she grabbed my arm, she said that Lucinda was brilliant, or something like that. I think she knew," said Niamh. "I feel like a freak now."

"Sweetheart, you are unique. I bet there is no one else in the world that is witch and Grimm at the same time. I don't even know what the Grimm's are. Grimm is a surname so they must be something magical like fairy, or elf, or goblin or something. You are special and one of a kind. You should be pleased," said May.

Niamh couldn't think of it as something to be pleased about but she did feel better after talking with May. A bed was made up for her on the sofa with a pillow and blanket, but she told May she had something she needed to do first, then she would be back for the night.

Niamh drove to Templestowe where she saw several expensive cars parked out the front of the Grimm house. She knew it was the Grimm house as the AirTag she had planted on the car showed her the exact location of where the vehicle was parked in the garage. Using magic, she punctured all four tyres on every car she suspected to be a Grimm car. As she was about to leave, she saw that each householder had their recycle bin and household rubbish bin sitting on the kerb waiting to be emptied early in the morning. Using magic, she upended the Grimm bins and scattered the rubbish across the street.

Feeling good with herself that she had achieved something worthwhile, she drove back to May's house for the night.

Chapter 71

GRIMM HOUSEHOLD 2018

After Tarren left the room, there was a dead silence for several minutes. Eventually, Justin left the room and returned ten minutes later to say his father had just caught an Uber. At this point, everyone started talking at once, surprised, horrified and shocked at the news he had just announced.

The news that Tarren was leaving and planning to divorce Marion was shocking enough but the fact that the young witch was his daughter blew their minds. No one saw that coming and many expressed disbelief that this could be true. One explanation expressed was that the alcohol Tarren had consumed over the past two decades had seriously addled his brain and he was now imagining things that were not true.

"Does she look like us?" asked Monica.

"Not at all," said Justin. "She looks like a witch."

"How can we find out if it's true or not?" asked Beaton's wife, Angela.

Everyone was silent as they thought on this predicament.

"Blood," said Anton. "That's it. You can tell by the blood. We can smell it, can't we? We can smell one of us if blood is spilled."

The others started an animated discussion about the blood, and all agreed it was the only way. They needed to confront her and somehow, spill some of her blood so they would know by the scent.

"How are we going to do that?" asked Beaton. "Punch her in the nose? Ask her nicely if we can cut her wrist or become blood brother and sister?"

"If we so much as touch her, Dad will be all over us," said Justin.

"But he won't know until afterward, and he may thank us if we find out she's not his daughter," said Anton.

"She can sense us a mile away. How are we going to get anywhere near her to do this?" asked Justin.

Anton looked at his two brothers, Justin and Beaton. "I think it's going to take both of you to do this. One to hold her, one to cable-tie her hands and legs and cut her arm just a little. We can't hurt her unless we find out she doesn't have our blood. Then it's open slather."

Justin and Beaton looked at each other and agreed.

"There's one more thing," said Monica. "Dad said the young witch was not to be harmed. He didn't say anything about the old witch." She smiled at her recollection.

The three brothers smiled at each other, knowing their assignment just became more exciting.

"Right. We wait for the two of them to leave the house and grab them on the street. We get them in the back of a car and take them to a quiet location. Does anyone have a gun?" asked Beaton. No one did.

"I think the old witch is the key as she is old and slow. If you grab her from behind and threaten to cut her throat with a knife, the young witch will do whatever you want," said Anton.

"How much magic does she have, the young witch? Does anyone know?" asked Monica.

"Can't be too much. She was only bestowed a few weeks ago and it looks like she is learning from scratch," said Beaton.

"We need to do this pronto," said Anton.

All agreed.

Chapter 72

NIAMH FLYNN 2018

Niamh showered at May's house the next morning and thanked May for her hospitality. It wasn't that she was totally avoiding going home and seeing her mother, but she wanted some time to think about the situation and talk to people. She was already feeling more positive from discussions with May and now, she planned to visit Emma. She'd sent Emma a text and they were going to go out driving in Lola.

"Thank you, May. I'll come around tomorrow. Today I'll see Emma and then go home and see what's going on there," she told her, voice dropping when she mentioned home.

Emma was waiting out the front of her house and was in raptures about Lola. She thought Lola was so perfect for Niamh and the two girls excitedly set off for a drive, chatting furiously. After a few minutes of discussion, it was decided to drive to Bendigo and back. Bendigo is an old gold mining town two hours north of Melbourne and the plan was by the time they drove to Bendigo, ate lunch and drove back, most of the day would be spent.

On the way, Niamh told Emma the latest fiasco with Tarren Grimm being her father, or supposedly so and how her mother and Tarren were planning a life together. Emma listened carefully, asked a few thoughtful questions and then stated that she thought Niamh was in an ideal situation.

"How so?" Niamh asked.

"Well, you have the best of both worlds, don't you think? You are a witch and still learning, but it sounds like you will be one with strong abilities. Plus ... you have Grimm blood and surely, no Grimm would touch one of their own."

Niamh hadn't thought that way, and maybe that made sense. Would a Grimm harm their own blood? Maybe Tarren would let his son know that they were half-siblings and then he would back off and leave her alone. What if the sibling was only a half blood? Did that make a difference?

They reached Bendigo around 11am and sat at a lake, eating a Subway sandwich and throwing pieces of bread to the ducks and geese. It wasn't long before the two of them were forced to stand on top of the picnic table to escape the aggressive geese and then make a run for the vehicle, squealing and giggling as the geese chased them.

Once safe inside Lola, the two of them laughed so hard, that their sides ached. It was just what Niamh needed. They headed back to Melbourne and Niamh dropped Emma back at her house around 3pm. Emma had calmed and reassured Niamh as she always did, and Niamh was thankful for having such a staid and steady friend.

There was nothing else now except to head home and face her mother. She wasn't looking forward to it though she knew it was time. It had been so much easier to delay the event and just talk about it, but she knew it was time to confront it. She parked Lola out the front, pleased to see the BMW was not present.

She found her mother in the kitchen, packing pots and pans into boxes. Her mother stood and wiped her brow.

"Oh good. I've been worried about you, Niamh. Are you ok?" she asked.

"Yes. I'm fine. I stayed at May's the night, and spent the day with Emma today," she explained.

Her mother nodded. "Is there anything you would like to ask me?"

Niamh thought for a moment.

"Did you ever think of having a termination when you found out you were pregnant?" she asked.

"No. Never. Tarren was the love of my life, and even though I found out afterward that he was married, and a Grimm, it didn't stop me loving him. You were conceived in love. Please remember that."

Niamh looked at her mother, and saw her eyes focused on Niamh. She looked honest and genuine, and Niamh in that instant, believed her story about loving Tarren. If it were not the case, wouldn't she have made an appointment to terminate?

"I still don't know what to think of it all, mum," she told her mother honestly.

"It's ok. There's no hurry. I'm just glad you know now. I'm sick of secrets."

"Have you told your sisters yet?" asked Niamh.

"Errr … no. Not yet. I 'll do that today."

Niamh wondered in the Grimm household, if her existence was still a secret or if it had blown open.

Chapter 73

LUCINDA FLYNN 2018

Niamh left for the day mid-morning, announcing she was on her way to visit Maddy before heading to May's. Lucinda invited Bethany and Arabella around to her house in North Ringwood at 11am. She spent the night awake, rehearsing how she would tell her sisters about Tarren. She worried that this news was not going to go down well and the last thing she needed was to be estranged from her sisters. It was difficult enough trying to manage Niamh's reaction to the news of her father, but she felt they may have turned a corner in acceptance.

Her sisters arrived within minutes of each other in their brightly coloured bohemian clothing and again, without pre-planning, the three of them looked like peas in a pod. Different coloured dresses and different coloured hair and yet so similar, that it was uncanny. Any neighbour hearing their overlapping chatter would have thought they were speaking another language.

Lucinda sat the two of them on stools in the kitchen this time as it seemed more practical for this conversation. Other times, they had sat in lounge chairs in the open plan living area but today was different. Lucinda placed coffee in front of them and a plate of Anzac biscuits she had just baked.

"How's your packing going?" asked Arabella, glancing around at the boxes scattered around the room with half packed items.

"It's getting there. We should be done in a week's time, I hope," answered Lucinda.

"How's Niamh doing? Is she still seeing May each day and learning how to witch?" asked Bethany.

"She is the regular witch these days, and has become really close with May," answered Lucinda.

The two sisters shared a glance and took a sip of their coffee. "So, you called us here for a reason, we assume," said Bethany. The two sisters thought Lucinda had called them to a meeting to discuss some formality about renting the house at 20 Liddle Street in Coburg.

Lucinda put her cup down. She was standing on the kitchen side of the bench while her two sisters sat on stools on the outer side.

"I did. I want to tell you of a recent development," Lucinda said, glancing from one to the other.

Two sets of eyebrows raised, no doubt thinking that after finding out Niamh was a true witch and bestowed, what other development could there possibly be.

"It's about Niamh's father," said Lucinda. She had decided to tell them in small pieces at a time rather than just spill the whole story in one go.

Both sisters put their coffee cups down. All they knew of Niamh's father was that Lucinda had enjoyed a brief and passionate affair with a married man, became pregnant and he had paid for their rent or supported the two of them for all of Niamh's life. There had never been any further mention of him by Lucinda so as far as they knew, he had never seen his daughter or had any further contact with either of them. She had their full attention now.

"He and I are going to pursue a relationship."

"Pursue a relationship? No wife on the scene anymore?" asked Arabella, voice a little smug.

"No. His children have grown up, and he has left his wife. I was never prepared to break up a marriage especially when there were children involved," said Lucinda.

The sisters glanced at each other again. They had not been aware that there were children involved.

"Have you seen him in the past twenty years or so?" asked Bethany.

"No. Not since Niamh was born. I told him he could not be part of her life," said Lucinda and saw her sisters' sharp intake of breath.

"That's pretty harsh, isn't it, Luce? Refusing to let a father see his child, even if they had another family," said Bethany.

"I had to be harsh," Lucinda said firmly. "I had to protect Niamh, no matter what." She could see the puzzled look on her sister's faces.

"Has Niamh met her father yet?" asked Arabella.

"Yes. She met him two days ago. It didn't go particularly well, but there's plenty of time for her to get to know him. We're going to take our relationship slowly and see how it goes. After this long, we need to get to know each other all over again," said Lucinda.

"There's a complication I want you both to understand." She paused, looking at each of them and seeing them wide-eyed with puzzlement and waiting for the revelation.

"His name is Tarren." She paused to brace herself for the onslaught. "Tarren Grimm."

The silence lasted approximately two seconds.

"WHAT?" cried one of them, and both jumped to their feet.

"LUCE, ARE YOU JOKING? YOU CAN'T BE SERIOUS."

"WHAT ARE YOU SAYING? A GRIMM? DID YOU SAY GRIMM? FOR REAL?"

"WHAT THE FUCK?"

The two sisters had stepped back a few steps in shock and Arabella was sucking in air as if she was having trouble breathing and was going to pass out. Bethany was the first to calm down a little and turn back to Lucinda.

"Luce, are you telling us that Niamh's father is a Grimm?" she asked.

Lucinda nodded. This was how she had imagined they would react.

"Why would you do that? Why would you have a relationship with one of them? Oh my God! I can't believe this. Oh my God," said Bethany. She bent over as if to be sick.

"I didn't know he was a Grimm when we started a relationship years ago, or that he was married." Lucinda started to say.

"Nice guy, eh?" said Bethany, sarcastically. "How could you not know either of those things?"

"But ... I fell in love with him. I still love him, and I always have," Lucinda said softly.

Arabella had calmed and joined the conversation. "So, Niamh has just found out that she has Grimm blood in her veins?"

"Yes. As I said earlier, it didn't go down very well at first, but I think she's still digesting it," said Lucinda.

"I bet," said Bethany.

"Poor Niamh," said Arabella. "What a thing to find out. The shock ... Oh my God."

"Luce, he could be the Grimm who stabbed May or the one who killed our father. Did you ever think of that?" asked Bethany.

"Our mother killed his father and brothers. His father is the one who stabbed May. He investigated it and although not condoning the deaths, felt his family had been the instigators," replied Lucinda.

"He could have started this with you as a retaliation, a way of getting a foot in the door. He could be wanting to get rid of us all," said Arabella, starting to panic a little, eyes darting around the room.

There was a knock on the front door. Lucinda looked at her sisters.

"I asked Tarren to come here and meet you both."

Chapter 74

NIAMH FLYNN 2018

Niamh picked up Emma in Lola and the two of them headed over to Maddy's house. Plans were afoot for the four of them to attend a local café. Maddy was still black and blue and with a cast on her arm, but her mother had thought she would be fine to coffee with her friends locally. She thought it would be beneficial for Maddy to enjoy her friends and escape the house for a short time.

Rather than force injured Maddy to climb through the collapsed forward front seat to reach the back seat of Lola, Emma had agreed she would climb in the back with Lee, and Maddy could sit in the front passenger seat. Lola had never driven so many passengers, and it was the first time Lee and Maddy had seen Lola. They too were absolutely in love with her. Lola had never enjoyed such a fan club as she did at the ripe old age of 48 years old.

"She's practically vintage," said Lee who was very into vintage clothing and accessories.

They drove a few kilometres away and parked near the café at North Ringwood where the four of them found a table in the sunshine out the front of the shop. Maddy was vastly improved from when Niamh had last seen her but still looked beaten. Her lips revealed less swelling but still exhibited scabs from the injuries, her tooth still chipped, her eye and cheek bone was now a strange shade of yellow, but she appeared more cheerful and more Maddy-like.

Niamh had spoken to Emma beforehand to ensure that there was no mention in conversation of the Grimm family and what it meant. She didn't want Maddy to know anything about the Grimm's and that her assault was in retaliation for not being able to get to Niamh. She was prepared to discuss her father suddenly arriving back on the scene, but no detail. One day, she would admit to Lee and Maddy that she was a witch but today was not the right time.

Ice coffee, latte and cappuccinos were ordered and the girls laughed and caught up on gossip from their time apart. All agreed Maddy was vastly improved from the last visit and Maddy agreed that she was beginning to feel like herself.

When the most topical of conversations was over, Niamh judged it a good idea to bring up the situation where her father had appeared.

"So, guys, it turns out my father has come back on the scene and is seeing my mother again," she told them.

"Really?" asked Maddy. "Have you met him before?"

"No. Apparently, he saw me in hospital when I was born but I've never met him before."

"Wow. What's he like?" asked Lee.

Niamh glanced at Emma and pursed her lips thinking how to answer that question. "Well, he seems friendly enough, I guess."

"Is he going to move in with you guys when you move to Coburg?" asked Maddy.

"I don't know what's going to happen with that. My mother said they need to get to know each other all over again so I don't think he would be moving in with us any time soon, and I don't want a strange man living in the same house as me, to be honest," Niamh said.

Maddy shivered. "No way. You don't know anything about him or what he could be capable of."

The other three girls looked at Maddy, realising that she was thinking of her assault. Lee put her arm around her and gave her a squeeze.

Niamh looked away, deep in thought. The person who assaulted Maddy was the son of her father, her own half-brother. She could never tell Maddy or Lee this information. She could barely think of it in those terms herself.

She didn't know if she would ever be able to accept and resolve the fact that her blood father was one of the witch's deadliest enemies, a Grimm family member.

Chapter 75

LUCINDA FLYNN 2018

Bethany and Arabella stared at each other in shock at the news that Tarren Grimm was at the front door, and there to meet them. They had been standing back a few steps from the stools they had previously been sitting on. Now, they stepped backward until there was a wall behind them and were holding each other's arms to give each other courage.

"NO, Luce. NO!" said Bethany, loudly.

"We don't want to meet him," said Arabella, fear evident in her voice.

"It's ok. It really is. He's lovely and kind. It will be ok. Trust me," said Lucinda, heading toward the front door.

"Luce, no. Luce ... Luce." Arabella was virtually in tears.

As she reached the front door, Lucinda took one last look at her two panic-stricken sisters and then pulled the door open. She saw the handsome face of Tarren as he took her hands in his and walked through the door. He closed the door and then turned to Lucinda, leaned in to her and they touched foreheads, holding for a few minutes.

There was not a sound from the sisters in the living room/kitchen area. They were wide-eyed and watching every move he made, not able to believe what was happening.

Lucinda and Tarren pulled apart and she smiled at him. “Come through,” she said to him. Taking his hand, she drew him in to the area where her two sisters were standing still holding each other’s forearms.

“Bethany, Arabella, I’d like you to meet Tarren,” she said, formally.

The two sisters stared at his face but didn’t move. They saw a tall, handsome man in neat casual attire with the trademark blondish hair and dark eyebrows, but not hostile or evil looking as they had anticipated. His face seemed serene and tentative, waiting for their response.

A minute ticked past and Tarren knew better than to offer his hand to them or make a move closer. He held his position, smiling lightly at them.

“Pleased to meet you,” he eventually said and nodded his head in greeting.

Bethany nodded her head in response, but Arabella was still just staring.

Tarren turned back to Lucinda. “How’s Niamh been since we met?”

“Oh, she stayed with May the first night, but she was here last night. She’ll be fine,” said Lucinda.

“I suspect she was in my street the night before last. Every car belonging to the family had every tyre punctured,” he said and gave a small laugh.

“What? No. That couldn’t be Niamh. She wouldn’t even know where the family live,” said Lucinda.

“I think she has a lot more initiative and gumption that you give her credit for,” he said and laughed again.

Lucinda saw that Arabella and Bethany had let go of each other's forearms which was a sign that they were relaxing a little more. Things were silent for several minutes and Tarren sat casually on a kitchen stool, trying hard to look relaxed, harmless and shorter.

"How many children do you have?" asked Bethany, eventually.

Lucinda was secretly pleased that she was making an effort at conversation.

"Four," Tarren answered. "Twins, a boy and girl, and two other boys."

"Do any of them look like Niamh?" Bethany asked.

"Errr ... no. She certainly looks like your side of the family," he said, casually.

There was a silence for a few minutes, then Bethany spoke again. "How can we trust you?" She said it with such honesty and sincerity that Lucinda caught her breath.

Tarren thought for a moment and then replied quietly and seriously. "You need to stop looking at me as the enemy. Don't think of me as a member of the Grimm family. Think of me as the man who loves your sister and wants to be a father to your niece."

The two sisters looked at each other, silently seeking the other's thoughts. They looked back at Tarren and answered honestly. "We can try," said Arabella.

Chapter 76

NIAMH FLYNN 2018

After a great morning of laughs with her friends, Niamh dropped Lee, Maddy and Emma home and headed to Coburg to visit May. She was eager for Emma to meet May and planned to arrange a day and time with May where she could bring Emma over. She sang along with songs on Lola's radio as she drove the back roads through Warrandyte, and as she was so close to Templestowe where the Grimm family lived, she couldn't resist turning Lola into their street.

It was only two days ago that she had driven down this street and identified which house belonged to the Grimm family, along with using magic to puncture their car tyres and upend rubbish all over the street. It had been night and dark at that time, whereas now it was light and daytime and she knew the bright blue of her car stood out. She convinced herself that it was a free country, and she could drive wherever she wanted to.

Pulling over to the opposite side of the road, a few hundred metres before the Grimm house, she looked around and there was only one vehicle parked out the front, compared to the many she had seen a few nights ago when she let down all the tyres. The rubbish she had strewn everywhere from the rubbish bins had been picked up and she hoped they enjoyed that little activity ... not.

The house looked quiet and fortress like and she decided she couldn't just drive away and leave no sign that she had been there. She looked around trying to decide what she could do to show her displeasure, and then she saw a bird land on a fence near her. That gave her the idea. She closed her eyes and concentrated on summoning all her friends, the birds to come. For five minutes, she continued calling them and pushing with her mind, and after she was satisfied that she had called every bird that was in flying distance of where she was, she opened her eyes.

Across the road, at the Grimm property she could see hundreds and hundreds of birds. They were sitting quietly on the parked car, on the fence, on the gate, on the house roof and in the trees, silent and watching Niamh, waiting. She could see small birds such as wrens and sparrows and larger birds including magpies, crows, seagulls, rosellas, cockatoos, kookaburras and hawks. She even saw a few pelicans, swans and a crane.

Niamh smiled at them and clapped her hands in delight, sending out silent thank you to her friends. Then she closed her eyes and gave them the signal they were waiting for. With a screech, the birds rose into the air and attacked the vehicle and the windows and door of the house, flapping their wings aggressively, scratching with their talons and pooping everywhere. The screeching of so many birds was so intense that neighbours came running out into the street wondering what was happening. A few people filmed the episode on their mobile phones and others stared in amazement as this phenomenon was only happening on the one house.

After five minutes of attack, Niamh sent a thank you to the birds and they stopped the destruction, rose into the air, and slowly dispersed in all different directions, disappearing as though they had never been there.

Niamh turned Lola around and left the street the way she had entered, pleased her session of destruction had been successful. It didn't escape her attention that this family shared the same blood as her, and she was guilty of sabotaging her own family. She also thought there was a good chance that the quick fuse to anger she had always carried and her mild desire for destruction was probably inherited from the Grimm bloodline. Her family of witches were reasonably mild-natured and kind people in general, although her grandmother had been guilty of extreme vindication when provoked. She decided she quite enjoyed causing mayhem and destruction, and now that she knew she was half Grimm, she had an excuse for it. No more guilt!

Niamh's thoughts turned to her grandmother as she drove the rest of the distance to Coburg. She had heard many stories from May, her mother and aunts about how her grandmother was a different person after her husband was killed. She had morphed from a fun, bubbly and kind person to a withdrawn, sullen and angry shadow of her former self. Everyone thought it had happened because she lost the love of her life in such tragic circumstances, but Niamh wondered if it was from the extreme retaliation she had carried out; the burning of a man in a car, and then the burning of a house resulting in the death of a man and two boys.

The murder of four people including two children would haunt anyone, especially a loving and kind person. Niamh thought it likely her grandmother had nightmares and a guilt complex for the rest of her life from what she had done.

Enjoying mayhem and destruction was not the same as murder and torture and she hoped she would never have to find out if she was also capable of what her grandmother had done.

Chapter 77

MAYBELLINE CONNOR 2018

"May, how strong do you think the Grimm family are with magic?" asked Niamh.

The two of them were sitting in May's drawing room again and Niamh was telling May all the latest news of her family, friends and the fun she had caused with the birds in Templestowe. May shook her head in wonder at the courage and confidence that Niamh displayed. She thought back to when she was eighteen years old and never would have been brave enough to venture into the heartland of enemy territory and do something so outrageous.

"Well, I don't really know but I've always thought they were not as strong as witches. Agatha and I sometimes talked about this topic, and we thought if they were strong enough then they would enter our property without invitation, or flush us out in some way. There must be hundreds of ways of getting to us and yet, after years of stalking us, the best they could do was attack me with a knife while I was walking down the street. They were unable to open the doors that terrible night when Agatha visited them," she said.

Niamh nodded her head thoughtfully. "I wonder what they can do," she said.

"I know they can control inanimate objects such as causing the hoist drop which killed your grandfather," said May, referring to the death of Ciaran. "I assume they can forecast stock markets or tattslotto because they all seem to have a lot of money," said May. "Other than that, I really have no idea. I wasn't brought up in a witch family either. Agatha thought I was adopted and perhaps, she was right. I never investigated it. So, I had to learn everything from scratch like you did. I never got to hear the history of the enemies of witches, only what Agatha told me."

"What did she tell you about it?" asked Niamh.

"Don't forget she was from Ireland so the situation changes depending on which country you're in and even what state or county. She explained that as well as witches, there are other magical beings such as leprechauns, fairies, goblins and elves that live among us."

"No way!" said Niamh, pulling a ridiculous face.

"Why would that be any stranger than witches and the magical Grimm family? Some of these beings don't get along with each other and some do. She thought that witches were the most powerful and that was why some enemies tried so hard to get rid of us. Obviously, that is what happened with the witch trials all over Europe hundreds of years ago, with our enemies spreading stories to make the village people afraid of us and wanting to eliminate us. They killed many women during that time, witches as well as normal women."

"Every time I visit you, I feel that there is someone out in the street somewhere watching. I feel it but I can never see them," said Niamh.

May looked at Niamh, concerned. "You are so much more powerful than I am. I don't feel their presence unless they are right up close. I think my magic has waned over the years, like my body." She smiled as she joked about her appearance.

"I'm trying to understand why your house is being watched. Are they after you or me? If me, why are they watching you?" Niamh asked.

May looked shocked and Niamh felt guilty for scaring her. Thoughts of her attack years ago must be running through her mind. "I would've thought you'd be safe now that the rest of the Grimm family must know you have Grimm blood too. Surely, your father would have told them, so they'd leave you be."

Niamh blanched a little at the word 'father'. "Maybe they don't believe him, or maybe they don't care. They may consider my witch blood overpowers the Grimm, or something," said Niamh. She had been thinking of this too. "You are I are the only true witches left in our little group now that my grandmother has gone. Maybe they have decided it's time for the two of us to be out of the picture."

May nodded and looked worried. Niamh wasn't sure exactly how old May was, but she had to be close to seventy years old and despite being overweight, was fragile and arthritic. Niamh was keen to move into the house at 20 Liddle Street so she would be closer to May and able to protect her.

"May, I want you to be super careful when I'm not here. No going outside your property without me. Do you understand?" Niamh asked firmly.

"Of course, love. We'll stick together, us witches," May smiled at her protégé.

"Is it still ok to bring Emma around to meet you tomorrow?" asked Niamh.

"Oh, yes. Looking forward to meeting her," said May.

Chapter 78

JUSTIN GRIMM 2018

Justin parked his car out the front of his house on the street and banged his fists on the steering wheel in anger. Here he was, pulling up at home again at the end of the day with no exciting news for the family and nothing to show for all the hours he was putting into this witch watching.

How had Beaton managed to weasel out of all the boring stuff? He had agreed to help Justin with this task and yet, where was Beaton when Justin was putting in all the hours, doing nothing but watching a house? No doubt Beaton had just vocalised his assistance in front of the family to be a hero when he had no intention of doing anything.

Justin stepped out of the car and then stopped dead in his tracks. Something was wrong. He couldn't quite understand at first but then his eyes focused on the scene around him, and he made an exclamation of horror. The footpath he was standing on was covered in bird poop, so much bird poop that the path was almost white. The car parked in front of him, his grandmother's car, was marbled with white and as he walked up to it, he saw that it was covered in scratches as well, the dark paint was disfigured beyond recognition.

Totally shocked and with no understanding of what could have happened, he looked around the neighbourhood and could see nothing wrong in the rest of the street. No white bird poop on the footpath in front of any other house and no other damage to cars. He turned and with a press of his remote control, the large gate opened, and he walked into the front yard of the house. The windows of the house were covered in bird poop, with scratches all over the wood beams of the front porch and front door, the driveway and pavers were covered in thick bird poop. What had happened? It was like a horror scene out of *The Birds*.

"Excuse me."

Justin heard a voice call out and he turned to see a neighbour standing at the gate. He walked over and opened the gate. He didn't know the neighbour's name, but she lived across the road, slightly down the hill.

"I've been waiting for someone to arrive home. There were hundreds and hundreds of birds going nuts on your place today," she said.

"You saw it?" asked Justin.

"I sure did and I filmed it." She pulled her mobile phone out of her jacket pocket and held it out to him.

Justin took the phone and stared at the small screen displaying the most birds he had ever seen, squawking and screeching and all over the house, the fence and the car.

"Oh my God," he said, horrified. "This happen to anyone else in the street?"

"Nope. I rang the police, and they said they wouldn't come because they can't arrest hundreds of birds," she said.

"Bastards. Thanks for letting me know," said Justin. "Weirdest damn thing ever."

He headed into the house, but he was starting to analyse the incident and realise what had happened. No one was home and he guessed his mother had gone out shopping with his grandmother and missed all the action with the birds.

"Beaton, you'd better get your arse over here," he said into his phone.

Beaton arrived the same time as his mother returned with his grandmother in tow. The next thirty minutes were spent viewing the damage, cursing the mess and wondering what on earth had occurred.

"The young witch must have done this," said Justin.

"What do you mean, she was here wrecking our place while you were in Coburg waiting for her?" laughed Beaton.

Justin fumed silently as he always did at Beaton's digs. "I can't watch the young witch at the same time as the old witch. You were supposed to be helping me, remember?"

"This was supposed to be over by now," said Dora.

"The problem is that the old witch barely ever leaves the house, and we can't go into her place uninvited," said Justin.

"Uninvited," repeated Beaton. "I've got an idea. Let's get invited."

Chapter 79

NIAMH FLYNN 2018

Tarren Grimm had been present for dinner at her house the night before and she had seriously contemplated eating dinner in her bedroom, but decided she was curious enough to sit at the table with him and her mother. He had been polite to her and interested in everything she said, saying the right words and asking the right questions. She hated to admit that he seemed very charming and genuinely interested in her, but perhaps that was part of the decoy, a charming persona hiding an evil spirit. She kept remembering what May had said about the Grimm's possibly being leprechauns, elves, goblins or fairies, and every time she looked at Tarren, she had to not picture him as a little green monster.

After dinner, she excused herself and headed for her bedroom while Tarren and her mother watched a movie. She was pleased he had the good grace to leave after the movie was over and not stay the night. She was not ready for the daddy sleep over yet.

This morning, she awoke excited to be introducing Emma to May this morning. She couldn't believe how much she hoped they would genuinely like each other. They were both such an important part of her life and she was positive Emma would love May too.

Emma sat in the passenger seat and when Niamh started the vehicle and the music channel sprung to life, Emma broke into laughter.

"What's with the old songs?" she asked.

"Well, Lola is a 1970 car, so I thought it only appropriate that I learn songs from the 1970s," Niamh answered.

"Oh, cool. I love music from the 70's. My mother plays them all the time," she Emma.

For the rest of the journey to Coburg, they sang at the top of their voices to the songs they knew some of the words including *Smiley* (Ronnie Burns), *The Wonder of You* (Elvis Presley), *Whole Lotta Love* (Led Zepplin), *Who'll Stop the Rain* (Credence Clearwater Revival) and *Close to You* (The Carpenters).

Niamh drove slowly and stopped outside 20 Liddle Street to show Emma the house that she and her mother would be moving into shortly. Across the road, she could see a white tradesman's van in front of a neighbour's property. It was a habit now that she always scanned where she was to determine who was about and what vehicles were in sight.

Niamh then drove down to the far end of the street, turned around and parked out the front of May's house. The house appeared quiet, and Emma remarked on how attractive the cottage was and loved the colourful plants and flowers neatly displayed in garden beds.

"Wait until you see the back garden. It's extraordinary with large trees and so many herbs, bushes and flowers," said Niamh.

"Whoever would have thought you'd be into nature and plants," said Emma, mocking her and the two of them laughed.

They stepped out of Lola and Niamh opened the front gate, stepping back for Emma to walk through first. Emma walked over to smell a David Austin rose that caught her eye and Niamh followed, stepping off the path to the front door.

Suddenly, Niamh stopped and the hair all over her body bristled.

"Oh no. Oh no. Something's wrong. Oh, Emma. They're here."

She turned to look at May's front door and she knew it was already too late. The Grimm's were inside May's house.

Chapter 80
JUSTIN GRIMM 2018

Justin and Beaton stood outside the white tradesman's van they had borrowed from one of their employees and viewed each other's outfits. They were both dressed in bright orange high visibility vests, workman boots, baseball caps and were complete with a clipboard and pen. They appeared no different to the average tradesman seen every day working around commercial or residential premises with their blonde hair hidden under the cap. Perfect, thought Justin as he glanced at his watch. It was 7am in the morning and the plan entailed the two of them being visible in the street for the next two hours.

They especially wanted to be visible to Maybelline and for her to assume they were workers from the electrical company. In case she wasn't outside during the nominated hours, they intended to be loud and vocal, calling out to each other while positioned on the street. If they were loud enough, the hope was that she would look out the window and see the men in high visibility vests.

They had prepared official looking cards and were dropping them in everyone's letterbox in the street informing the house holders there would be work underway on the smart meter box of each house and the workman may need access to the property.

At 9am Monica, their sister, made a phone call to Maybelline. Monica had been roped in to the scheme the night before via a phone call once the two brothers had nutted out the logistics of the plan.

"Good morning. Is that Maybelline Connor?" she asked.

"Yes, it is," said May's friendly voice.

"This is Mary Winter calling from Melbourne Emergency Contractors. I hope you're doing well this fine morning. We have been called to repair an emergency problem in Liddle Street in Coburg and I believe you are at number 14. Is that correct?"

"Yes. That's correct," said May.

"You may have seen we have tradesman working in the street this morning. They will have placed a card in your letter box. Have you checked your letter box this morning?"

"No. I haven't."

"We are replacing a faulty switch in the smart meter of each house in the street. The current switch has a high risk of sparking an electrical fire. Will you be home for our tradesman to enter the property and replace the switch this morning?"

"Ummm ... oh. Yes. I guess so."

"Please check your letter box so you have the details of the repair. So, just to confirm, you are Maybelline Connor of 14 Liddle Street, Coburg and you give permission for our tradesman to enter your property and repair the faulty switch in your smart meter. Is that correct, Mrs Connor?"

"Yes. That's correct but it's Miss Connor."

"Oh. I'm sorry. Miss Connor. Thank you for your time. Goodbye."

"Bye," said May, hanging up then making her way out to the letterbox.

She took the card and could see a man in an orange vest further up the street so walked back in the house, reading the card.

Monica phoned Justin and Beaton. "All done. You have permission to enter the property."

Chapter 81
NIAMH FLYNN 2018

Niamh stood statue-still as she quickly evaluated the situation. She was positive there was an enemy presence from within May's house and she could feel it was strong, either a powerful person or two people. Two people with magical power equated to one powerful person if unseen. Although she had never been in this situation before, her witch instincts kicked in and she listened to what it was telling her.

Despite her distress, she tried not to show the depth of her alarm regarding May's safety due to Emma's presence. She felt a strong, protective urge over both Emma and May and fought to remain calm and logical. Emma had moved back on to the path and was now standing directly behind Niamh, drawing in closer as her alarm increased.

Quickly and without moving too obviously, Niamh reached into her handbag and retrieved her mobile phone, turning the phone to mute and then pressing redial to phone her mother. She left the phone in her handbag and hoped her mother would answer and hear what was happening.

"Emma, stay behind me," she instructed in a calm, steady voice. "The Grimm's are inside May's house and we're going to walk in the front door, calmly. Ok?"

She looked back at Emma and could see from her expression and the pale colour of her face, that Emma was terrified. She nodded quietly, trusting Niamh and what she thought should happen. Niamh suddenly became the protector, the alpha and the true witch.

Slowly and with deliberate steps, they made their way the extra ten metres to the steps, then up the steps to the door. Niamh again looked at Emma to ensure that she was following and calm enough. She could see the terrified look on Emma's face, and though she tried not to show it, inside she was just as terrified. Confident that they were ready, she opened the door and walked in.

The door opened into the hallway with the lounge room to the right and the kitchen and drawing room area at the far end of the hallway. Niamh looked in the lounge room to ensure it was empty, but she knew they would be in the kitchen/drawing room area. Slowly, they made their way down the hallway, Niamh trying not to panic, walking slowly and cautiously with Emma close on her heels.

As they reached the far end of the hallway and entered the open plan kitchen and drawing room, she could detect the scent of a Grimm. She turned to the left and could see May sitting down on a chair with the blonde guy with dark eyebrows she remembered from the city, standing behind her. He was the one she had called caterpillar eyebrows. He was staring at Niamh and Emma as they entered the room and Niamh could detect a slight grin on his face.

Her eyes went back to May to check on her condition, and she was concerned by a strange look on May's face. Her eyes were not the bright, wide eyes she was used to seeing. These eyes were cast downward a little and were trying to look up to see Niamh. May was wheezing slightly and having a degree of difficulty getting air into her lungs. Niamh couldn't see any obvious injuries though she could faintly smell blood. May's wrists were tied together with cable ties and Niamh wondered if the faint blood smell was from the cable ties cutting in to her skin.

Niamh tried to focus on May's eyes to read them and judge how she was, but May seemed to be having trouble holding eye contact. She hoped May was not having a heart attack or something similar. It was not a promising start and she felt panic rising up in her which she tried to quell.

"Ah, the young witch. Niamh Flynn, or should I call you, little sister?" caterpillar eyebrows said in a bright and mocking tone. "Come on into the party. Oh, you've brought company. How nice."

Niamh stepped forward a few steps with Emma shadowing her. Movement behind them caught her eye and Niamh spun around to see another blonde man with dark eyebrows. He had entered the front door and followed them down the hallway, effectively blocking an escape. She hadn't been aware of his presence, so focused on May and caterpillar eyebrows. This guy looked a little older and more mature than caterpillar eyebrows, obviously a brother or closely related.

"This is another of your brothers, Beaton. Oh, and by the way, I'm Justin," he said.

"She doesn't look like one of us," said Beaton, staring at Niamh for the first time ever.

"No. She doesn't. She looks like a witch," said Justin.

"Are you sure she's our half-sister?" asked Beaton.

"That's what Dad said, but I don't know. Hmmmm. Not sure."

He looked Niamh up and down as if sizing up a prize steer to be slaughtered. "There's one way to find out," Justin said.

Niamh had been quiet, listening and trying to decide what to do. She had Emma and May to consider so she could not risk getting into a magic fight with these two, not even knowing what their magical abilities were like, plus there were two of them and one of her. Not only that but she was still learning and quite emotional with her magic. May looked to be out of action and Niamh was concerned about her breathing.

The lights in the room started sizzling and dimming as Niamh's emotions took over. The two Grimm's seemed not to notice.

"We need to bleed you," said Beaton, looking at her and producing a knife.

Justin stepped away from the back of May closer to where Niamh stood. Were they going to manhandle her and draw blood? She gently pushed Emma toward May, and immediately Emma raced over and sat with May, placing her hand on May's forehead and checking she was ok. Niamh wasn't able to give any attention to May and her condition so she trusted that Emma would look after her as Niamh gave her full attention to the two Grimm brothers.

Niamh stood guarded while the two men approached slowly from either side of her. Both now had knives in their hand held out in front. Niamh desperately looked around trying to decide what to do. She saw May had candles lit in the kitchen and there was a slight flicker from the flames. Using magic, she threw a candle at Justin's face and the other one at Beaton's face. The hot wax hit both in the cheek and they squealed in shock, swiping the candle aside where it crashed landed to the floor.

"That's not very friendly of you, little sister," said Justin, his face and voice restrained with anger contained.

"We just want to verify that you are our half-sister," said Beaton.

"Our father told us not to touch you, but if you're not his daughter, then we can do what we like with you. Wouldn't that be fun? You do know what I did to your friend, the normal friend?" said Justin. He grinned as he remembered the enjoyment of the episode.

Niamh pulled a furious face unwittingly. She didn't want him to see that his words were affecting her, but she couldn't help it. He was deliberately trying to provoke her. With no control over what she was doing, an electrical bolt hit Justin in the knife hand, causing him to drop the knife. He squealed and quickly retrieved the fallen weapon.

"If you aren't our half-sister, when we finish having fun with you, we can have fun with this normal friend of yours, and maybe the old witch too," said Justin, seemingly not perturbed by the lightning bolt hitting his hand.

Why was he trying to provoke her? Was it because he desperately wanted to harm her and if he provoked her enough to retaliate, then he could tell his father that she caused it?

"Grab her, Beaton. I'll cut her," said Justin.

Beaton lunged at her and she jumped back out of his reach, the same time as Justin swiped at her with the knife. She threw up her arm in defence and the knife hit her forearm cutting down to the bone. She felt the knife hit the hardness of her bone and the jolt as the blade hit the target. Blood sprayed and dripped down her clothes, but she didn't feel any pain. Vaguely, she was aware that the pain would come later.

She grasped her injured arm with her good hand to stem the bleeding. Emma screamed, a long, loud shrill and the sound of the scream filled the room. May was struggling to stand up and kept falling back on to the chair, too weak to stand.

Niamh looked at her two assailants and could see the blood lust, particularly in Justin. His eyes had a gleam that showed he was enjoying the blood and violence and would like to continue. She braced for another attack from the two of them when suddenly, they both stopped and were still.

Chapter 82

NIAMH FLYNN 2018

The knives remained in their hands pointed toward her but the brothers were still as if frozen in time. She stared from one to the other, waiting for something to happen but there was just this strange frozen stance. They were still breathing, and their eyes were still looking at her but there was this strange stillness as if they were caught in a trance. Had she frozen them in some way she was unaware of? Did she have the ability to turn them into stone?

Taking advantage of the pause, Niamh looked over at May and Emma and could see May trying to stand up from the chair with her hands cable tied. Emma was next to her, holding her arm and trying to keep her from standing. One of the times when May straightened up, in her attempt to stand, Niamh saw there was blood stain down the right side of her chest. It was under her breast, hence hadn't been noticed earlier. With shock, she realised that May had been stabbed and that was why she was having trouble breathing. Her large breasts had hidden the wound and blood from her seeing it.

"MAY!" she screamed with a terror she couldn't describe and rushed over to her.

Niamh gently pushed May back on the chair by the shoulders, hushing her and telling her it was ok, she would be fine. She saw the look on Emma's face and realised that Emma had also seen the stab wound on May and the blood stain. Could she heal her? She had never done it and never been told how to do it. She tried to place her hand over May's wound but was distracted by the two Grimm brothers.

They had been silent and still, and she realised that they were smelling the air like an animal smells a scent, like a wolf would smell a bloodied rabbit. The two of them were standing almost side-by-side, still with knives in their hands, and their noses in the air and nostrils dilated inhaling. With a start she realised they were smelling her blood, and it sent a shiver up her spine. This was the strangest thing she had witnessed, and she wondered if there was a blood lust coming on. Were they part animal and would turn rabid at the smell of blood?

The two brothers stared at each other as if reading each other's mind. As much as Niamh was desperate to turn her attention back to May, she knew that if she turned her back on them now, it would be her demise and the demise of Emma and May. She needed to be aware of what they were doing and planning to do.

"So, you are our little sister, it seems," said Justin. He looked mildly surprised and yet, he still stood as did Beaton, with the knife in their hand.

Niamh discreetly looked around the kitchen for a weapon she could use, still not aware of what type of magic she had and what she could call on quickly. Her eyes fell on a saucepan of water sitting on the wood stove and she focused on it, asking the water to boil, which it did within 20 seconds. She fervently hoped this time that the saucepan would not shoot up to the ceiling and embed into the paintwork up there as the cup had when she first tried to boil water. She focused on the saucepan asking it to hit Justin over the head as he was the closest.

With a crash, the saucepan flew across the room and hit Justin on the side of the head with a thud, causing him to scream out in pain. Boiling water sprayed over his face and neck, and he screamed louder, throwing the knife to the floor and shielding his face with his hands. He ran backwards, crying and rubbing at his face as Beaton stared at him and then turned back to Niamh aggressively.

Beaton screamed in anger and charged at her, knife held in front of him. Using magic, she threw a kitchen chair in front of him at lightning speed. He hit the chair hard and toppled over, crashing on the floor in a heap. With grunts of pain, Beaton climbed back to his feet as Niamh stood, ready to defend again.

A strange sensation reached her and she stopped to look around and identify what was happening. She couldn't control her nose which had gone into over-drive, and she suddenly felt like an animal smelling the trail of an enemy. With a stark realisation, she understood that the saucepan had cut Justin on the side of the head when it hit him and there was a small but steady amount of blood sliding down his face. She could smell the blood, and it was the most alarming thing that had ever happened to her. She could detect that he was family, and he had the same blood as her. It caused her to pause and be still as it had done to the two brothers only minutes ago.

Using this pause to his advantage, Beaton charged again. She didn't have a chance to avoid the charge this time, her complete senses absorbed in the blood smell of a family member. He hit her full on and they both fell backwards in a tangle of bodies, the knife slipping from his grasp and sliding across the floor. Niamh had been hit full in the stomach and was winded. She gasped as Beaton disentangled himself from her and was trying to pull himself up on a chair.

She managed to scramble on to her knees, gasping for air when she heard a strange sound that sounded like *whack, whack, whack, whack, whack.* She didn't have the breath to turn and see what the sound was but the sound continued while she gagged and sucked trying desperately to fill her lungs with air. Despairing of being able to breathe ever again, suddenly, it was over and she was able to suck in a large lungful of air.

Whack, whack, whack, whack, whack, whack, whack.

She maintained the position for a few minutes frantically inhaling and exhaling to maintain consciousness. She could see Justin over at the kitchen sink, with the water tap running, throwing cold water over his scalded face. He had his back to her and was concentrating on his own injuries.

Whack, whack, whack, whack, whack, whack, whack.

Feeling she could breathe satisfactorily again, she sat back on her haunches and turned to look at where Beaton was. He was lying on the floor nearly ten metres away from her unmoving. She thought she was seeing things when she realised that the sound of whacking she could hear was the old-fashioned witch straw broom whacking Beaton all by itself.

Her mouth fell open in shock at the sight of an old straw broom suspending in the air thumping a man on the floor as if he was a bad boy and getting a hiding. Immediately, she spun around to look at May knowing she was the only one who could do this.

May's eyes focused on Niamh's eyes with a twinkle and the whacking stopped. May had just saved Niamh's life.

Chapter 83

NIAMH FLYNN 2018

"MAY!" Niamh screamed and raced over to her again.

The act of using her magic to whack Beaton with the old straw broom had taken every sap of energy that May had in her body and she was spent. Her eyes stayed on Niamh, but they were struggling to focus. Niamh reached May and gently pushed her back to relax in the chair. Emma was right there soothing May and rubbing her arm in support.

"May, oh, May," Niamh said, gently, wrapping her arms around May's shoulders and holding her cheek against May's cheek. She could smell the herbal scent of the spices and organic material May used to make soaps and creams.

"I'm sorry, May. They wanted me and they've hurt you. I'm so sorry," Niamh cried.

"No," May's voice came out raspy and in a whisper. "They tried before. They wanted all of us witches dead. Not your fault, love."

Niamh felt the tears wet her face as she held her cheek against May and hugged her. "You'll be ok. May. You'll be ok." She pulled back slightly and looked at Emma.

"Em, can you call 000 and ask for police and an ambulance?" she asked.

Emma jumped to her feet and walked a few steps away, fishing her phone out.

Suddenly, there was movement and sound, and Niamh turned slightly to see Tarren Grimm and her mother explode into the room from the hallway. Both stood, looking around and trying to assess what was happening.

With a scream of anguish, her mother ran over to May and Niamh and started looking for injuries.

"What's wrong? Who's hurt? Where's this blood coming from?" her mother cried out.

Niamh looked at her mother, tears and blood all over her face. "Oh mum, it's May."

Her mother grabbed a few cushions from the chair next to May and lay them on the ground. "Come on Niamh, let's get her flat on the floor," she said.

Niamh gently took May's shoulders and pulled her down to the floor as gently as she could. May's breathing was laboured, and her eyes had a pained look in them. They lay her flat with her head on the cushions and her mother could see the blood stain down the side of her chest. Her eyes caught her mother's eyes, and they acknowledged that May was dying. Her mother had tears running down her face as well.

Vaguely, Niamh could hear Emma on the other side of the room, talking with Tarren and the two of them were checking Beaton and forcing Justin to sit down so they could look at his scalded face. She discounted what they were doing to focus on May.

"May," she whispered to her. "May, can I heal you? Tell me what to do. Please. Tell me how to fix you." She ran her finger gently down May's face affectionately.

"Too late," she heard May whisper back.

"Is the ambulance on its way?" she heard her mother call out to Emma and Emma confirmed it was.

"No. May. It's not too late. Tell me what to do. Please. I'm strong. I can do it," she whispered.

Niamh looked down and placed her hands where the blood on May's chest was. She closed her eyes and focused, wishing for the wound to heal. Come on, she begged. Heal. Come on.

"Too late, love," May said again.

"NO!"

"Luce, glad you're here. Loved you girls like you were my own," rasped May, her voice coming out in a series of puffs as she struggled to get air into her lungs.

"We love you so much, May," her mother said and buried her head against the side of May's head, crying.

"Niamh," May said. Niamh leaned up close to May's lips to hear what she was saying. "I bestow on you. You're the one. Niamh, I bestow on you."

"NO!" Niamh cried out and sobbed as she realised May was saying goodbye. "NO. Don't go. Please, May. Don't leave me."

Niamh kissed May's cheek and then realised that May was no longer breathing.

Chapter 84

NIAMH FLYNN 2018

Total despair and heartbreak filled Niamh as tears ran down her face and sobs erupted uncontrollably. The lights in the house exploded into tiny fragments of glass which tinkered as they landed on the floor.

BOOM!

The outside electrical conductor exploded, and sparks flew in all directions, taking the power out in the entire Liddle Street.

Slowly, Niamh stood as if in slow motion, still sobbing, blood and tears marring her face. Her focus was on Justin who was now sitting on a lounge chair being attended by his father, Tarren.

CRASH!

The sound of loud thunder filled the room and continued for several minutes. Niamh reached her full height and took deep breaths as her magic spiralled out of control. Windows flew open and cupboard doors banged open and shut. A supernatural whirlwind erupted in the middle of the drawing room, spinning and twirling, sending candles, ornaments and vases crashing to the floor.

Niamh opened her mouth and a feral growling erupted and filled the room, turning everyone's blood cold. Heads turned to her and witnessed a wild banshee, eyes almost glowing in the semi-dark of the room, eyes fixed on a target. There was silence in the room as Niamh growled, and the sound of thunder could be heard.

Suddenly, Justin started convulsing and his body violently spasmed until he fell to the floor. Tarren and Emma who had been standing nearby jumped in alarm, unsure what to do. The thuds reverberated in the room as his body seized on the wooden floor, becoming more severe with every second.

Emma looked up at Niamh and realised the cause of the seizure.

"NIAMH ... NIAMH ... Look at me," Emma shouted to her. Her voice almost unheard over the sounds of growling, thunder, whirlwind and the thudding of Justin's body convulsing.

Emma rushed over to Niamh and took her by the shoulders, shaking her. "NIAMH. LOOK AT ME. NIAMH. STOP IT. DON'T DO THIS. STOP. STOP."

In desperation, Emma looked over at Tarren who was looking totally stunned by what was happening. He read her eyes and raced over to Niamh, pulling her body against his own and holding her in a tight embrace. He squeezed her into his chest and could feel her struggling to be released to continue the mayhem.

"Niamh, come on. Stop it now. You can stop it. Come on. Come on, Niamh. You can do it. What would May say?"

Hearing May's name stopped Niamh instantly. She took a deep breath and burst into tears, crying into

Tarren's shoulder. Justin stopped convulsing, the whirlwind wound down and disappeared and the thunder abated. Justin lay still on the floor for a few minutes, before climbing back to his chair, shaking his head as if he had no idea what had just happened to him.

Faintly, Niamh was aware of dogs howling outside in the neighbourhood and they continued for some time. The animals knew their friend had left the world and Niamh knew that life would never be the same now. She had only known May for a few weeks and yet, she felt that she had always known her. They had imprinted on each other, and she now had May's power as well, having been bestowed by May.

Niamh wiped at her eyes, pulling away from Tarren gently and kneeled down to sit with her mother at May's side. Her mother was sobbing and holding May's hand. Niamh bent over and kissed May on the forehead, noting that her forehead already felt cold, and she knew May was no longer there.

"Come on, love. Let us look after her," a male voice said in her ear and hands gently took her shoulders.

Niamh looked up and saw the medics had arrived, one of them helping her mother stand up. Reluctantly, Niamh stood and hugged her mother, united in their grief. After a few minutes, Niamh turned to see where Emma had gone.

She saw two uniformed policemen had Beaton sitting on a chair with his hands behind him, in handcuffs she imagined. Niamh wasn't sure if she was happy to see he was alive or not. She felt he was a nobody and inconsequential, a bug to be trod on and swept away.

Next to him and only a few metres away sat Justin, hands behind him and also on a chair. Emma was holding a damp white hand towel to his face being the kind Florence Nightingale that she was, and behind the chair stood Tarren overseeing the situation.

Justin was staring straight at her and she would swear he had a slight grin on his face and a cocky expression. She wondered if she was imagining it as he had just been burned by a candle, scalded by boiling water and almost had his brain fried when she turned banshee. How could he not be afraid of her? Didn't he realise how powerful she was, and that she still did not have full control of her magical abilities? He should be pissing in his pants and humble in front of her, and yet, here he was smug and unrepentant.

Beaton was looking down at the floor despondently, but Justin looked pleased with himself, pleased that May was dead. She couldn't help but focus on his smug face and she could feel her anger growing again. Realising she was looking at him, Justin called out to her.

"So, another witch down. Just you to go, little sister."

Two things happened at once; Emma screeched, pulled the hand towel away from his face and punched him as hard as she could, right across the nose. His head snapped to the side and blood spurted from his nose. Almost simultaneously, Niamh let out a roar of anger and thrust her hands in the air toward Justin. Electric charges zagged across the gap between them and hit Justin, his body jerking uncontrollably for a few seconds.

Emma ran into Niamh's arms and the two girls hugged, Niamh watching over her shoulder at Justin to ensure he was neutralised. When he glanced at her, she smiled smugly at him and gave him the bird, finger held high so he could not miss it.

A team of medics and police entered the room, and a medic began treating Justin's face which had a red, angry, scalded look to it. Tarren was talking to the police, explaining what had occurred and vaguely, Niamh wondered what he was saying. Was he protecting his sons? The thought of him protecting his sons made her angry. If she knew for a fact that he was guilty, she knew she wouldn't be able to control herself again. She looked at him through squinted eyes, feeling like giving Tarren a jolt of electricity but thought better of it.

"GET THEM OUT OF MY SIGHT!" She heard the firm voice of Tarren and saw he was walking away from the two handcuffed men and was heading toward her side of the room. She could see by the look on his face that he was angry and upset. This look reassured her that Tarren knew what was right and wrong, and she hoped he would continue to understand that his sons were guilty of a terrible and unforgivable crime.

She also knew that if Emma and Tarren had not stopped her earlier, she would have killed Justin. There was no doubt in her mind and she now understood, what her grandmother had felt on the fateful night of the fire, avenging her husband. She felt an affinity with her.

Emma let go of Niamh and stood beside her as Tarren reached out and touched her shoulder.

"Niamh, I'm so sorry. Are you ok? I should have got here faster."

He suddenly noticed the blood all over her arm and that she was cradling her injured arm.

"Medic," he called. "This girl is hurt."

He signalled for one of the medics and pointed to Niamh's arm. The medic pulled back her sleeve and asked her to sit down. She sat on a chair and everything felt surreal. A medic treated her arm and gave her pain relief as she watched Justin and Beaton Grimm being led from the room by the handcuffs. Justin didn't look as smug as he had not long ago yet she still thought his face showed disrespect and she longed to wipe the smug look from his face. She had to turn away to try to control her urge to cause damage and mayhem.

Tarren and her mother were hugging, and her mother was crying into his shoulder. Emma was sitting next to Niamh for support, but all Niamh could see from her vantage point was May. Her body lay on the floor and couldn't be moved yet as the room was a crime scene. Niamh looked down at her short, overweight body, dressed in a bright pink matching pants and top, saw the red, congealed blood on the side of her pink top, and her pale face framed by dyed red hair. She knew she would never see May again, and that May deserved so much more than this ending.

"The world has lost its sparkle today," Niamh said out loud to no one in particular.

Chapter 85

SIX MONTHS LATER 2019

Niamh lit the five candles and placed them around the kitchen and opened one of the windows to let fresh air flow through. Her guests would be arriving in the next ten minutes, and she wanted the house to be perfect. Scones, jam and cream ready to go and she opened the cupboard to check the Nespresso machine had adequate water in it.

Six months had passed since that terrible day when the Grimm brothers took May's life and so much had changed. From that day, she had refused to leave May's house and was still there. For an unknown reason, she could not leave May's house empty, not for a moment. It was not just important, but imperative that she stay there for those six months, and she couldn't explain the reason. Perhaps, when bestowing upon her, May had left silent and secret instructions for Niamh that she must occupy her home. Niamh had no idea, but she could not leave. There had been a witch living in the house for 49 years and that would not be ending any time soon.

It had taken several days for the police office and investigators to complete what they needed to prosecute the Grimm brothers for murder, attempted murder, stalking, assault, fraud and a number of other charges. Interestingly, Justin's DNA had matched the DNA on record from the assault on Maddy so he was charged with that assault as well.

Tarren explained that historically, the Grimm's were immune from any form of prosecution or justice due to their magical abilities. They were able to influence the prosecutor, or police and have records changed to keep them from any form of litigation or prosecution, but in this case, Tarren had used his magic to ensure that they were prosecuted.

It was a difficult situation for him as the two accused were his own sons, but he was adamant that they should pay the penalty for the serious crime they had committed. He had called another family meeting not along after the death of May, and had put the entire family on notice that he would no longer tolerate any anti-witch behaviour. He committed to make it his life-long duty to ensure the safety of witches in Australia. His commitment to the witches did not go down well with the Grimm family and he didn't feel confident that the feud was at its end. All he could promise Lucinda and Niamh was that he would monitor the situation and be their protector.

Tarren and her mother moved into the house at 20 Liddle Street Coburg several months ago and were deliriously happy. Tarren had the financial means for them to live in a much more opulent home, but her mother had insisted that she wanted to live in her old family home and wanted to be close to Niamh to support her, knowing how hard the death of May had hit her. Her mother was the one who shopped for Niamh and brought her groceries and anything else she needed. The only time Niamh had left the house at all was for May's funeral and Niamh insisted on lamingtons and champagne, not tea and biscuits.

Niamh had formed a civil and mildly friendly relationship with Tarren, though not a close father daughter relationship. After nearly twenty years, it would be difficult to fall into a close relationship and they both understood and were happy to let the relationship evolve over time. She did acknowledge that he was not a typical Grimm like the others she had seen, and did exhibit a kind and thoughtful character. She was pleased for her mother that this was the case, and couldn't help but smile when she saw them together and so in love.

The doorbell rang and Niamh opened the front door to welcome Emma, Tarren and her mother who arrived at the same time. Emma had caught an Uber even though she now had her licence, she was yet to purchase a car. Niamh could see her two aunts heading through the gate so waited to welcome them inside before closing the door.

After everyone had been served a Nespresso complete with scone, jam and cream, Niamh called the room to order with a small clap of thunder. Everyone jumped at the sound, so unexpected on a sunny morning, before realising that Niamh had caused the thunderclap.

"OK. Thanks for coming, everyone. This is the first time we've all been in the same room since we lost May," she began.

"I haven't been in this room since May lived here," said Bethany sadly. "You've kept it the same."

Niamh nodded solemnly. "I called you all here today for a few reasons. I wanted to thank you for being supportive over the past months. I've appreciated the kindness you've shown me and I'm sure May would be pleased with how we've come together. Thank you especially to my mother for the super support she's provided."

Her mother smiled in acknowledgement.

"I've made a few decisions regarding my future and I wanted to bring you all together to thank you and to tell you what my plans are."

She paused and looked at the people assembled. All eyes were on her.

"I've decided to follow in May's footsteps and become a public psychic and herbalist. I won't be 'Marvellous Maybelline' though, I will be 'Cailleach' in honour of my grandmother. I know May left her estate to the three of you."

She indicated her mother and two aunts. "I hope you'll allow me to remain here and use her home and garden for this purpose."

She could see smiling and nodding from the three Flynn sisters.

"But ... there is something I need to do first."

All eyes were on her and she deliberately paused to create a touch of drama. She grinned at the expressions on everyone's face.

"I want to go to Ireland, to the old cottage our ancestors lived in. I want to experience Ireland and the way of life my grandmother did before arriving in Australia. I want to pay respect to our ancestors at the family cemetery."

Surprised looks from most of the guests. They weren't expecting this.

"And ... Emma had agreed to come with me to Ireland. As you know, she was present on that terrible day that we lost May. She has since paused her university studies indefinitely and this trip away will do her the world of good."

She didn't need to mention that Emma had suffered terrible ongoing post-traumatic stress and had nightmares and depression. Most of those present in the room were aware of this fact. The trip to Ireland was intended to be a fun and relaxing time for Emma to find herself again.

"I'd like to ask my mother to maintain May's house and garden while I'm in Ireland as I wish to return here and be based here."

Her mother nodded and smiled. Niamh knew her mother was elated that both of them had bonded and were as close as they had ever been in recent months. Losing May had brought them together in grief and they had supported each other since.

"Great. That's it. I wanted you all here to tell you this exciting news. Thank you again. We're planning to leave within the next few weeks."

Emma stood and the two girls hugged. The aunts stood to ask Niamh and Emma a few questions about their trip to Ireland when Niamh's mother cleared her throat for everyone to pay attention. Everyone turned to face her. She was standing holding Tarren's hand affectionately, and she looked so happy and youthful.

"While we have you all here, there is some news we'd like to share with you as well." She looked at Tarren and the two of them exchanged a look. She turned back to the face the people waiting for her news and excitedly announced, "We are having a baby."

There were a few surprised gasps and congratulations, but her attention was on Niamh to see how Niamh was handling the news.

The sneaky smile that sprang to Niamh's face indicated that she already knew.

THE END.

About The Author
L.J. Fox

L.J. Fox holds a Bachelor of Adult Education, Master of Business Administration (Internet Marketing), as well as qualifications in Information Technology. She has worked as a computer programmer, taught business computing at a TAFE College and managed the online presence for a number of corporates as well as the State Library of Victoria in the role of Web Manager. She has now retired to the mid-north coast of NSW where she grows Clivia plants and independently publishes novels in the light fantasy/paranormal/horror genre.

'I am a storyteller from Australia and my primary writing goal is to entertain you, to keep you turning those pages not anticipating what will come next, not to mention - the story must involve something a little morbid or downright weird. If you found the stories easy to read, fast-paced, interesting, enjoyable and little bit quirky then my work is done.'

L.J. Fox

For more books and posts, visit the website and join the mailing list - https://ljfox.com.

www.ingramcontent.com/pod-product-compliance
Lightning Source LLC
Chambersburg PA
CBHW070638310726
48982CB00001B/329

* 9 7 8 1 7 6 4 4 1 3 6 2 6 *